PRAISE FOR T

"This is an absolutely 5-star read for me. I am mind-blown."
—Arevik Heboyan, *Biblioanalytic.com*

"Wow! What a fascinating concept. A truly thought-provoking and satisfying read."
—Grant Leishman, *Readers' Favorite*

"A fascinating and illuminating historical reconstruction that takes us vividly into the world of Jesus' first followers. The reader will come away from this easy-to-read remarkable work with a far better understanding of just what was at stake."
—Barrie Wilson, PhD, Professor Emeritus, Religious Studies, York University, Toronto. Author of *How Jesus Became Christian; Searching for Messiah*.

"Insightful and beautifully written."
—Patrick W. Andersen, *Author of Second Born*

"I loved the way [the disciples] were portrayed. They weren't larger than life, they weren't perfect to the point of unattainability. They were ordinary people with fears and low self confidence and wondering if they were doing the right thing."
—Jeannie Langston, *The Pen Is Mightier*

"Interesting and fast moving. Ms Duarte has crafted a very likely account."
—Patrick Carmen, *NetGalley Reviewer*

THE HOLY CONSPIRACY

the HOLY CONSPIRACY

· KRISTI SAARE DUARTE ·

Conspicuum Press

A detailed Author's Note may be found on page 267.

This is a work of fiction. Names, characters, places, and incidents are a product of the author's imagination. Locales and public names are sometimes used for atmospheric purposes. Any resemblance to actual people, living or dead, or to businesses, companies, events, institutions, or locales is completely coincidental.

Published in the United States of America by Conspicuum Press
The Holy Conspiracy/Kristi Saare Duarte. — 1st ed.

Library of Congress Number: **2020902272**

Publisher's Cataloging-In-Publication Data
(Prepared by The Donohue Group, Inc.)

Names: Duarte, Kristi Saare, author.
Title: The Holy Conspiracy / by Kristi Saare Duarte.
Description: 1st ed. | New York, NY: Conspicuum Press, 2020.
Identifiers: ISBN 9780997180749 | ISBN 0997180749 | ISBN 9780997180756 (ebook)
Subjects: LCSH: Jesus Christ—Fiction. | Jesus Christ—Disciples—Fiction. | Mary Magdalene, Saint—Fiction. | Paul, the Apostle, Saint—Fiction. | Christianity—Origin—Fiction. | LCGFT: Religious fiction. | Historical fiction.
Classification: LCC PS3604.U837 H65 2020 (print) | LCC PS3604.U837 (ebook) | DDC 813/.6—dc23

ISBN-10: 0-9971807-4-9
ISBN-13: 978-0-9971807-4-9
eISBN: 978-0-9971807-5-6

For information, please contact:
Conspicuum Press
PO Box 231
New York, NY 10027
info@ConspicuumPress.com
KristiSaareDuarte.com

Cover design by Damonza.com
Author photo by EDuartePhotography.com

For Eduardo

Introduction of Characters

For the sake of authenticity, the character names used in this novel are as close to the original Aramaic names as possible. Aramaic was the language spoken by Jesus and his disciples in the first century. The universal language spoken in the Roman Empire was Greek. Hebrew was only spoken by the priests and the highly educated.

Below is an overview of the characters of this novel. A more extensive "Who Is Who" can be found on page 268 at the back of this book together with a detailed Author's Note.

Biblical characters:
- **Andreas** (Andrew, disciple)
- **Bar-Tôlmay** (Simon Bartholomew, disciple)
- **Barzebedee** (James, son of Zebedee, disciple)
- **Iosa** (Joses, younger brother of Jesus)
- **Kephas** (Simon Peter, disciple)
- **Levi** (Levi/Matthew, disciple)
- **Mariamne** (Mary Magdalen, Jesus's wife, disciple)
- **Mother Maryam** (Mary, mother of Jesus)
- **Phillipos** (Philip, disciple)
- **Saul of Tarsus/Paulus** (Apostle Paul)
- **Shimon** (Simon the Zealot, disciple)
- **Taddai** (Jude Thaddeus, Jesus's nephew, disciple)
- **Tau'ma** (Judas Thomas, Jude, Thomas Didymus, identical-looking younger brother of Jesus, disciple)

- **Yakov** (James the Just, brother of Jesus, disciple)
- **Yeshua** (Jesus)
- **Yohannah** (Joanna, wife of Chuza, disciple — in this novel: wife of Phillipos)

Other characters:
- **Abram** (Iosa's partner)
- **Michal**, (Yakov's wife)
- **Shemuel Bar Azai** (visitor from Provence, Gallia)
- **Talitha** (Yakov's servant and lover)
- **Yudah Tzaer** (Jesus's son)

● CHAPTER 1 ●

Capernaum, Galilee, AD 30

The executioner slammed a nail into Yeshua's wrist. Streams of scarlet blood drove rivers down the crossbeam and dripped onto the moistened soil. All around him, women wailed, called out for mercy, and pleaded for God to save the innocent from their brutal punishments, while the temple priest nodded for the executioners to continue. And they did, as if merely completing another mundane task before returning home to their wives and a hot meal, oblivious of the onset of Pesach at dusk. When the soldiers raised the cross, Yeshua's body slumped forward, forever pinned to its prison of injustice.

Yakov steadied his hands on the workbench and jerked his head to chase the memory away. Strands of his tousled brown hair got caught in his mouth, and with a sigh of frustration, he swept them back. Six new moons had come and gone since his brother's execution, but fear still consumed him like a droning mosquito, refusing to give in.

He blinked to regain focus in the soft light of sunset that filtered through the open window and painted his carpentry workshop with strokes of gold: the bench littered with tools, the half-finished doors leaning against a wall, the stack of wooden planks piled up in the back. Even the rusted metal parts of the saw and the plane glistened when caught in the amber rays.

His mother had thrown herself at the executioners' feet, begging them to release her son. But they had kicked her away.

A shiver snaked up his spine. He mustn't think about the past.

What good would it do? Instead, he returned his focus to the chisel in his hand and pressed the tool into the grain of the oak plank that formed the back of a chair.

But how could he ever forget? He could still hear Yeshua's voice asking Yahweh to forgive them all before his chin had dropped to his chest, he had closed his eyes, and just like that, he was gone.

Yakov's cheeks stung with shame. Here he was, safe and sound—and, most importantly, alive!—while his brother's corpse lay rotting in a rock-cut tomb in the hills of Jerusalem. He should have protected his brother, fought off the soldiers when they came to arrest him. Instead, Yakov and the other disciples had scattered like frightened salamanders, running for their lives. But what could he have done? His fists wouldn't even have left a dent on the Romans' shields. They all would have ended up dead.

Despite the weight in his chest, a ray of pride warmed Yakov's heart when he stepped back to look at his work. The carved flowers that formed the backrest of the chair were exquisite. A work inspired by God. His customer, the Roman prefect, would not be disappointed. And his wife, Michal, would gleam with appreciation when he presented her with a leather purse heavy with denarii.

A knock on the door interrupted his musings.

Yakov stared at the door, heart thumping. Who would visit his workshop at this hour? He quickly blew out the flame of the oil lamp and slumped against the back wall. Panic rose in his throat. Had Herod's men finally found him? But what could he have done to arouse their suspicions? He hadn't spoken of Yeshua. Hadn't met with the other disciples. How had they found him? Had they finally arrived in Galilee to finish them all off?

Another knock, this time more demanding.

Yakov buried his face in his hands and wished they would go away.

"Come on, open up. I know you're there."

Yakov peeked at the door through his fingers. He knew that voice:

Kephas, one of Yeshua's disciples. Heart still pounding, he rose from his seat and approached the door. But then he stopped short, yanked back by the memory of the last time he had seen his friend.

"We've got to talk," Kephas said through the door.

No. They didn't need to talk. What was in the past was in the past. No need to dig up old issues, tear open wounds that had already scarred. Place themselves in the path of danger.

"Stop pretending. I heard you."

"Go away," Yakov whispered. "My hands are full..."

"Just open the door. I will claim only a moment of your time."

Resigned, Yakov unbolted the door and pulled it open. Outside, the red-cheeked Kephas leaned one hand against the wall. He tugged at his ginger beard with his calloused fingers. "Yakov, be good. We can't keep pretending nothing happened."

Yakov couldn't even look at him. He shouldn't have opened the door. "Nothing happened." He paused. "I mean, I can't..."

"We're all meeting at my house tonight, after supper."

"We? Who are *we*? I'm sorry, I'm busy. I have to finish this chair, a table. Tomorrow a customer is coming to collect a door, and I..."

"All of us. Andreas, Bar-Tôlmay, Phillipos, Levi..."

This can't be happening.

"... Tau'ma, Barzebedee, Shimon." Kephas listed the names of one disciple after another. "Taddai, too."

Yakov's hands twitched. Panic pulsed through his body. "Not Taddai. You can't have my son."

"Taddai's a grown man. He will do as he pleases."

"And Yudah?" Yakov asked. He stared provocatively at his friend. "Have you called upon him, too?"

"No."

"*All of us* means Yudah, too. If he's not there—"

Kephas's smile dwindled. "No, my friend, not Yudah. We don't know, we still haven't... Nobody's heard a word."

Yakov looked at his hands and saw they were shaking. He grabbed on to the edges of the workbench to still them.

That fateful day, he had dragged the bruised and bleeding Yudah away from the other disciples, who were kicking him senseless. In the moment of terror and despair, they had forgotten that Yeshua had beseeched them to forgive the man who would betray him. Yudah had loved Yeshua more than life. He would never have betrayed Yeshua of his own accord. He was only doing Yeshua's will. But where was Yudah now? Yakov hadn't seen him since he'd left him to the care of an innkeeper in Bethania. When Yakov returned a few days later to collect him, Yudah had disappeared.

"So you will come?" Kephas said.

Yakov shook his head. Nothing good could come from this.

Kephas placed his hand on Yakov's shoulder, as if to transmit some comfort that Yakov didn't need. Didn't want.

"You'll come, Yakov. Yeshua chose *you*."

"Ha, you know my brother: he was full of antics, and…" Yakov swallowed to keep the bile down that was threatening to erupt. "Look, he spoke out of jest. I could never…"

Kephas didn't seem to hear him. "After supper. My house. Be there."

As soon as Kephas disappeared around the corner, Yakov's knees buckled and he sank to the floor.

They were going to trap him.

Moments later, Yakov joined his family for their evening meal in their snug courtyard, where they all sat on cushions around platters of grilled fish and carrot stew. Yeshua's pregnant young widow, the lustrous Mariamne, sat by his mother's side and fed her bread soaked in milk, while rubbing the fragile old woman's throat to coax her to swallow. She wiped the corners of Mother Maryam's mouth and spoke to her softly, although the old woman's clouded gaze was forever lost in another world.

Yakov watched them warily. Had Mariamne heard about the reunion at Kephas's house? Was she even invited?

But the succulent taste of musht smothered in onions and honey brought Yakov back to the present. The fish melted in his mouth, and he closed his eyes to savor the taste.

"Good, yakiri?" Michal asked. She rested her hands on her ample waist, prodding for a compliment.

He grinned at his hearty wife. "Yes, my love. Delicious."

She giggled like a youngster and shimmied her hefty arms, making her tunic dance off her plump bottom.

Yakov laughed with her and tried to appreciate his good fortune. Here he was, still alive and healthy, surrounded by his children and three incredible women; his loyal wife, Michal; his brother's widow, Mariamne; and his mother. What more could an honest man wish for?

Taddai, the oldest of his six children, kicked his shin. When Yakov turned to scold him, Taddai raised an eyebrow as if asking, "*So?*"

Yakov averted his eyes. He didn't want to think about what lay ahead. It was true, then. Taddai had also agreed to the meeting among the disciples, as Kephas had said. They would all be there. Every one of them who had been too afraid to be seen together ever since Yeshua died.

Yakov pushed his platter away. He couldn't muster another bite.

Mariamne probed him with her deep blue eyes. He looked down and pulled at a loose thread in his mantle.

What were they thinking? Were they all prepared to risk their lives to fulfill a pointless promise to Yeshua? Had they forgotten how he died?

After the meal, Mariamne rushed to wash the clay platters, sweep the floor, and put Mother Maryam to bed. Although she was with child, her chores resembled those of a house slave, as was customary for a widow living with her late husband's family. Most days, Mariamne did not mind, but now that the disciples had agreed to get together, the eager whisper inside her had awakened. She was impatient to return to teaching. When she overheard the fisherman Kephas speak with young Taddai, she knew she had to join them, invited or not.

Mariamne hurried along the shore-side path to Kephas's house. A cool breeze from the lake carried the scent of seaweed and mud and a faint stench of fish from the dozens of nets that hung by the banks to dry. She stopped for a moment by the gate of the two-story house with whitewashed walls and listened to the hushed murmurs of voices inside. God had brought her here for a reason. Yeshua had trusted her. She had to make sure they made him proud. As she stroked the roundness of her belly, she thought of the child who would be born soon. How would she protect him in this cruel world where Jews had no rights, where men held all the power and women held none?

She was about to push the iron gate open when she noticed two men approaching. *More disciples?* She dove to safety behind a fig tree and peeked out at the passing men. She had to squint to make out their features in the shifting moonlight. They looked too short, too broad-shouldered to be Galileans. *Could they be Romans?* Blood rushed to her ears, and she fought the urge to flee. If they were plainclothes soldiers, what were they doing here? Could they be Herodian spies searching for zealots who were planning an uprising? Or had the day finally come that they were looking for Yeshua's disciples?

The men paused by the fishing boats, and in the light of the moon she saw the daggers that hung from their belts. Soldiers, then. They laughed over some joke she couldn't hear and pointed in the general direction of Kephas's house. Mariamne gasped. She had to stop them before they came closer, before they heard the multitude of voices inside. She clutched her hands to her chest. *Yeshua help me*, she pleaded. She closed her eyes, and suddenly she knew what she had to do.

Trembling with fear, Mariamne wriggled a ring off her finger, slipped it into the folds of her tunic, and stepped out of the shadows. She picked up a stone from the path, glanced at it closely, then threw it away. She walked along the path toward the soldiers, head bowed low and her gaze skimming the gravel path as she picked up stones here and there and threw them back.

"Psáchnontas gia káti?" one of the men asked in Greek. "Searching for something?"

Mariamne looked up.

"Can we help you?" they asked.

She passed them by, eyes still focused on the ground. "My ring," she said at last, and sighed dramatically. She twisted strands of her dark curly hair between her fingers and fluttered her eyelashes. "I've lost my grandmother's ring."

One of the men chuckled with disdain. "You should be more careful, kyría." He gazed back at the village, urging his companion to ignore the woman and to continue their mission.

But the other one, a younger man with plump cheeks and a friendly face, couldn't take his eyes off Mariamne. "We will help you look," he said and beamed at her. And then to his companion, "Wait, Quintus, what harm can it cause? Why don't we walk with her for a while, at least to the town gate? Then let's get something to eat. I'm hungry."

"You're always hungry," Quintus said, shaking his head. But at last he agreed to suspend their mission of searching for rebels, at least for tonight.

An hour later, after Mariamne had conveniently let one of the soldiers "find" her ring on the other side of Capernaum, and once she had seen them leave, she returned to Kephas's house. The gate creaked when she pushed it open, and the hushed chatter subsided. Inside the courtyard, the glow from a bonfire danced across the high walls and illuminated the faces of the men, who sat side by side, huddled in a comfortable conspiracy under the open sky. She shuddered. What would have happened if the soldiers had entered? They would have arrested them all—or killed them.

Yakov waved her close, and Taddai made room for her between them on their mat.

Kephas stood in front of a wall adorned by intricate mosaics of fishing boats and stormy seas. "My friends," he called out, unfazed by her presence. "Let's remember the holy glimmer of God that Yeshua showed us. He taught us to be courageous. Fear nothing! Because he'll stay with us forever, he'll keep us from harm's way."

Mariamne shifted in her seat. Should she tell them how close they had been to being arrested tonight? But Yeshua had saved them, hadn't he?

"I've something to share," she started, but Kephas hushed her with his stare. She lowered her eyes and tried to relax. The soldiers had returned to Tiberias for the night. They were safe. At least for now.

"Six new moons have come and gone." Kephas looked from one disciple to the other. "We can't remain idle any longer. We must finish what he started. He shouldn't have died for nothing."

Everyone nodded solemnly. Ever since Yeshua died, they had all delved into their former jobs with a passion that only fear can spur. They had all gone into hiding and continued to live in constant dread of being recognized as Yeshua's kinsmen, of being accused of lawlessness, of zealotry.

They had all let Yeshua down. Perhaps she more than anyone. Oh, what a coward she had been. But how could she have known he would just give up? She had expected him to leave, to flee back to Mesopotamia. Instead, Yeshua had succumbed to the Romans' threats and let them hang him from a cross like some common bandit. Mariamne bit her thumbnail to keep from tearing up. This was neither the place nor the time to show weakness.

"Do you remember what Yeshua called those who attack us?" Kephas asked. "He called them blind because they have no one to lead them. Isn't that right, Yakov?"

Everyone's attention turned to Yakov.

He laughed nervously. The courtyard grew silent, impatient, as they all waited for Yakov to poke fun at the situation.

Mariamne ached to put her arm around her brother-in-law, encourage him, but it would be unseemly for a widow to touch a man in public. She nudged him gently, hoping he would stand up and reveal something, act like his brother, their teacher, would have done. "Nothing worth having comes easily, does it?"

"S-sister," he stammered. "Y-you're the one who knew him best. Why don't *you* tell us what he talked about in those… l-last days?"

Mariamne couldn't shake the feeling that the other men didn't want her there. She glanced at Yakov, who had lowered his head and was scratching dry skin off his calloused fingers to avoid further attention. What should she do? Should she respond—or ignore the question?

Yakov elbowed her to nudge her on.

She shot him an angry look. But she did want to speak. She longed to be heard. She yearned to share Yeshua's words, to keep him alive. She shrugged off her discomfort and cleared her throat.

"Let me speak in earnest," she said, "and I'll share with you what I've seen since Yeshua left us. I had a vision."

The men erupted in a murmur of doubt. Mariamne drew a breath of courage and spoke more loudly, supported by the trust she had in him, in Yeshua. Her husband.

"He appeared to me in spirit and said, 'You're blessed, because the sight of me does not disturb you.'" Mariamne gazed across the frowning faces of her fellow disciples. "I asked him how it was possible for me to see him like this, alive before me, and he said, 'Because you don't see me with your eyes. It's your heart that sees.'"

"That's rubbish!"

"She's making it up!"

"Get the woman out of here!"

In the gloom, Mariamne couldn't tell who was saying what, but they all leaned forward, as if threatening her.

"Leave her be." Taddai stood to stare down the crowd. Taller than most, Yakov's son still looked like a boy, with his thin arms, lanky legs, and feathery beard. "If you can't listen with love, you're not listening with God. Let's hear what she has to say."

The murmur dissolved as their anger dissipated. Mariamne smiled gratefully at him. Then she closed her eyes and focused on calming her beating heart, as Yeshua had taught her. She connected with God. When she opened her eyes, ready to continue, she cast a loving gaze across the other disciples.

"Yeshua asked us not to mourn him, but to be glad he came. He wanted me—us—to remain in harmony. For he's still alive within us. All of us."

The baby inside her moved, as if to encourage her to be strong. She was on the right path. She placed a hand on her abdomen and let it rest there while she imagined a ray of love emanate from her heart and envelop everyone around her.

"When Yeshua passed away, his atman, the soul that had always accompanied him like an invisible garment, showed him the seven steps to God's Kingdom. We must rise through these seven climates: darkness, craving, ignorance... We must overcome jealousy, enslavement to the body, arrogance, and self-indulgence. The soul has to pass through each of these seven manifestations before it can awaken and release into Nirvana."

The other disciples watched her in complete confusion. Mariamne wavered. This wouldn't do. She had to use more familiar phrases, words they recognized, to keep their attention. "He asked us not to give up, to keep announcing the Good News like we used to do, whatever we may fear. God opposes the proud, but shows favor to the humble. Remember?" Her cheeks burned. They must know she was telling the truth. They had to recognize his words.

"And although we must abide by the laws he gave us, and those offered in the Torah, we should never become bound by them." With significant effort, she pushed herself up onto her knees. "He doesn't *want* us to remain in sorrow. Let's find comfort in his grace, in all he was, and still is. He prepared us for this!"

A veil of silence hung over the courtyard. She had said all she needed to say. She had spoken without fear. Yeshua would have been proud of her. She willed her heartbeat to slow, then she hung her head low and adopted the posture of a subservient woman, the way she had been taught to behave.

The fisherman Andreas, one of the older men in the group, stood up next to his brother Kephas. He scratched his graying beard, one hand on his protruding belly, and looked from one man to another, carefully avoiding Mariamne's eyes.

"Tell me, friends, what do you reckon of what she's told us?" He allowed for a lengthy pause while nodding with certitude. "I can't believe our Master would speak like this. What climates? What manifestations?" He laughed. "It's too different from what Yeshua used to say."

Kephas placed a hand on his brother's shoulder. "Should we believe that our teacher would appear only to her—a *woman*—and speak of these unfamiliar things?"

Mariamne bit the inside of her cheek to keep from cursing. How dare they speak to her like this? With a strength she didn't know she had, she pushed herself to stand and placed her hands resolutely on her waist, garnering strength from her abdomen before she spoke, in a voice both softer and stronger than her own:

"Kephas, Andreas, don't be foolish. How can you possibly think I invented this?"

Andreas's shoulders slumped, and his eyes looked down on his hands clasped over his old man's belly.

Mariamne sent him forgiveness from her core and added in her sweetest voice, "Would I lie about our teacher?"

Levi, a spindly tax collector who had joined the group only in the last months of Yeshua's life, cleared his throat and indicated for her to sit. He turned to Kephas.

"Are you repudiating her for being a woman? What has come over you?"

Mariamne couldn't help but smirk. Maybe she had a chance, after all, to lead the disciples. She could do it better than anyone else.

Kephas shook his head, unperturbed.

"If our teacher held her worthy," Levi continued, "who are you to reject her? Have you forgotten how Yeshua loved her? Let's bury our differences. He would have wanted us to continue to spread the Good News far and wide. And we can master that task, if we work together."

Yakov was about to shout out a "Hear, hear!" when he found Kephas staring at him. He had regained his authoritative posture, as strong as the rock after which Yeshua had named him.

"Levi is right," Kephas said, clutching his fists. "We owe it to Yeshua to work together. And how can we do that? Well, let me tell you. First, we decide which of us men is potent enough—*man* enough—to take the reins from our beloved Yeshua."

"Bah! Have you forgotten?" old fisherman Barzebedee asked in his thunderous voice, and he raised his finger to point at the men around him. "You were there! In that room. You all heard Yeshua say that if we are ever in doubt, to go to Yakov, because he'll know what to do."

Yakov squirmed in his seat. He didn't want the responsibility, the burden. And above all, he didn't want to die. "I-I already told you, Yeshua often said things like that, things h-he didn't mean."

If only Taddai would stop grinning at him. How could he even think his father was the right man for the job? Yakov was a simple carpenter. He liked to joke and drink and sing out loud. He didn't like to speak in front of crowds. He wasn't a leader. And he definitely was not interested in adopting Yeshua's Nazirite lifestyle: no more wine, no meat. His wife would not be thrilled.

"What do you say?" Barzebedee asked. "Will you lead us?"

Yakov's head throbbed. He buried his face in his hands. How could he get out of this? Then... *Wait!* Hadn't Yeshua said something about Kephas? *What was it?* The memory shot him to his feet. With jubilance, Yakov handed them the answer they were looking for.

"Ha, I say he chose *you*, didn't he? T-that's why h-he named you Kephas, the R-rock."

The nods and hums around him eased some of Yakov's fears. He didn't have the makings of a leader. He didn't yearn for attention.

Unlike Kephas, who hiked up his shoulders and feigned bashfulness. He coveted the position, Yakov could tell. He already appeared five inches taller, his chest wider.

"How so?" Kephas tugged at his ginger beard, unable to hide his satisfaction.

Yakov gladly took the bait. Kephas needed to hear why he should be their new leader, have it smothered all over him like fragrant cane oil. "D-don't you remember? That evening when he first named you Kephas? H-he was very clear about it, wasn't he?"

Andreas lit up: "I do! His exact words were something like, 'You are a solid friend, a rock, and on this rock I will build my community.' That's what he told us."

Yakov glanced at Mariamne. Andreas hadn't even been present that night.

"Remember that, Kephas?" Yakov insisted. Of course he didn't remember, because Yeshua had said none of that, but Yakov was more than happy to play along.

"Yes," Kephas mumbled, frowning. Then, with more conviction, "Yes, I do."

Yakov chuckled, delirious with relief. Kephas's pride had won. Now everyone would agree that Kephas was the man to lead them from here. And Yakov could return to his life in safety and comfort in his carpentry workshop and hide from all the prying eyes that haunted him.

"Well, I propose Mariamne as our leader." Levi gestured at the beautiful woman beside him.

Yakov squirmed. *Oh goodness, Levi. Just leave her be.*

"She was Yeshua's closest companion, his most beloved," Levi continued, watching Mariamne with adoration. "She's the one he trusted the most. She should lead us from here on."

Kephas looked like he was choking on a sour grape. As if he couldn't believe how someone could suggest a woman leading men.

Mariamne laughed that brilliant, pearly laughter of hers, fresh and divine like summer rain.

"I accept," she said. Her entire face radiated with love. "I will take the lead, if you'll allow me, and I will serve you well."

Yakov couldn't help but chuckle to himself. She was exactly like Yeshua, with that same cocky determination. That fearlessness. The ambition to lead and to teach. The absolute confidence that she knew right from wrong.

The room broke into a cascade of voices and hoots of disapproval. The buzz grew louder as all of them fought to be heard, to argue and disagree, to settle or agree.

"Hear, hear now, fellows. Let's have some stillness, please?" Andreas called for everyone to sit and stop talking. "We've got to agree on this. Aren't we all in favor of Kephas as the leader of—?"

"Yes!" Yakov exclaimed too quickly, too loudly. Mariamne shoved her elbow into his ribs. But Yakov just shrugged. What else could he do? Mariamne didn't stand a chance among this crowd of headstrong men. Kephas, on the other hand, would be an excellent leader.

The bickering grew louder and drowned out any other outbursts.

Andreas stepped onto a bale of hay, cupped his hands around his mouth, and shouted, "Silence, fellows. What are we, barbarians? Romans?"

The rumble fizzled into a quiet murmur.

"That's better. But listen, we can't go on like this. We have to make a decision. While we all sit here on our tender behinds, time passes by, and soon we'll have forgotten everything we learned. It's already been too long. We owe it to Yeshua—*to us*—to carry his message farther. We owe it to God."

"Andreas is right," Yakov said, more loudly and with more strength than he had ever mustered. He would do anything to take the pressure off himself. "Kephas is the best man to take the helm."

"Let's cast lots!"

Yakov didn't have to look around to know who had shouted out the suggestion. The low, manly tone didn't fool him. *Mariamne.* Why had he even brought her along? Only he hadn't. She had sneaked in, uninvited. Why couldn't she be like Michal, like other women, quiet and obedient?

"Cast lots?" Kephas had joined his brother on top of the bale of hay, as if a physical height would emphasize his superiority. "Let's not be foolish, friends. We're not electing a high priest, we're looking for a man among equals, someone who will gently lead and advise the others. Someone righteous and decent—"

"Like Yakov," someone called out from the back.

"No. Kephas!"

"Yakov!"

"Mariamne!"

Another rambunctious squabble rose and wrangled around the room, unifying and separating the men into islands of conformity, until it grew and morphed into a unanimous call:

"Cast lots, cast lots, cast lots!"

Kephas stepped down from the bale of hay, defeated.

Yakov ran his hand through his thinning hair and wiped the cold sweat off his forehead. What was happening? What they asked of a leader was not child's play. They lived in a world ruled by greed and power, where boorish Romans and imperious temple priests reinforced each other's supremacy. Where fighting either was synonymous with a death sentence. Why would he ever volunteer to step into the arena where Goliath always defeated David?

Andreas dug a small hole in the ground where the lots would fall, while Levi used the tip of his curve-bladed dagger to etch letters into three flat stones: *Kaph* for Kephas. *Yudh* for Yakov. *Mim* for Mariamne.

"Have we agreed on these three? Yakov, Kephas, and Mariamne?" Levi asked.

This time they all nodded.

"Blessed are you, Mariamne, Kephas, and Yakov." Levi held the three stones in his cupped hands and stretched them toward the sky. "May our beloved teacher direct these lots and show us which of these noble disciples should become our holy example and courageous leader. Yeshua, we pray for your guidance. We promise to honor your choice with love and respect. As I cast these lots, may your chosen leader land on top. Amen."

Yakov held his breath as Levi cast the stones up in the air and watched them fall into the pit, one by one, as if time had halted to a standstill. He closed his eyes. *Please, Yeshua, I don't want this. Haven't I suffered enough for you?*

When he opened his eyes, everyone was staring into the pit where the three stones lay pancaked, one on top of the other, as if meticulously placed there by hand. Andreas reached down and grabbed the top stone. Holding it between his thumb and middle finger, he showed them the letter.

Yudh.

A few nights later, Mariamne found Yakov sitting cross-legged in their courtyard, staring into the frostbitten sky. Lost in his thoughts, his eyebrows knitted over his crooked nose, as if dreading a destiny he could not escape.

She knew she should leave him alone, cover herself with a warm blanket and curl into bed like everyone else. But the quiet sadness in his eyes captivated her and wouldn't allow her to abandon him. She longed to help him.

Ever since that evening at Kephas's house, Yakov had buried himself more deeply in work, barely leaving his workshop. He always had to finish one more project, he said. Surely tomorrow would be a better day to reunite with the disciples.

Always tomorrow.

If only he could gather his courage and be the same confident man he was when surrounded by his own family. At home he never failed to find the correct words. He never stuttered. He spoke of God with clear and convincing parables. Yet as soon as he stood among the other disciples, his tongue swelled and his spirit waned.

Mariamne took a step toward him, but stopped. Perhaps she should let fate run its course. Let Yeshua's message wither and die like a delicate spring flower in the advent of snow. But she couldn't!

She knelt by Yakov's side and followed his gaze. The stars glittered with nascent hope in the glacial sky, the luminous rays Yeshua had called "hosts of heaven."

"Here you are," she said, and she let her hand rest on his knee, urged by an acute desire to offer him comfort. "You're an honorable man, Yakov. You never fail to show gratitude to The One, he who created the glorious lights."

"What do you want?" Yakov brushed her hand away, like dirt.

She should have known better. He didn't want her here. She leaned onto her arms to raise herself up, but an inexplicable force within her guided her down again. She was here for a reason, and even though he might not be aware of it, he needed her. Mariamne let her heart fill with a silent glow.

"I know what you're going through," she said. "You're exhausted and confused. Tired of those who think they know better than you, who aim to advise you. But you don't have to listen to anyone. Listen to what God says when he speaks to you. Yeshua always said the wise shall shine like the brightness of the sky, and those who teach others about righteousness shall illuminate the world forever and ever."

Yakov closed his eyes, as if willing her to disappear.

"Yeshua chose you, Yakov. It upset me at first, I'll admit. But he was right. Only you are wise enough to lead us."

"Go to bed, Mariamne."

"I can help fill you to the measure of our fathers. You don't have to find your purpose, Yakov. Just *be* your purpose."

Yakov laughed with disdain. "Leave me alone. What do you know, anyway? You know nothing."

Mariamne put her hand on his knee again and squeezed it. She didn't care if Michal saw them. This was the first time since the night in Kephas's house that they had spoken in this direct manner. She looked straight into his eyes. "I know everything."

Yakov stood abruptly. "You're a fool, Mariamne," he said without looking at her. "First you lead my brother to his death, and now you will grant me the same favor?"

Mariamne wanted to take his hand, comfort him, but she could tell he didn't want to be touched.

"We've fed you," he said. "Cared for you. Provided a roof over your head." He raised his hands and whispered, his voice scarred with pain, "Oh, Yeshua, how could you have been so thoughtless?"

Mariamne struggled to her feet and placed her arms around him. "I can help you. Trust me."

At last, Yakov's teary eyes met hers. Her words had permeated his hardened core.

She took his hand and pulled him along with her toward the shore.

"Let's take a walk, and I'll explain."

At first, Mariamne's idea had appeared ludicrous—a simpleton's dream—and Yakov couldn't help but push it away. Why would they move to the heart of hatred in Judea? And why Jerusalem, of all places, where they risked being recognized by the temple priests and by the Roman soldiers who had arrested and executed Yeshua?

But then one early morning, as Yakov sat meditating on a flat rock by the lake, a bubble of a once-dormant dream floated up through his abdomen into his chest and eclipsed his heart. What if the other disciples were right? Perhaps he could carry Yeshua's torch farther. Continue his mission. Even complete it. If only he could conquer his fears, he could be as good as Yeshua.

His whole being filled with a sparkle of hope, a yearning. He had lied to himself. It wasn't true he didn't want this. It was all he had ever dreamed of.

"If we think of them as holy, perhaps we can succeed," he said to Mariamne later that day as she helped him clean his tools and arrange the workshop for the day.

"Who?"

"Pilatus, Herod Antipas, their lot. Yeshua always emphasized that they're not separate from us, they are also one with God."

"Yes!" Mariamne said. Grinning, she held up the two iron nails she had measured for size and looked from one to the other. "And in Judea we can hide in the open, not live in fear of persecution like here."

Yakov shivered with a mixture of fear and excitement.

A few nights earlier, she had told Yakov about the Roman spies she had encountered outside Kephas's house and how she had intercepted them. At first her story had paralyzed him. The Romans had no morals. They would arrest anyone who fit the bill of possible rebellion. And Galileans, known as troublemakers who opposed the current regime, were at the top of their list of suspects. But then it had dawned on him: they were no longer safe here in Capernaum. They had to leave.

That same night, Yakov finally called all the disciples to meet in Kephas's house, leaving two boys to stand guard outside and warn of anyone approaching.

"In Jerusalem we'll b-be one of many groups," Yakov said, his mouth dry, heart pounding in his chest, and cheeks aflame. He closed his eyes to gather strength. These were his friends. There was nothing to fear. When he looked up again, he drew in the benevolence that radiated from them. His heartbeat slowed, and he cleared his throat. "Everyone around Lake Kinneret knows us. Th-they remember how we traveled with Yeshua from village to village, a-announcing the Good News."

"It only takes one envious person to betray us," Taddai added. "Perhaps someone whom we couldn't heal, or someone who wanted to join Yeshua but for some reason couldn't. If anyone reports us to Herod Antipas, or the Romans, and tells them we're planning an uprising... Look at what happened in Bethsaida last week. Three dozen innocents killed."

"Those people were terrorists, sicariis," Andreas called out, shaking his head.

"No, they weren't," Mariamne said. "They didn't even carry weapons, for goodness' sake. Some were farmers."

"How's that different from what happened to Yeshua in Jerusalem?" Kephas asked. "We'll place ourselves in the path of danger."

"It *is* different." Yakov didn't want to argue. Why couldn't they believe him?

"Remember the Baptist?" someone said. Yakov shaded his eyes with his hand to see who had spoken, who had thought it wise to bring up the beheading of their cousin Yochanan, but in the dim light, he couldn't tell them apart.

"Antipas had it out for him," Taddai answered. "The Baptist insulted him. We're different. We don't judge."

Mariamne lounged against the wall, her belly jutting out like an overgrown watermelon. She looked at the men around her. "Antipas sent spies to Bethsaida. What makes you think he doesn't have spies here, too? And the Romans. People are getting arrested and murdered all around us. Honorable people."

"Jerusalem's too dangerous!" The ever-brooding Shimon jerked his head so fiercely he sent his woolen curls bouncing.

"*Capernaum* is too dangerous," Yakov said, emboldened by the feeling that they had no choice.

"Don't you think our neighbors have noticed we keep meeting here?" Mariamne said. "You think they don't talk? Luck has been on our side thus far, but what about the next time? What if the spies—Antipas's men or the Romans, whoever it might be—lean against the gate to eavesdrop, and hear something they might deem incriminating?"

"And you think we won't stand out more in Jerusalem? A pack of poor Galilean preachers?" Kephas chortled.

"N-not if we conform to the law," Yakov said. He drew courage from his core and continued. "If we act like any other Jews. Keep Sabbath, kosher, circumcise our sons, pay our respect to the high priest... As long as we don't openly, verbally oppose the Pharisees, the Sadducees, or the Herod family, we'll blend in."

Yakov couldn't believe the strength of his voice. Never before had he spoken so clearly, with such conviction. His heart beat so fast, it nearly bolted out of his chest. But he had spoken his truth. Now it was up to them to decide if they would join him or not.

"And how will we survive in Jerusalem? Have you thought about that?" Kephas asked. "Where shall we live?"

A wide grin spread across Yakov's face.

"I have a plan."

Jerusalem, Judea, AD 31

Four months later, Yakov and his fellow disciples sat cross-legged beside their newly built mud-brick houses in a fertile valley of the Jerusalem hills. The fresh breeze of spring caressed Yakov's nostrils with a scent of rebirth, and his soul filled with the contentment that only Sabbath could bring.

Someone shoved him in the back, interrupting his peace of mind. When Yakov glanced over his shoulder, he saw Mariamne glaring at him, eyebrows raised. *Go on*, she prodded with her eyes. *Get up and speak.* But Yakov shrugged helplessly and turned his attention back to Kephas, who stood proudly in front of the group, ready to speak.

"Let's lift our cups in gratitude to God and to the memory of Yeshua, our teacher," Kephas said and straightened his back. He raised his cup of pomegranate juice and observed his companions, eyes blazing with conviction.

Yakov raised his cup, relieved. Ever since they had arrived in Judea, Kephas had eagerly agreed to deliver the daily sermons. His voice rang clear and determined, more brazen than Yakov's could ever sound.

But when Yakov glanced at Mariamne, she rolled her eyes. Why couldn't she accept he wasn't ready yet? Tomorrow would be a better day, he promised her. If she would only wait one more day, surely he would find his voice and feel more confident. More ready. Besides, why shouldn't Kephas take control for now? It wouldn't be forever, just now, in the beginning. One day Yakov would feel ready. Just not yet.

"We offer our gratitude to our Father," they all recited in unison, "for the holy vine of David, which you made known to us through Yeshua. May your glory last forever."

Kephas beamed with pride. Everyone had memorized the words. "And the bread," he added.

The disciples raised their flatbreads with both hands and said, "We thank you, Father, for the knowledge you taught us through Yeshua. May your glory last forever."

"When this broken bread was scattered upon the mountains," Kephas continued, "you brought us together and made us one. Let's gather the crumbs from the ends of this earth and unite them in your Kingdom, because yours is the glory and the power for all time to come."

"Amen," they mumbled, their heads bowed in reverence.

"Yakov, we'd love to hear what *you* have to say now," Mariamne said too loudly. Yakov wanted to press her mouth shut, but he couldn't, of course. He shouldn't. It wasn't her fault he found himself in this situation. He had agreed to come here, to continue Yeshua's work.

All the other disciples watched Yakov with eager anticipation. There was nowhere to hide.

Kephas waved him closer, hiding his jealousy behind a toothy grin.

Reluctantly, Yakov stepped up to Kephas's side. His heart beat wildly. What could he say that would make any sense to them?

"Re-re-remain eager for the word of God, b-because…" *Because what?* His voice dwindled. He cleared his throat and took a deep breath to strengthen his resolve. If only he could open up to receive the words of God. Let spirit speak through him. "Th-the first expression of the w-word is faith," he said, forcing a smile. "The second is love… and the third, it's the w-work you do. Life emerges from your good deeds, and G-God's love will shine upon you."

Sweat trickled down his spine, and his cheeks burned with uneasiness. His gaze rested on Michal, his dear, obedient wife, who sat in the back among the other women. She had been reluctant to move, hesitant to leave the village where she had lived her entire life. And she had raged in anger when she realized she had no choice. But like any dutiful wife, Michal had finally accepted her fate. Like his dear mother, a mere shell of the woman she once had been, who had remained oblivious as Yakov carried her out of the house and placed her on the back of their old mule for their five-day trek to the Holy City. Did she even know she was here?

Yakov surveyed the dozens of brave disciples around him. Seventy of Yeshua's closest men had accompanied them to Jerusalem. Kephas was there, as was his brother, Andreas. But many of Yeshua's disciples from Galilee had refused to upend their entire existence, sell their belongings, and resettle in the volatile Judea, no matter how hard Yakov tried to convince them. They refused to spend the rest of their lives in an ascetic community where they had to share all their income and all possessions. "A pit of serpents," they called Jerusalem, "the home of Roman demons," "slaves of mammon," "forever stripped of its holiness." Yakov had—unsuccessfully—asked them to replace their hatred with forgiveness and to see the misdeeds of others as an opportunity to heal, but to no avail. They would never return to the place where they had been robbed of all their hopes, they said, where a pungent scent of death would forever accompany their steps.

Despite this, a new group had emerged, and a solid one. With the donations of their families and the inheritances of the wealthy widows among them, the group had settled on a large lot of land flowing with milk and honey in a hidden valley not far from the road to Jerusalem. They built a village of houses made of mud tiles, mule dung, and straw at a safe distance from the eyes and ears of any spies.

They had all vowed to work together and contribute to the welfare of the new community, every one of them with a set range of chores. Tau'ma assisted Yakov in their makeshift carpentry workshop, while others tilled the land and planted enough barley, wheat, beans, lentils, and vegetables to feed them all. Kephas and his wife tended to the beehives. Levi and Andreas took care of the sheep, goats, and chickens they had brought for a constant supply of milk and eggs. Yakov's brother Iosa and his partner, Abram, wove the wool from their flock of sheep and tailored garments for neighboring Judeans. As a community, they were far from rich, but they would never starve. They had even had enough to share with the orphans and widows who lived nearby. Yakov smirked to himself. Yeshua would have been proud—a life of simplicity and austerity that allowed their minds to focus on nothing but God.

"As Yeshua always said," Kephas continued after waiting out Yakov's long, drawn-out pause, "the beginning must come from you. From us. We've come here for a reason. Will you agree, Yakov?"

Yakov scanned the faces in the crowd before him, well aware that they were growing impatient with his indecision, with his avoidance of accepting the yoke of leadership with all its duties. Halfheartedly sharing the responsibility with Kephas wasn't enough.

"Together we have the knowledge," Kephas continued, with a smug twist to his mouth, "to rid the masses, our fellow Jews, of their ignorance. Remember how Yeshua always worried whether we could reach his height of wisdom? But when his seeds of enlightenment sprouted within us, he saw what we can achieve."

Yakov shook his head. This wouldn't do. This wasn't how Yeshua would have spoken. But how could he clarify his brother's thoughts?

Speak! a voice in his head demanded. *Speak up, Yakov!*

With his heart pounding and his cheeks flushed, Yakov drummed his fingers on his thighs. He had to say something, or they might as well return home. They had come this far, now they must make the best of it.

"Yes," he said, a smidgen too loudly. "You are correct, K-kephas. We arr-arrived from thoughtlessness."

Mariamne nodded, prompting him to continue.

"W-we trudged through mud and traced the steps of our teacher." Yakov swallowed hard and blinked for a moment. *Focus*, he told himself. *These are not your enemies.* He pulled the sides of his mantle wide, like wings, and laughed. "But look: our clothes didn't get dirty. We weren't inundated with the filth of others. Th-their shadows never enveloped us. And why? B-because the light of heaven… b-blazes like the midday sun in each of us."

Something had helped him speak and make himself understood. He exhaled and ran his fingers through his thinning hair. These wonderful, loyal men and women around him, they deserved to be reminded of the lessons Yeshua had taught, not hear an altered message that would make them feel superior to others.

"Yakov is right. We have all the knowledge," Mariamne said. She stood tall, stroking her pregnant belly. "We shouldn't dwell in the suffering of others, but we can help lift them up. Share what we know."

Kephas pushed her aside, gently, so no one would notice. He brought his palms together to signal to the assembly of disciples that the sermon had ended.

Yakov's heart expanded with love when he looked at Kephas, and at Mariamne, and at all the men and women around him.

He owed them all so much.

Interminable days of hard work passed by as the village grew into a compound of stables and workshops and fields to be plowed and planted. Everyone toiled together from morning to midnight, without uttering a single word of complaint. No clouds of worries passed in the skies, no rains of disagreement fell upon them. Peace had made its home in their midst.

Until one day, when Taddai came storming into the shed where Yakov was sawing planks into stakes for the fences around the animal enclosures.

"Father, come. Quick!"

At the back of a muddy field, Mariamne had crumpled to the

ground. She clutched her belly, moaning, her face contorted with pain.

It could mean only one thing.

Yakov rushed to her side. He hooked his arms under Mariamne's torso, and, together with Taddai, helped her back to the house where they placed her on a straw mattress covered by a clean linen sheet and made sure she was comfortable. Then they left the women to handle the rites of childbirth.

Outside, the powerful wind ripped at the woven fabric that covered the open windows. To calm his nerves, Yakov squatted against the wall of the house and picked up a piece of olive wood from his pouch. He pressed the tip of his dagger into its firm veins. A few feet away, a child fathered by Yeshua was about to enter this world. Yakov's skin prickled with anticipation and fear, and he pulled his headscarf tighter around his head.

Hours passed.

When the newborn child's screams finally pierced the air, Yakov wept with gratitude. This time he would make it right.

On the morning of the eighth day, the rabbi arrived for the newborn's circumcision ceremony.

"Praised be Adonai." The rabbi lifted the infant high over his head for all to see. Then he placed him onto a table covered with a white cloth.

Trembling, Mariamne watched as the rabbi raised the sharpened knife, its blade catching the rays of the rising sun.

The baby wailed.

Mariamne's eyes flooded with tears. *Soon,* she thought. *Soon, my child, your suffering will come to an end.*

With a quick snip, the rabbi removed the foreskin, wiped blood off the baby's penis, then handed the whimpering child back to Yakov.

The worst is over.

"B-blessed by the creator, who…" Yakov said. He focused his gaze on the child in his arms, "wh-who sanctified Abraham, his companion, and wh-who established the law within his flesh…"

"And formed this proof of a holy covenant with all his descendants," the rabbi continued, impatiently.

The crowd echoed in unison: "This child has entered into the agreement."

The rabbi blessed a jug of pomegranate juice, placed a drop in the baby's mouth. "Creator of the universe, may you grant a pure and holy heart to…" The rabbi paused. "His name?"

"Yudah," Yakov said, and smiled at Mariamne. "Yudah Tzaer, our little Yudah."

Everyone gasped, their faces darkened with disbelief.

"To Yudah Tzaer," the rabbi continued, unaware of the commotion the name had caused. "May he learn and teach, and may he fulfill your commandments."

A local trio of wandering musicians set up to play: a lyre player, a harpist, and a flutist. Michal and her daughters brought out trays of grilled carrots and beet salad, semolina cakes and flatbreads, apples and cheeses. And in no time, even the grumpiest of men danced, sang, and clapped their hands in time.

But among the disciples, a whisper could be heard. It spread from one mouth to another: she named him Yudah, after the man who betrayed her husband. *How could she?*

Mariamne withdrew into the principal house of the compound, the one she shared with Yakov and his family, away from the crowd, from their accusing stares, and settled to feed her son. As she watched him eagerly suck her nipple, she wondered how the others could have forgotten that their friend Yudah had once saved them all. Ever since Yeshua had stirred up trouble in the temple last year, it had marked the disciples as a band of rebels. Only afterward had Yeshua realized what he had done, and he felt guilty. He had placed them all in danger, and especially Tau'ma, his younger brother who looked so much like Yeshua that few people could tell them apart. Therefore, Yeshua had begged Yudah, the bravest of all disciples, to approach the Romans and point Yeshua out, mark his cheek with a kiss, so they would arrest him, and leave Tau'ma and the others alone. The night before his arrest, Yeshua had told her he was tired of running, tired of always being afraid.

Mariamne sighed. How could they still blame Yudah? Yeshua had told them what would happen, what he had asked Yudah to do. But no one had seen Yudah since Yeshua's arrest, and perhaps it was for the best. If Yudah had dared to return, the other disciples would have beaten him up, perhaps even stoned him. Everyone except for Yakov. He understood perfectly why she had chosen that name, and he had condoned it:

Yudah: the praised one.

"It's time we face our fears," Kephas said a few nights later as the members of the community sat around a bonfire, singing songs from home. "We came this far, and for what? To sit here and lament our destiny, hidden away in the hills of Judea?"

Yakov shivered. He didn't like where the conversation was going.

"God is still our God. The temple belongs to us Jews," Kephas continued. "Even the rabbi said so: if we don't visit the temple, we can no longer call ourselves Jews."

"We can't go back!" Yakov said, surprised at the strength of his voice. Then he added: "The priests will recognize us. Come after us. Maybe even kill us!"

"Kephas is right," Mariamne said. "The time has come to step out of the shadows. We mustn't waste our lives in hiding any longer."

Yakov watched them incredulously. Were they out of their minds? This was not what they had agreed upon when they returned to Judea.

Kephas studied Yakov's face. "You want to be a leader and you're afraid to visit God's abode?"

"I-I'm not afraid," Yakov said, but his breaking voice betrayed him. He was shaking with fear. He didn't want to go back. Ever.

"Then show us you're not the weakling you appear to be." Kephas patted Yakov's shoulder. "Because I'm going back to the temple tomorrow. Who's coming with me?"

Yakov didn't want to go. He had sworn never to set foot in the temple again. But if everyone else was going, he had no choice.

In the late afternoon of the next day, Kephas, Mariamne, Yakov, and all the other members of their community made their way to the temple. Nervously, they pulled their headscarves down to shield their faces before they climbed the temple stairs, passed the soldiers who kept guard, and entered the Court of the Gentiles. After they made sure no one was paying them any attention, they congregated in the shade of a colonnade on the far eastern side of the temple called Solomon's Portico. Behind the white pillars and under the cover of the roof, they found protection from the weather and from the field of vision of any temple priests and the Roman soldiers stationed at the Antonia Fortress.

"Come closer, kind men. Let us help you leave your misguided path," Kephas urged passersby.

"Shh!" Yakov hissed. His heart beat so wildly, he could barely breathe. "They'll hear you."

Kephas looked at him. "And if they do?"

"I'm serious," Yakov said. "You'll place us all in danger."

The others watched him, their faces stricken with fear.

"This time we'll be quiet," Kephas agreed reluctantly. "But only this time."

Yakov's gaze traveled around the courtyard. He scanned the faces for any reactions, anyone who might recognize them as followers of Yeshua the Nazarene, but no one even looked their way. Exactly as Mariamne had predicted, in Jerusalem they were just one group of many. No one remembered them.

Every day, Mariamne tried to persuade Yakov to speak before the other disciples. And although the progress seemed slow and arduous, when he did speak, the words flowed more easily and more clearly.

"Yeshua's spirit dwells within you," Mariamne insisted. "Why don't you speak to him if you're in doubt. Because Kephas is right, we have to keep announcing the Good News to all who have ears—carry his message across the world. That's why we came here."

Yakov couldn't help but agree. Their movement had become stagnant and tired, like the old skin a snake has left behind. They had given up their entire lives to hide in the safety of Jerusalem, but the daily prayers at the temple weren't enough to keep the energy of the movement alive.

"Perhaps we should travel again," Yakov suggested to Mariamne one day on their walk back from the temple. The others had rushed ahead, but he adapted to her pace as she carried baby Yudah Tzaer in a sling on her back. "We could walk in pairs to avoid suspicion, go out on the road like we used to, visit villages in Judea, places we never reached before. It will lift our spirits. Like the old days."

"I'm a mother now, Yakov. I can't slack my hand from my responsibilities. From my son."

Yakov hung his head. She was right. Mothers didn't venture onto the roads where bandits and rebels threatened from behind every cliff.

"But I'd like to go," he heard himself say. The thought, the words, had been waiting to escape for the longest time, but duty had kept him fettered.

"You're not Yeshua, you know."

Why would she say something like that? Not a single day passed that Yakov didn't try to live up to his brother's perfect image, be half the man that Yeshua had been.

But Mariamne's remark was a word of compassion, not disrespect. And she was right. Yeshua was the restless one, the one who ran away whenever he was unhappy or didn't get his way. Yakov always stayed.

"We need you here," she said. "Please be patient. The right time will come."

She kissed his cheek, and he shuddered, involuntarily, at the surge of heat that passed through his body from his face down his spine and awakened the dormant beast in his groin.

He turned away and sped up his steps before she detected his shameful reaction.

Jerusalem, Judea, AD 32

Mariamne squatted by the fire pit, where skewers of squash and onions roasted over restless flames. She stoked the coals, then turned the skewers sideways to ensure the vegetables cooked evenly, and she inhaled their sweet scent.

Beside her, Michal sat cross-legged, and cleaned out stones from the basket of wheat on her lap.

"The food is nearly done." Mariamne said to her sister-in-law. "I'll prepare the platter."

Michal gawped at her, as if nothing Mariamne ever did was good enough.

"They do look tasty, don't they?" Mariamne said, and she sent Michal love from her heart. "I know it's not always easy here. And God knows I would have arranged things differently, if only fate had allowed it. But we're women, you and I, we're destined to live in the shadows of men. We should work together. Help each other." She reached out and rocked the basket where her baby was napping.

Michal ignored her. Somehow, happiness had failed to burrow its claws into Michal. She wore that permanently dull expression of those who had lost everything. But what had Michal ever lost? Michal still had a husband and six healthy children. What oil of joy had ever spilled from her?

At least Mariamne had Yudah Tzaer now, her miracle child.

When Mariamne first moved into Yakov's house after Yeshua's passing, she had attempted to make friends with Michal. She went out of her way to clean and cook for the family, to wash and feed their mother-in-law, to do anything possible to ease Michal's burdens. Still, Michal always turned her back on Mariamne and said nothing. Not a word. As if Mariamne was to blame that Yakov had abandoned his wife and children all those years ago and followed Yeshua around the countryside.

At that very moment, Yakov entered the courtyard with his son Taddai and his three daughters. "Ah, squash!" His face broke into an irresistible grin. He kissed his wife on her forehead and winked at Mariamne before he took a seat on the dining mat and waited for the meal to be served.

Mariamne smiled at Michal, hoping they could share the joy, but Michal quickly covered her face with her scarf. She filled a basin with water, and together with her daughters, they washed the men's feet and hands.

There was nothing Mariamne could do. Instead, she arranged the food in tidy heaps on the clay platter: slices of roast squash and onions, a salad of beets and raisins, steamed bulgur, olive relish, and a basket of bread cakes.

She placed the platter in front of the men and then she settled next to Michal and the girls. The family enjoyed the meal in silence, grateful for all that God had given them.

Until Yakov handed Mariamne a piece of flatbread and their hands brushed. As if hit by a current, their eyes met. Mariamne's heart fluttered. But when she leaned forward to scoop up some lentils with her right hand, she found Michal's gaze boring into her.

What on earth was the matter now?

Michal shook the empty breadbasket in Mariamne's face.

More bread. Of course.

Mariamne got up and walked over to the oven. She swung her hips just to bother Michal. She knew she shouldn't, but she'd had enough of this jealousy. She had done nothing wrong.

When she handed Yakov the basket with bread, he didn't even look up.

Michal chuckled.

"God asks only one thing from us," Kephas announced to the men and women seated around him in the shade of Solomon's Portico a few days later, "and that's to love our neighbors as ourselves."

Mariamne fanned herself with the sleeve of her tunic, stirring up dust particles from the ground. The scorching summer heat burned through her headscarf and parched her throat, and she longed for the sermon to end.

"When the Holy Spirit guides us," Kephas said. He basked in the glow of the leadership role he still claimed as his, "we understand that separation is an illusion. We are all one and the same. Only when we stop valuing what makes us individual, can we discover we're not only *of* God, but *are* God."

Mariamne startled when Yakov squatted by her side to hand Michal a skin of water. The heat of his presence surged through the air, and Mariamne longed to share a word, a moment, with him. It had been days since they had spoken. She wasn't sure what Michal had told him, but whatever it was, it seemed designed to make Mariamne appear guilty.

Michal grabbed the pouch with both hands, raised it to her lips, and gulped the water down. Then she offered the skin to another woman, not to Mariamne, and shone with eager gratitude at her husband.

When the water skin finally reached Mariamne, only a few drops remained. Michal chuckled as Mariamne jiggled the skin to squeeze out the liquid that was no longer there.

Kephas cleared his throat. "The Good News Yeshua brought us is a message of joy. It's not a message about the Messiah, or someone who will sweep in and save us from our troubles."

"And from those foreign fools who think they rule us," Yakov added in a loud whisper, winking at the Roman soldiers stationed at the gates of the temple yard. The disciples around him laughed.

A shade of sadness passed over Kephas's face, and for a moment Mariamne felt for him. All Kephas wanted was to be respected and loved. But however wise his words, the other disciples always sought Yakov out for advice, exactly as Yeshua had foreseen.

"Don't waste your time searching for a savior," Kephas continued, "someone who will appear magically and carry your burden."

"Yes, that's rubbish, won't happen," Yakov muttered, and everyone laughed again. He hinted at three white-robed men who had approached to listen in. "Perhaps the Messiah is already here, one of these fine priests."

"Right," Kephas said, and he pretended to laugh along with the others, but his flushing cheeks didn't fool Mariamne. The man was fighting for survival in this community, swimming against the rising tide of Yakov, a man who had shrugged away from his given responsibilities but whose measured words always soothed the others like honey.

The temple priests moved on, satisfied that the group was not blaspheming against God or the high priest.

"We need to find the savior *inside* us." Kephas patted his chest. "And until the day we discover this limitless force within, we'll be ruled by a fear that can grow dense like fog and make us all blind. It can convince us beauty and influential positions and wealth are important. And that we all need them——"

"W-we all *want* them, you mean to say?" Yakov interrupted. "B-but instead, we've all chosen to live a simple life. Why?"

"Because this fear," Kephas said, and he nodded at Michal, "is nothing but an illusion. A replacement for truth. Because truth is God, and God can never change. God is always love."

Michal beamed. She and Kephas had always had a special bond.

"B-blessed are those of you who... who remain faithful during trials," Yakov said after Kephas had finished his sermon. Although Kephas remained the principal speaker, the other disciples always asked Yakov to stand up before them and share a few words before they returned to the compound. It was one thing to joke and share witty comments, but an entirely different matter to stand up before an audience to speak words of wisdom.

Although his heart thundered in his chest and cold sweat formed on his brow, Yakov gathered all his courage and spoke. "B-because those who pass the t-trial, they w-will receive..." He closed his eyes. *Guide me*, he pleaded, *help me*. When he opened his eyes, he spoke quickly before his doubts caught up with his voice. "They will receive the life God has promised us. A-and if we are tempted by trials, despite our best efforts to remain p-pure, we must not blame it on God. Because God isn't the one who tempts us."

Later that afternoon, on their walk back to the compound, he didn't wait for Mariamne, like he hadn't waited for her ever since Michal caught him smiling at her and raised hell. He was a married man. He had to do what was right for his family, for the sanctity of his marriage. Tomorrow he would ask Mariamne to leave his house, build a hut for herself at the other end of the compound, and she would no longer bring discord into his family.

He had to prove to Michal where his loyalty lay. They had once accepted Mariamne into their family because of what she had lost. And because she was expecting Yeshua's child. But now that the child had been born, and they all lived in the same tightly knit, isolated community, there was no need for them to share their living quarters.

"Father, what's the matter?" Taddai had caught up with him on the peak of the hill and used the strength of his adolescent body to yank his father's elbow and hold him back. "What's gotten into you?"

"What?"

"Don't do this. You'll regret it."

"Your words make no sense."

"Father, don't feign ignorance. Why are you letting Mariamne walk alone? Why are you so rigid all of a sudden?"

Yakov shook him off. "*I'm* rigid?"

"Abba, what did she do?" Taddai forced him to sit on a patch of grass under a blossoming almond tree. "Tell me what she did. Did she try to seduce you?"

"Me?" Yakov let out a laugh. "You must be blind. She'd never try to seduce me."

"What, then?" Taddai said.

Yakov sighed. Taddai was still too young to understand matters of the heart. A good wife would set him straight, but until then... "Don't be foolish."

Yakov squatted down to untie and retie the laces of his sandals, stringing them tighter around his calves. He shouldn't have a conversation like this with his son. What would Taddai know about women and their competitive jealousy?

"Abba, even if Mother minds all the time you spend with Mariamne, why does it cause you such bother? The two of you are allies. Friends."

Yakov stood and looked into the distance, across the hills. "Your mother will have supper ready—it's time we go home."

"She can't help that she's a beautiful young widow. Why does she cause such a storm in your belly?" Taddai elbowed his father and laughed, as if he understood anything at all about how the world worked and what was right and wrong.

Yakov started walking along the slope, but Taddai caught up with him. "If she hasn't tried to seduce you, she has done nothing wrong. Her hands are clean. Don't abandon her."

"Your mother has lifted her heel against her."

Taddai picked up a stone, aimed, and threw it as far as he could. It bounced twice before it hit the trunk of a tree. "How can you be surprised that Mother wants her out? You think she enjoys living with another woman, one who is more attractive than she ever was?"

Yakov stopped and stared at his son, surprised.

"Every man she passes turns and looks at her," Taddai said. "That's why Kephas wanted to ban her from joining us, you know."

"No one is looking at her."

"I am."

Yakov frowned. His son had known his aunt Mariamne all his life. How could an adolescent look at an older woman and feel—lust?

"Just don't let Mother's jealousy destroy the bond you have with Mariamne."

The boy was right. It might not please Michal, but so be it. Yeshua's son had the right to grow up under the same roof as his uncle, his only father figure.

Yakov let out a sigh, as if a heavy burden had dropped from his heart.

"It's her or me. You hear?" Michal's screechy voice made the walls of their house tremble. She tore at his mantle, her eyes swollen with tears. "We don't need a dirty harlot among us, do we now? She already seduced Yeshua... Who's next? Is it you? Or Taddai? Will you let a harlot seduce your own son?"

Yakov's face burned with frustration. "Leave Taddai out of this."

"You're nothing but a coward, Yakov. That's what you are. She has broken your teeth."

"Hold your tongue, woman!" He lifted his hand to slap her, but drew it back. This was not the kind of man he was.

"Weakling," Michal hissed between sobs.

Yakov left her whining in their alcove and rushed out the door.

Surely God had made a mistake when he created Eve from Adam's rib. Men would have been much happier without women.

Jerusalem, Judea, AD 33

In the year that passed, Mariamne found that no matter how much effort she put into making friends with Michal, her sister-in-law grew increasingly cold toward her. She never missed an opportunity to fling a sarcastic comment at Mariamne, as if putting her down raised her own value. And although they had never been close, Michal's frigidity made Mariamne's life harder, lonelier, especially now that Yakov had distanced himself from her to please his wife. She missed Yakov's companionship on their daily walks to and from the temple.

Instead of joining the others for the daily temple sermon, Mariamne filled her days with caring for Yeshua's ailing mother and spending time alone with baby Yudah Tzaer in the hills, meditating. She taught her son how to sit still and focus on his breath, how to visualize a bright golden light around him, and how to chant the sacred word *Om* and recite the Gayatri mantra she had learned from Yeshua. And even before baby Yudah Tzaer could speak, he would lay his hands on anyone who fell ill to ease their pain. Like his father, grandmother, and great-grandmother, he was a natural healer.

Whenever Mariamne joined the others at supper, she sat as far away from Yakov as possible, and spoke only to the women, careful not to stir any trouble. Kephas, on the other hand, took advantage of the situation and forged a new companionship with Yakov. They were a solid pair now, Kephas and Yakov, leaders of the community, like oxen yoked together, pulling the plow through clay-filled soil, preparing the fields and planting seedlings of faith. Mariamne could only sit back and watch as she was replaced and pray that one day Yakov would speak to her again.

Jerusalem, Judea, AD 36

Years came and left without change and eventually, when the pain of rejection in Mariamne's heart finally eased, she rejoined the others in their daily journeys to the temple. One day, at the end of the summer, Mariamne found herself listening to Kephas's monotonous voice, imagining that Yakov was speaking to the crowd before him. She longed for his wise words, to hear the visions and parables Yeshua had once shared. But despite all her efforts, Yakov still resisted his rightful position. And these days, she no longer held any sway over him, although she never doubted that he cared for her, deep inside. Their love for Yeshua, his brother and her husband, would always unite them. And the faith Yeshua had placed in each of them. Nothing and no one could break that cord.

Mariamne opened her crown chakra and connected with God and Yeshua and every person around her.

"Those who focused on the physical world couldn't perceive the light Yeshua emitted," Kephas said. He patted the head of a toddler by his side. "But we did. We heard God's words spoken through his mouth."

Startled by a shadow that fell on her face, Mariamne jolted back to the present. When she looked up, she saw a temple priest standing above her. He had weaseled into the crowd and snaked his way between the women. She smiled up at him, hoping to disarm him with friendliness, but when she recognized him, she gasped. Six long years had passed since she'd last laid her eyes on him, but her heart held no doubt that the man who stood at her side and leaned in to hear better, was the same priest who had reported Yeshua as a troublemaker to Caiaphas only days before his crucifixion.

The skin on Mariamne's arms prickled with fear. Her chest cramped. She wanted to get up and warn Kephas, but how could she stop him without drawing attention to herself? She looked around. Where was Yakov? Now was the time for him to take over, to change the subject as he always did when Kephas's message became too bold.

When she found Yakov among the men, she closed her eyes and sent a warning to his mind. *Say something, Yakov. Pause him. We're in danger.*

Having noticed the priest, Levi cleared his throat. Shimon coughed. Bar-Tôlmay rose halfway, as if ready to bolt up to hush their teacher, but before he could move, his brethren pulled him back to restrain him. They had all prepared for this; they understood how to avoid arousing suspicion.

Kephas continued, unperturbed. "Yeshua taught us how to hear God and understand him better than any priest. He showed us how to draw strength from his spirit and—"

"God's sweetness," Yakov said, taking the word out of Kephas's mouth. He patted his friend's shoulder with an innocent grin on his face. "Well, that's what they say, anyway. What do we know?"

Mariamne exhaled with relief. It had worked! With a tilt of her head, she raised her chin toward the priest beside her.

"My friends," Yakov continued, as he guided Kephas gently to the side. "The heat of the day has beaten the strength out of me. What do you say? Let's return home and—we'll meet here again tomorrow?"

As the crowd scattered, the priest continued to the next group of devotees sitting around another preacher. They weren't targeted this time.

Not today.

On her way back home, Mariamne dragged little Yudah Tzaer firmly by the hand up the steep Mount of Olives. If she didn't pull him along, her five-year-old would stop and smell every flower and inspect any ants, butterflies, and bumblebees they passed. At that pace, they wouldn't get home until long after sunset.

Mariamne pointed to a mother swallow that was nudging her babies out of the nest for their first flight, and Yudah Tzaer's big brown eyes lit up. She tousled his sandy-brown hair. Oh, how she loved the little boy. More than she had ever imagined possible.

"Hold on, wait for me!" someone called.

Mariamne's heart skipped a beat. *Yakov?* She turned around and struggled not to laugh with glee when she saw her friend rush up the hill toward her. Panting, Yakov pressed his palm to his chest while he caught his breath.

Mariamne laughed. He was speaking to her again. At last!

"Go on, run to the other boys," she said to Yudah Tzaer.

The boy didn't hesitate for a moment. He sprinted away, taking immediate advantage of this unexpected freedom.

Yakov invited Mariamne to sit beside him in the shade of a twisted olive tree and offered her his skin of water. She paused before she took a seat and tried not to appear too eager. It had been years since they had spent time together. Time alone.

"What a frosty day—can you believe it?" Yakov said playfully as he wiped sweat off his forehead with the back of his hand.

Mariamne chuckled. "Freezing."

"I can't remember it being this scorching hot before. Ever."

She couldn't either. But there were more important matters to discuss now than the weather.

"We can't pretend there's no threat," she said, hoping he would listen. "This new high priest, Yonatan-something, he's relentless."

"Yonatan bar Ananus," Yakov replied, deep in thought. "But he'll be replaced before you know it."

"Don't count on it."

"Kephas says he won't last long. His younger brother's more likely to take over."

"The man is a fool with uncircumcised ears."

Yakov laughed out loud.

Mariamne lowered her head. She should know better than to judge others. Be more compassionate.

When Yakov placed his hand on her shoulder, she leaned her cheek against it and found comfort in its familiar roughness. Her entire being filled with peace. She had missed him so.

"You should teach again, Mariamne," he said, and gently withdrew his hand. "I heard you speak to the women a few nights ago, back at the compound. You bear far too much knowledge to bury your wisdom under the rocks. They need you, like you've always said. And we do, too, Kephas and I."

"Ha. Kephas needs no one but himself." She stood and brushed the soil from her tunic. Her heart raced in her chest. Yakov's touch had awakened something within her, a feeling of... desire? But how could she possibly harbor such feelings? He was a married man, her brother-in-law. Yakov was her friend, nothing more.

"I've got to go," she said, and started the long trek back to their house. She stayed a few steps ahead of Yakov, trying to clear her head.

Teaching, that's what she should focus on. That's all she wanted. She would be silly to dream of love at her age.

Her days of amorous adventures were long over.

CHAPTER 10

Jerusalem, Judea, AD 39

Light snow dusted the temple courtyard where the disciples had gathered for the afternoon sermon under the cover of Solomon's Portico. The snowflakes danced in the air before they settled like downy feathers on the whitened ground. Despite the chill, Yakov nudged Kephas to move a bit to the side, but Kephas planted himself firmly at his side, unwilling to move an inch. Yakov scrunched his nose. The man smelled like he hadn't washed for days.

"When you pray," Kephas said, as he pulled his mantle closer around him, "you must have no doubts that God hears your prayers."

Eight years of practice had made Kephas's words flow more smoothly, more confidently. He spoke with the certainty of a man who had suffered no misgivings in his entire life.

"Indeed, because God hears your prayers!" Yakov added.

"If you waver," Kephas continued, "you'll be like a wave at sea, blown hither and thither by the wind. If you are unwilling to believe, you won't receive an answer."

Andreas nodded, forever supportive of his brother.

On the other side of the seated group, Mariamne huddled among the women. She kept watch to warn of any priests or other eavesdroppers. Ever since the high priest Caiaphas had passed away three years ago, the city had erupted in anti-Roman attacks and turmoil. As Kephas had predicted, Theophilus soon replaced his brother Yonatan as the high priest, and now he seemed to balance on a tightrope of pleasing Emperor Tiberius while keeping his Jewish underlings under control. Yakov flinched. A few days ago, Theophilus had even allowed some visiting gentiles entry into the most holy sections of the temple. An unforgivable act! That kind of contamination of this sacred space could only end in God's punishment, like so many times before. When were the Jews finally going to learn to avoid provoking God's wrath?

As Kephas was speaking about how they all were powerful kernels of God, Yakov noticed that Mariamne had shadowed her eyes with one hand and was gazing up at the fringe of golden triangles that crowned the Holy of Holies structure in the center of the temple yard. It was their agreed-upon warning signal that an undesirable person may have infiltrated their group. When she was certain she had Yakov's full attention, she tilted her head toward a man dressed like a Galilean pilgrim who stood leaning against the far wall. Although he appeared innocent enough, his stare gave him away. His gaze was too focused on the Holy of Holies, while his ear strained toward Yakov and Kephas. A temple informant!

Yakov nudged Kephas and cleared his throat. "B-be quick to listen, but slow to react," he said to change the subject, like they had practiced. "If someone b-bothers you…"

"… be slow to anger and pause before you speak," Kephas picked up the thread. "Remove the foreskins of your hearts. Accept all loving thoughts God plants within you, and you will find peace."

Nonthreatening words. Nothing that went against the rules of the temple or that anyone could possibly interpret as anti-Roman, anti-establishment rebellion. And it worked. The informant listened for a few moments before he shuffled away to the next group, leaving a trace of footsteps behind him in the desolate, snow-covered courtyard.

Soon after the informant had left, another stranger approached. Dressed like a Jew with fringes on his headscarf, but of short stature and with unmistakably Roman features, he greeted the disciples amicably before he settled down among them as if he belonged. Yakov raised one eyebrow at Mariamne. But she shook her head.

Not an informant, then?

The stranger clasped his hands in prayer and beamed at Yakov, exposing a perfect row of white teeth behind a neatly trimmed beard. Yakov smiled back hesitantly. The man looked familiar. Yakov could have sworn he had seen him before somewhere. But where?

"May peace from peace be with you," Kephas said to end the day's meditation. "Love from love, and grace be with you in your holy life. Amen."

Moments later, as Yakov, Kephas, and Mariamne descended the stairs from the temple, the familiar stranger approached them, joined by a tall nobleman in a thick black woolen coat.

"Saul, you came!" Kephas exclaimed as he touched the stranger's shoulder in salutation. "Yakov, brother, this is Saul from Tarsus. He's a great admirer of Yeshua's."

Who is this man? And how come Kephas knows him?

"Peace unto you, brother!" Saul saluted Yakov, his head at a slight angle, making his Roman nose seem even straighter in the long shadow of the afternoon sun. His clothes carried a sweet, citrusy scent of frankincense, a resin sold by Arabian merchants.

"And unto you, peace," Yakov responded pensively. This man was no Jew—couldn't be, not with those shoulders as broad as an oxen's. "You seem familiar. Have we—?"

Saul leaned back on his heels, his arms boldly akimbo, still musing. "I have frequented the temple on many occasions over the years. But I'm afraid we have not made our acquaintance before this eve."

Yakov frowned. "I see, I see. Well…" He struggled to find the right words.

"Tarsus, you say?" Mariamne asked, as she elbowed her way in between the men and used her feminine charm to fish for information.

"Tarsus. Yes, that is correct."

"How lovely. Near Damascus, isn't it?"

"Eh, no, it's the capital of Cilicia."

"I see. Many Jews there?"

With each question, Saul's face tensed into a deeper shade. He turned to Kephas. "Who is this woman?"

"My brother's widow. Yeshua's wife," Yakov said. "We call her the Magdalen, our tower of wisdom." He steered Mariamne in front of him to include her in their circle.

He turned to Saul. "You were saying, there are many Jews in Cilicia?"

Saul straightened his posture and tilted his head. He drummed his fingers on his waist. "Yes, yes. Many Jews. In fact, I'm a Pharisee from the womb."

"A Pharisee? How interesting," Mariamne said, undeterred by Saul's earlier outburst.

"Indeed. Circumcised on the eighth day."

Mariamne snorted in apparent disbelief.

She's right: if it were true, he wouldn't have needed to say it.

The tall nobleman had forced his way between them. "My friend is good man," he said in a thick foreign accent. "Maker of tents. Wealthy man."

Saul patted his shoulder. "May I introduce my associate Barnabas? We travel together."

Barnabas wiped his nose with a delicately embroidered handkerchief he pulled from his pocket, and he grinned eagerly, like a child begging for a piece of honey cake. "My friend, he wants to tell you a story. Very important, this."

"Is it?" Yakov said. "Then you'd better join us at my house this evening."

While Yakov gave Barnabas directions to their compound, Saul's attention had already shifted back to Kephas. With a quick nod goodbye, the two men walked away, heads together in deep discussion.

A cramp formed in the pit of Yakov's stomach. There was something disturbing about the Tarsian, but he couldn't quite determine what.

CHAPTER 11

That evening, Mariamne played the role of a submissive woman. She washed Saul's and Barnabas's feet and refilled the men's cups of pomegranate juice. Then she squatted by Mother Maryam's side and fed the feeble woman bread soaked in milk, at a sufficient distance to avoid attention but close enough to eavesdrop on the conversation.

"This way of yours," Saul said, as he made himself comfortable in a cross-legged posture by the fire pit, "the message you convey at the temple, I must confess I find it engaging. Exhilarating, even. In all my years of studies of the Torah, I have discerned nothing remotely similar to your... what would you call your faith?"

"Jews. We are Jews," Yakov said. He bit into a crunchy flatbread smeared with honey.

Mariamne watched the crumbs tumble down his chin and get caught in his beard.

Behind him, Michal lounged against the wall to absorb Saul's every word with wide-eyed fascination.

"Let me see if I understand: your folk are neither Pharisees nor Sadducees." Saul rubbed his palms together in deep thought. "If so, would you claim association with the Essenes or Nazirites?"

"No, not really," Yakov said. "We—"

"Our teacher, Yeshua," Kephas interrupted, "was a Nazarene. Well, in a way. He adopted some Nazirite rules but also made a few changes. People often called him the Nazarene, like a branch from King David's bloodline."

"He was not... We are not Nazarenes," Yakov insisted.

"Essenes, then?" Saul asked, eyebrows raised.

"No."

Saul leaned forward, as if to reveal a secret. "I see. But if you wish to spread your message far and wide, you must have a name for your mission."

Mariamne drew back into the shadows, trying to render herself invisible. She studied Saul's face and body language. He was an attractive man with his large brown eyes and long eyelashes, neatly trimmed beard, and high cheekbones. His mantle looked new, completely unpatched. And she had never seen such clean nails on any man. Besides, he didn't slouch for a moment, even as Yakov and Kephas leaned down on their elbows, glutted after finishing the last morsels of the stew. She had no reason to doubt he was educated, but could he be a Pharisee with a face like a sculpture of Caesar Augusts, and a nose as straight as a dagger? It was possible, of course. His pronunciation of Aramaic was almost flawless. And a man who spoke Greek, Aramaic, *and* Hebrew... Only Pharisees and Sadducees sent their sons to study the Torah.

"Will you tell me more about him, about Yeshua?" Saul leaned back and propped himself up on his elbow, adopting the posture of the other men.

Mariamne smirked. He was doing it on purpose, to lower their defense barriers. To win their trust.

Yakov sat up and scratched his chin as if to gather his thoughts. He grabbed a stick and pushed the coals around the pit, stirring the burning embers up in flight toward the round opening in the straw-covered ceiling.

"My brother... A funny man, but he always knew he wanted to be a priest. When we were children, I would always make fun of him. We were carpenters!" Yakov chuckled. "I told him that no synagogue in the world would allow a lowly carpenter to become a priest, not even a rabbi. But Yeshua, he was stubborn. He spent all his free time with our village rabbi, pestering him with a thousand impossible questions..."

Mariamne looked up. Had she detected a smidge of envy in Yakov's voice?

"I used to tease him, drive him mad. And he was such an easy target. I told all the grown-ups that Yeshua wanted to be a priest, and then I laughed at their shocked expressions. Imagine that: a carpenter's son with such high aspirations."

Yakov raised his palms. "Then again, he was kind and an unselfish man, Yeshua was. He loved one and all. He treated his foes with the same respect as his closest friends and family."

"And this was in Judea?"

"No, no, we were raised in Galilee."

Yudah Tzaer crawled up into Yakov's lap.

"The very seed of Yeshua," Yakov said, and he gently pushed the boy down from his lap to sit beside him.

Mariamne sighed. Would Yudah Tzaer never learn? An eight-year-old boy should not behave like a toddler. But the boy had grown up an affectionate child. He always sought out human touch, especially from his uncle, who was already teaching him how to file soft woods and make simple furniture. But like his father, Yudah Tzaer was terrible at woodwork.

Saul raised his eyebrows as if the mellow child didn't fit into his image of Yeshua.

"We grew up in a lakeside village, Capernaum," Yakov continued, ignorant of the confused look on his guest's face. "That's also where we met Kephas and the other fishermen. In Galilee."

"Where *I* met Yeshua," Kephas said, as if eager to emphasize the importance of his relationship with their teacher. "He arrived at the shore one day and told us all we had to do was believe in a bigger catch. Nothing else. And, lo-and-behold, that day our nets overflowed with fish. We even had to throw some back in the lake because we didn't have enough space in the boat." He laughed. "Like wizardry!"

Saul fingered his beard. "Fisherman? I see. Yeshua was a fisher of men…"

"No," Yakov interrupted, confused. "A carpenter, not a fisherman."

Mariamne's gaze met Yakov's across the room. When she found Saul staring at her, she lowered her head. But she sharpened her ears to make sure she didn't miss a word.

"A craftsman?" Saul sounded as if he were interrogating them.

"N-not... no. Or-or perhaps yes." Yakov's voice sounded unsure now. "As a child, yes, he was a carpenter. B-but then, as an adult..." Yakov snickered to himself. "He was useless with a chisel."

Mother Maryam moaned. For a moment, everyone's attention veered toward her before returning to Yakov.

"He was more of a one-thumb-blue-the-other-bleeding sort of craftsman," Yakov said. "I made him sweep the floor. He was rather handy with the broom."

"And when did he become a preacher?" Saul's voice.

"When he returned from Parthia. Or was it the Kushan Empire? I can't exactly recall where, but that's when." More insecure laughter.

Why was Yakov being so truthful? This Saul could be an infiltrator sent by the temple priests.

"Hmm," Saul said. "Are you certain it wasn't the Roman Empire? Or Arabia? Perhaps Syria?"

Long pause. Mariamne lifted her head and peeked over her knees. Yakov fiddled with the laces of his sandals. Her heart thumped against her chest. One evening with this man, and Yakov had returned to the same insecure man he had been when they first arrived in Judea.

"He was a wonderful teacher," Kephas interjected. "Everything he said came from the heart. From God. A powerful man."

Saul assented, not taking his eyes off Yakov. "A carpenter. Well, well. What do you know—an incompetent carpenter evolves into a mighty hand: a preacher. What a remarkable story. Almost inconceivable."

The uncomfortable silence that followed could have made a mule blush.

Kephas rubbed the back of his neck. His eyes shifted from one man to the other, as if desperate to find something to say.

"Not the easiest child, my brother," Yakov said, his gaze focused on the fire. "But remarkable, yes, that he was."

"God's son." Barnabas's eyes brimmed with awe.

Yakov turned to look at Barnabas, as if he had forgotten he was there. Then he brushed the soot from his fingers and stood from his mat. "It's late, fellows. Yet another day tomorrow."

A current of relief shot up Mariamne's core. Yakov was of no small power, but they had to talk about everything that Saul had said and digest the conversation before they continued.

"Bless the night," Yakov said and patted Saul's shoulder. "Thank you for bringing the cup of gladness to our home. You will join us again tomorrow at the temple?"

As soon as Kephas, Saul, and Barnabas had withdrawn, Mariamne extinguished the last cinders and returned to her room for the night.

She lay awake, listening to the wind flapping the carpet that covered the entrance of their house, and she thought about tonight's discussion. Yeshua had never spoken much about his childhood or why he had left home. Even though she had enjoyed Yakov's story, she had noticed all the words left unsaid. The pain that had eclipsed Yakov's voice. Where did it stem from? What had Yeshua done?

"I had a vision," Saul said to Yakov when he entered the compound with Barnabas a few nights later. "I must confess, that is the genuine reason for my visit." He brushed fresh raindrops off his mantle as he stepped into Yakov's house. "I met him."

"Who?" Yakov asked. He indicated for Saul and Barnabas to take a seat next to Kephas and him by the fire pit.

"Yeshua."

"No. Wait," Yakov said, confused. "Haven't we told you, Yeshua died?"

"He told me to carry his words to your heart." Saul's voice was soft. Kind, even. "Try as I might, I could not shut my ears from this message."

Yakov's heart raced like a wild horse. Pearls of sweat formed on his forehead. He didn't want to hear this. He couldn't stay in the presence of this man. But there was nowhere to run, no way to escape this encounter.

Michal knelt by his side and placed a comforting hand on her husband's shoulder. "Accept the fruit of his mouth."

Yakov glanced at his wife. As much as he hated to admit it, she was right. He owed it to Yeshua to hear this man out. He took a deep breath to still his heart. "Perhaps I can spare a moment, but don't make it too long."

"I was on my way to Damascus," Saul said. His gaze rested on Yakov to make sure he had his full attention. "Many years ago. Yes, I should have come sooner. I am quite aware of the damage my absence may have caused. But please trust my confession: my heart was fearful. You see, many years prior, I had accepted a position of great consequence. In fact, I have come to understand that the period of my employment may have coincided with the time when your teacher was arrested."

"My *brother*. Yeshua was my older brother." Yakov surprised himself. He wasn't sure why he felt the need to emphasize his close relationship with a man who didn't differentiate between family and others. But something about Saul didn't add up. It wasn't only his Roman features and his reluctance to speak about his past. Every word he spoke rang false, like a shofar blown by an apprentice.

"Oh yes. At the time I was contracted by the temple, by Caiaphas." Saul raised his gaze toward the round opening in the ceiling where drops of light rain entered and glistened for a moment in the light before they fell smattering into the flames and evaporated.

The orange gleam from the fire illuminated the contours of Saul's face, and as if hit by lightning, Yakov remembered where he had seen Saul before. The man seated by his hearth, in his own home, had been present at Yeshua's crucifixion. He had stood among the temple guardsmen. Yakov jerked his head, trying to erase the vision. But how could he forget the look on Saul's face that day? That demeaning expression of pure revulsion. Of superiority. How could he forget how Saul had raised a sword to Yakov's neck and shoved him away?

Yakov couldn't breathe. Saul had been an accomplice to Yeshua's murder. Whether it was Pontius Pilatus, the high priest, or whoever was in charge, who had employed him, it didn't matter. The man who sat here in his own home, ate of *his* food, and drank from *his* cup, had been present at his brother's death. Saul had been employed to guard against any riots.

But it couldn't be. He must be mistaken. Neither Kephas nor Mariamne recognize him. And if it were true, how would Saul dare to show his face around here? Yakov rubbed the spot between his eyebrows to force the thoughts away.

"I was not stationed in Jerusalem, or even Judea," Saul continued. "My employment brought me much farther, out into the northern regions: Syria, Cappadocia, Asia. Believe me, my heart bleeds with shame at what I must confess. But I was once in charge of pursuing and arresting thugs and bandits, zealots and sicariis, and any false prophets who threatened the peaceful order of the Roman Empire."

"You were there," Yakov said.

"Where?" Saul looked lost.

"At my brother's execution."

Saul laughed. "Oh no, I never placed my feet at any crucifixion. I was purely a man of the written word, not of violence."

"Ha! Then how did you know they crucified him?"

Kephas looked at Yakov, shoulders raised, as if to say, *I had no idea.* This was madness. Yakov couldn't stand to hear another word. He had been right, then: this man was an interrogator, an infiltrator.

"Just leave!" Yakov pointed at the door. "Both of you."

"Your *brother*, Yakov. It was your brother who brought me here," Saul said softly.

Bile rose in Yakov's throat, and his knees buckled beneath him. "Go!" He wagged his finger at them.

Michal grabbed Yakov's finger and lowered his hand. "Let him speak, yakiri. He means well. Look at his fallen face."

"You must've confused him with someone else," Kephas said, incredulous at what was happening.

Reluctantly, Yakov sat down. *If we are all one, then so is this man,* he tried to tell himself, but at this moment, those words meant nothing. Still, he knew what he must do: first hear what Saul had to say, and then ask Yeshua to forgive him. And he would forgive him, too.

Unbeknownst to everyone else, Mariamne had tiptoed into the room and was squatting by the water vat. She gestured to Yakov with a slight wave of her hand to let Saul continue.

"As a Roman citizen, I had a duty to—"

"You told us you were a Jew!" Yakov almost dashed up again, but Kephas held him down.

"He *is* a Jew, Yakov. Let the man speak before you judge. You won't want to criticize his clean hands, believe me."

"Kephas is right," Saul continued. "I am a Jew, but also a citizen of the empire. As I mentioned, I'm a Pharisee from the womb, and as the beginning of my father's strength, I was educated in the Jewish law."

Yakov tried to listen without prejudice. Yeshua always said not to judge, no matter if the person worked as a tax collector, a harlot, or an enforcer of gentile law.

"My entire life transformed some years ago on the road to Damascus. Antipas, the tetrarch, had ordered my division to break up a faction of anti-Roman rebels who were plotting an uprising. My assignment, specifically, was to search for a group led by a man called the Nazarene who were poisoning the minds of peaceful Jews around the empire." Saul paused, and he lifted his chin slightly. "Obviously, I had no knowledge of Yeshua at the time, and didn't know he had been… you know, had passed away. As I approached Damascus, exhausted from walking for days, a blaze of lightning came upon me. Right through my cranium. The entire world flashed in a mist of the most heavenly light. I raised my eyes and heard a voice."

"The Yeshua voice," Barnabas added, and he nodded eagerly at Yakov.

"Yes, Yeshua's voice." Saul spread his arms wide to emphasize his amazement. "He spoke to me and said, 'Saul, Saul, why do you persecute me?' I fell onto my knees and gazed upon the divine being before me. Stunned, I inquired, 'Who are you?' because, honestly, I did not know. He said, 'I am Yeshua, the Nazarene. You were set apart for me, chosen before you were born. Rise onto your feet and proceed to the city and continue my work.' And that's what I did."

Saul closed his eyes and clutched his hands to his chest, smiling blissfully.

Was Saul telling the truth?

A muffled chuckle erupted from the corner where Mariamne was squatting, but Yakov's heart pounded too hard to pay her any mind. *Had Yeshua really appeared to him?*

"Then what?" Michal eyed Saul like a smitten adolescent.

Yakov looked from Mariamne to Michal to Saul. Would Yeshua appear to a stranger, when he hadn't even appeared to his own brother? And what now? Should he accept Saul into their midst and forgive him for whatever actions might be in his past?

"I remained paralyzed three days and three nights," Saul continued. "I could neither eat nor drink. Wasting away, truly, in a humble wayside inn. But the proprietor's wife watched over me and wouldn't allow me to perish."

A tear ran down Saul's cheek, and he wiped it away with a manicured finger.

Yakov scoffed. This man surely knew how to tug the heartstrings of an audience.

"One day, a visitor came by, one of Yeshua's disciples. He laid his healing hands upon me and brought me back to life. As soon as I recovered, I found my heart filled with love. From then on, I could no longer persecute any zealots, least of all Yeshua's disciples. All I wanted was to know him. And that is the reason I came this way."

Yakov thought of arguing against being called zealots, but there were more serious issues at hand. His lips creased with suspicion. "Who was it, then, the man who healed you there in Damascus? We haven't sent anyone that way."

"His name, I was told when I awakened, was Ananias. But I never met him again."

Yakov scratched his beard and tried to remember if he had ever met anyone with that name, but his mind came back blank. "You came straight here from Damascus?"

He caught the quick exchange of worry between Saul and Barnabas before Saul's gaze settled back on him.

"At the time, my life was complicated. As I have divulged, I am a Roman citizen. I had a duty, first and foremost, to report to my superiors and to resign from my commitments. As soon as they released me, I made my way around Damascus proclaiming Yeshua's gospel. I told one and all that he is the Son of God, our savior."

"*One* son of God," Yakov corrected him. "And what gospel can you possibly have been spreading? You knew nothing about Yeshua or his message."

"With Yeshua's help, I spoke with such clarity and conviction that the local rabbis considered me a threat. They expelled me from Damascus—they even sought to end my life!"

"You came straight to Jerusalem, then, to meet us?" Yakov asked. He grew increasingly confused as the story unfolded.

"I needed time. Alone. You must understand, I had to digest all I had experienced. I did not even contemplate to seek anyone's advice. Instead, I traveled to Arabia, where I stayed for many years and taught the nomads in the desert about Yeshua's gospel."

"Years?" Yakov couldn't believe Saul had waited so long to meet the family of the man he now viewed as his teacher. "But you knew *nothing*! We spent three years with Yeshua, learning all that he—"

"But I did! I know him in my heart. With all my soul. Believe me when I admit that the knowledge I've acquired directly from Yeshua is more profound than anything he may have taught you. He spoke to me in spirit, and he still does. I understand him."

Mariamne had burst into quiet giggles. But Michal watched their guest in silent awe.

The story was outrageous, shocking even. Even so, Yakov couldn't simply dismiss him. Hadn't Yeshua always claimed God spoke to him, ever since he was a child? And if that were the case, why had Yeshua never spoken to *him* in spirit?

"I've come to share his vision, help you spread his gospel to Jews and gentiles alike. With a unified voice, we can conquer the world."

"I beg your pardon," Yakov said, and he rose from his seat, frustrated. He looked down at Saul and shook his head. "You fainted from exhaustion. You saw a *vision*! And now you think you can come here and teach *us*?"

Saul shrugged. "I'm aware how painful truth can appear to the oblivious. Surely you must know you have failed in your endeavor. You aimed to replace your teacher Yeshua, is that correct? But look at you! You lack the wisdom, and even the courage, to make your message heard. If you were such a prominent leader as you claim to be, surely your following would have grown. Still, you preach only to your own friends and family, the same people Yeshua gathered around him years ago."

Yakov brushed the dust from his mantle, shaking with indignation. "We followed him for three years! Day in and day out, we listened to his speeches, learned his healing practices, gained insights into the inner dimensions of the Torah. What on earth could you ever share with us that we don't already know?"

Saul just raised his hands in surrender. He grinned up at Yakov, like a father would a fussing child.

He wouldn't listen.

CHAPTER 13

Early the next morning, as Mariamne went to collect water at the brook, she found Saul sitting on the stone wall by the compound gate, waiting for her. He followed her down to the stream.

"Why do I sense you do not trust me, Magdalen?" he asked, and took her hand.

His hand felt warm and moist in the frosty morning.

When she tried to yank her hand away, Saul pulled her closer. His hot, sweet breath met hers. But the overwhelming scent of frankincense forced her to turn her face away. He must have bathed in perfume.

"Yeshua trusted me," Saul said. "He sent me here, to you. And you would do well to obey your husband's will."

His touch, the closeness of his body, nauseated and thrilled her. Still, her acquired wisdom compelled her to view him with the eyes of God: as an equal. Besides, she didn't know what to make of Yakov's insistence that Saul had been present at the crucifixion. Surely Yakov's memory had played tricks on him.

"Why are you here?" She looked straight into his long-lashed, seductive eyes. "If you already know it all, why come to Jerusalem?"

"Yeshua demanded that I come," he said. "Yakov needs my help. And *you* need me."

Mariamne chuckled. *The nerve.*

"I observed you watching me last night," he said, and cocked his head, musing.

Yes, she had watched him. And yes, despite the outrageous story he had woven, Saul intrigued her. At the same time, she couldn't forget how he had spoken to Yakov, ridiculed him in front of the other disciples.

For a moment, Saul's grip relaxed, and she pulled her hand away. She had barely retracted one step before he was upon her again. He grasped both her hands and rubbed them warm between his. Then he brought her palms to his lips. Before she could protest, he pulled her close and locked her into his arms in a manner no man should hold any woman besides his wife.

"Yeshua insisted that I claim you as my bride." He said, his mouth so close to hers that his beard tickled her chin.

Mariamne let out a laugh. But it wasn't funny.

"You need a husband, and I need a woman by my side."

Mariamne pressed the clay jar between their bodies and pushed Saul away. "Michal's waiting for me," she said. "I must hurry back with the water."

She removed her sandals and stepped barefoot into the icy stream.

"I will marry you, Mariamne the Magdalen. I'd like you to be mine. I will love you and honor you."

His eyes burned across her body, scanning her breasts, her torso, her calves, as she lowered the jar into the water.

"I made a promise to Yeshua to stay his forever," she said, not looking up. "Besides, I've vowed to care for Mother Maryam."

She raised the jar onto her head, slipped her sandals onto her feet, and started walking back to the house, careful not to spill.

"Woman, the world is coming to an end—any day now," Saul said, keeping pace with her. "We all need to be saved before the last day arrives. And I am confident Yakov's wife is quite able to care for his mother on her own. But a widow like you, you need someone to take care of *you*. Let me be the man who saves you." He blocked her way, his eyes full of love. "Your Yeshua, he commanded me to wed you."

Would this man never stop? Mariamne turned to face him as calmly as she could. "Yeshua speaks to me, too. Never forget that."

The surprise on his face gave her all the confidence she needed. He would leave her alone now.

"Saul asked me to marry him," Mariamne told Yakov when he finally settled down for breakfast after his morning walk in the hills. She could hear her voice shiver, the tones of uncertainty, of confusion. But she had to let him know. "Of course I declined."

Michal rolled her eyes.

Yakov dropped his bread onto his lap and looked at her. "Maybe he means well. He sees you're lonely and wants to help. Kephas trusts him. And Barnabas couldn't admire him more."

"But you don't."

"I've been thinking," he said. "Maybe I've been wrong to judge him."

"It doesn't bother you, then? He thinks he knows Yeshua better than you."

Michal stood to clean up after their meal, hinting at Mariamne to follow her.

"In a moment, Michal," she said, not ready to give in.

Michal snorted. "In a moment," she mocked and made a grimace. "You'll want me to do everything in this house."

"Did you know he wasn't born a Pharisee as he claims?" Mariamne continued, ignoring Michal. "Phillipos says that Saul converted to Judaism."

Yakov gave her a blank look.

He didn't believe her.

"Maybe you *should* marry him," Michal said. "There's not a law in the entire world that says you must stay a widow for all time to come."

Mariamne stared at her. Then she stood and grabbed a broom to sweep the floor.

Yakov slouched down and rested on his elbows. He watched Mariamne with a concerned frown.

"Apparently, Saul was in love with a girl from a prominent Jewish family," Mariamne said. She swished the broom around the floor as if she could sweep away her worries. "He asked for her hand in marriage, but since he wasn't Jewish, her father refused. So Saul traveled to Jerusalem, studied at the temple with Caiaphas, and became a Pharisee."

"One is either born a Pharisee or not, as you well know," Yakov said in his sweetest, kindest voice. "Whoever told Phillipos that must have misunderstood."

The softness of his voice bothered her more than she would admit. "But remember," she said, as she rested her chin on top of the broomstick, "Saul was employed by Caiaphas. He had clout."

Michal nudged in between them and snatched the broom from Mariamne, shooing her away. "Caiaphas is dead."

What did Caiaphas's death have to do with anything?

"Caiaphas was not like that," Yakov muttered.

"Oh, leave it, Yakov," Mariamne said. "You know as well as I that Caiaphas could be bought."

"If that is true, then why isn't Saul married?"

Mariamne's heart jumped. At last he was listening to her. "Once Saul returned to this young lady's court a few moons later, she had married another man. A purebred Jew."

"It's just a rumor, then. You can't believe all that people say."

"Admit it: the story makes sense," Mariamne insisted. "How, otherwise, could someone be both a Roman citizen and a Jew? He had to have been a Roman first."

Yakov seemed to agree. But then he stood, brushed the bread crumbs off his mantle, and added, "That doesn't make him a wicked soul, if he went through all that trouble for love."

"That's what I said!" Michal leered at Mariamne. "You should marry him. Well, you can't stay here forever, if that's what you thought."

"Michal's right," Yakov said. He studied Mariamne's face. "You *could* marry him."

Mariamne's heart sank. He still wanted her gone?

*

That afternoon, Saul joined the disciples as they congregated in the temple courtyard for the pre-sermon meditation.

"I've been thinking about this proverb," Kephas said after they had all returned to their awareness. "'As you teach, so you shall learn.' When we teach others, God's voice is often speaking to *us*. Instead of offering advice to others, we are in fact offering advice to ourselves. Keep your ears open and listen to what comes out of your mouths. You could well be amazed."

"My brother Yeshua called upon all of us to be teachers," Yakov added.

Mariamne smiled. There it was again, the emphasis on the word *brother*. When would Saul finally understand he could never know Yeshua as well as his own family and his disciples did?

Saul used the pause to stand up and address the crowd. "Master Yakov, Kephas, I have noticed how the Holy Spirit speaks through you, like he speaks through me. But I fathom you cannot hear him as clearly as I can." Saul's eyes bore into the men and women seated around him, his arms stretched wide, as if to include every one of them. He motioned at Yakov. "And you may not comprehend yet that the Holy Spirit urges us all to prepare for the end of the world."

Saul had claimed his space. No one questioned him because he stood right next to Kephas and Yakov. "And when the last day arrives, Yeshua will return upon a silvery cloud to save us from eternal damnation."

"All Yeshua requests of us," Saul continued, "is that we accept him as our savior. Why don't we join forces, go out in all the towns and villages around the world, and save both Jews and gentiles in the name of our Lord, Yeshua?"

"Lord?" Yakov said, confused. "My good man, let's not blaspheme in the holy temple. The Lord our God, the Lord is One. No man shall ever be called Lord."

"Let him speak." Kephas placed his arm around Yakov's shoulder. "I want to hear what Saul has to say."

Yakov snorted. "What has come upon you, Kephas, that you turn your back on me and the brethren who have supported you all these years?"

Kephas pursed his lips as if he had no idea what Yakov was saying.

"And you!" Yakov wagged his finger at Saul. "What right do you have to weasel into our midst and pretend you know more than we do? You called me spineless!" Yakov's voice trembled with frustration. "You said I have no voice, no courage."

Saul raised his palms in defense. "Brother, you must be aware I meant no harm. But you speak in whispers, in stutters. You hide behind your fellow disciples. What am I supposed to say? Kephas here has been your true leader. He has kept your community united. And he, for one, understands that I know the real Yeshua."

"Kephas?" Taddai interrupted. "Yes, we have provided a platform for him to speak, and gracefully he accepted. But we all know uncle Yeshua chose my father, Yakov, to lead us."

"And how, if you may please explain to me, will your movement survive here hidden away in Judea?" Saul asked Yakov, ignoring Taddai's outburst. "You cower in a remote corner of the temple where no one will ever see or hear you. Do you not realize that all the young men who have grown up in this poor people's assembly will leave you for more inspiring teachers one day? And the older people? Well, they will perish with you. In the end, you will find you have accomplished nothing. When you die, all this will be lost."

"Death meant nothing to Yeshua," Yakov said. "He urged us to unite with God while we're still alive. That's the only point of access to God's Kingdom: you must deny the material world, see what's invisible, and unsee what's visible with our eyes. Only by appreciating that we are all part of the All-Knowing, of God, can we ever reach the kingdom. Because nothing real can be threatened, and nothing unreal exists—"

Mariamne observed the disputing men. The charismatic, broad-shouldered Saul, who spoke with such grace, and such conviction.

And Yakov, the lanky laborer, the best of men, whose charm sprang from the goodness of his heart and his kind eyes. Oh, how she wished Yakov would see Saul for what he was: a lesson in staying calm, in recognizing his own reflection in all men.

"I already told you," Saul interrupted. "The gospel I bring you is not of human origin. My words are not faint memories of words spoken by a brother or a friend. I did not receive my gospel from any man; I received it in a revelation from Yeshua himself: the Lord, our Savior."

The disciples stirred, unsure what to make of Saul.

Yakov smirked. "There it is again, that word: *Lord.*" He stepped away from Saul and walked through the crowd of disciples who had followed him for years, laying a hand on their shoulders as he passed.

Kephas's gaze shifted from Saul to Yakov, and back to Saul, perplexed.

"Let me make myself clear," Yakov said, his voice strengthened by his faith. "I wouldn't use that word here in the temple, lest you find yourself arrested for idolatry. Instead, let's remember what Yeshua taught us: maintain peacefulness within, endure pain, if necessary, and always forgive wickedness. Remain gracious and abundant in goodness toward every man, woman, and child."

Mariamne wanted to rise up and applaud.

"Yeshua," Yakov continued, "never claimed superiority—or greatness. Quite the contrary. He insisted he was equal to all, even those who despised him. Through acts of kindness and forgiveness, he showed us how to become perfect. Holy. Doers of his word, not simply listeners, nor speakers."

Mariamne beamed at him. When Yakov spoke like that, to a large crowd, he outshone any man in the entire world.

"Therefore," Yakov continued, as he stepped through the crowd, "we shall never doubt that *ours* is the true testimony. When you understand you're one with God, you'll know your soul does not need to be saved, and you have received the unfading gift of living in God's

Kingdom." He gazed up at a group of strangers who had approached to hear the debate, and waved them closer, his cheeks ablaze with energy. "Come, one and all, come closer. Many years ago, our community, the Jerusalem Assembly, chose me as their leader. And for too long, I resisted the responsibility. But that era has ended. Kephas, we are forever grateful for your service, for your friendship. From now on, however, I will speak in the temple every day, and when I tire, I will gladly accept your assistance."

Yakov squatted amid the seated disciples and rested his hands on the shoulders of the two men at his side. "Let us close our eyes, sit in stillness, and unite with God."

Mariamne squinted through half-closed eyelids and watched Saul whisper something in Kephas's ear before he stood and left the portico, followed by his men.

Finally, Yakov had stepped up and accepted his responsibility.

Her entire being filled with love.

The same night, as Yakov was having his evening meal with his family, Saul barged in, followed by Barnabas.

"Who do you think you are?" Saul raised his finger at Yakov. "Who gave you the authority to own Yeshua's words? Certainly not God. Or Yeshua."

Yakov spat the seeds of an apple into his hand and made space for Saul and Barnabas to sit by his side. "Come join us. Have a drink of hot milk, friends."

Barnabas sat, but Saul didn't move, hands firmly parked at his waist.

Yakov gestured to Michal to bring the men their cups.

"You're both wise men, this I cannot deny," Yakov continued. "But you mustn't forget that you never knew my brother. You never even met him. What you speak of, the words you claim Yeshua revealed to you, differ from everything Yeshua believed. Your faith will move you farther away from God, not toward him. Why don't you stay for a while and learn more about Yeshua and his message? As you suggested earlier, we can join forces."

Saul scratched his head in disbelief. "I do know Yeshua. Much better than you do. *So* much better."

"You don't, Saul," Mariamne said.

"Don't you start!" Saul pointed a threatening finger at her. He squatted next to Yakov and poked his chest. "And *you*! What you fail to understand is that the Holy Spirit appointed me and offered me superior knowledge to whatever it is you and your fellows believe. Yeshua is my Lord. I need no further certification for my mission."

Michal's cheeks flushed with excitement. She gleamed at Saul and nodded encouragingly at Yakov, as if prodding him to accept Saul's words.

"I respect that's what you believe." Yakov raised his cup to Saul in reverence. "But you seem to think this is some kind of competition. Listen, as much as you try, you can never reach enlightenment—salvation—until the day you accept that you are one with everyone around you. And with God. You can find salvation only in the present moment. No faith in a Lord Yeshua, or any other Lord whom you've met—no faith in a person—can save you."

"Not person, the God Son," Barnabas tried.

Yakov waved to his wife. "Yakiri, bring our friend a slice of honey cake."

Michal rushed on her pudgy legs to cut a generous slice of the fresh cake and held it between her hands as she offered it to Saul, head lowered in submission.

But Saul stood abruptly and pushed her out of the way, sending the cake flying to the floor.

Michal's eyes filled with tears.

"Barnabas!" Saul demanded, with his eyes still peeled at Yakov. "Go pack our mules. We are leaving this godforsaken place, these ignorant people."

As if they had expected the command, Saul's servants immediately appeared at the compound entrance with their mules.

"I arrived here in good faith," he said to Yakov. "I came bearing a gift of salvation, a favor to you and mankind. But if you want to stay blind, stay blind."

Saul raised his hand in a contemptuous wave before he slammed the gate behind him.

"I fear that's not the last we will see of him," Yakov said, deep in thought.

Jerusalem, Judea, AD 41

In the years that passed, Yakov strengthened his stature in the Jerusalem Assembly by taking a stand more frequently to deliver the daily temple sermons. On the quietest days between the Sabbaths and holy days, a few of the temple priests sometimes joined the disciples in prayer, and Yakov soon learned to speak with words that indulged them. Because by now, Solomon's Portico had become the disciples' sanctuary in an increasingly volatile world, where violence had surged since Emperor Caligula's murder and Claudius's subsequent rise to power.

The only cloud that remained in the clearest of skies was caused by a relentless rumor that echoed from many directions that a nobleman in Syrian Antioch was preaching about a magnificent savior called Lord Yeshua. Still, Mariamne and Yakov considered Saul harmless. He might have gained some fame, but he was still only one of hundreds of preachers spreading news about yet another savior. And the significant distance between Judea and Antioch meant that any stories Saul taught his gentile followers could not affect the message Yeshua's disciples taught. Besides, Yeshua was one of the most common names across the continent. They had found no solid proof that Saul was speaking about their own teacher.

But when a traveling merchant from Aegyptos brought word that Saul in fact preached in the name of Yeshua the Nazarene, Yakov had to wonder if he had underestimated Saul.

"I have this idea," Yakov said to Kephas one morning after many sleepless nights, when his friend entered the carpentry workshop. "I'd like to send a few men out in different directions to see how people receive our message these days."

"No harm in teaching the uninformed," Kephas said. He picked up a wooden chip and cleaned his fingernails with it. "Whom did you have in mind?"

"I was thinking... Barzebedee, Shimon, Taddai, and Tau'ma: I'd like them to travel through Samaria to the Decapolis. And you, why don't you visit Syria, perhaps Antioch?"

"Me?" Kephas gave Yakov a sour face. He folded his arms in front of his chest like a defiant child. "I have no wish to travel. I'm quite comfortable here in our compound. Tell me, what have I done to deserve this honor?"

"You're our *rock*," Yakov said without looking up. He continued to file on a window frame he was preparing for one of the temple priests. "Yeshua would have sent you. He trusted you."

"And you? Do you also trust me?"

Yakov sneezed. The air in his workshop was stuffy with sawdust, and it didn't help that Kephas had pulled the blanket shut in front of the entrance, hoping for a private chat. He studied the stubby man before him. Strands of gray now made his once-ginger hair look dull, but despite the wrinkles the years had painted on his face, Kephas embodied a youthful spirit.

"Of course I do. And Saul will welcome you—that's what's important. You were his confidant, his ally." Yakov wiped his nose. "Besides, I know you'll do the right thing."

He spoke the truth. Yakov trusted few people more than Kephas. They had spent half a lifetime together, preaching Yeshua's message—The Way, as they now called it. Kephas knew Yeshua's message by heart, and more importantly, he understood it. "You're perfect for this task, that's all there is to it. And you're a free man. You don't even have a set job at the compound."

"I keep bees."

"Yes, I know. But your wife can manage the beehives." Yakov placed his hands on Kephas's shoulders and looked into his eyes. "Be good, Kephas. You've got both the time and the wisdom. And Yeshua loved you."

Kephas wrung his hands. After a lengthy pause, he said, "You can trust me. I won't let you down. I will do what's needed, what's best for us all."

Yakov took a deep breath to quiet the storm of worry that was brewing in his heart.

The day before Kephas left, Yakov asked him to speak before the Assembly to reassure the other disciples that Kephas was the right man to infiltrate Saul's followers and gauge what level of success Saul had gained. Although Yakov would never admit it to the others, he still feared that Saul might pose a serious threat to them. And now he wanted to lay his worries to rest. As soon as Kephas returned and confirmed the rumors about Saul were false or exaggerated, he could go on with his life. But until then...

"If you always act from goodness," Kephas said to the crowd before him, "who could ever harm you?"

It was a rhetorical question. Nevertheless, several disciples responded. Kephas mused as he scratched his graying beard. "As long as you approach others from a perspective of love, nothing in the world can cause you pain."

Yakov relaxed when he saw how comfortable and inspiring Kephas still was in a teaching role. He had been preaching the Good News for a long time, ever since Yeshua sent their small group out to sow the seeds of knowledge among the poor in Galilee. There was no need to worry.

"Remember to love all men and women as your equals." Yakov put his arm around Kephas's shoulder. "Never respond to attacks. Acknowledge their suffering and bless them instead. Because only those who experience pain will seek to hurt others."

"That's what I'll tell Saul," Kephas said later at night as Michal and Yakov watched him pack the traveling sack he would carry on his long walk to Antioch. "I'll quote the scripture, 'To enjoy life, you mustn't speak evil or tell lies. Instead, strive for peace with all your heart.' If I say that, he'll listen. I know he will."

Yakov hoped he was right. But he couldn't help but agonize about all the tricks Saul must have amassed by now.

Mariamne was about to start the morning fire in the courtyard when she heard Andreas's and Kephas's hushed voices outside. She pressed her ear to the wall.

"Will you be well, brother?" Andreas asked.

Silence.

"Do you trust him?" Andreas again.

"Saul? Yes, I think so. I don't believe he means harm."

"You don't think he was there, then, at the crucifixion?"

"Of course not. I didn't see him there."

Long pause.

"Me neither." Andreas sounded unconvinced.

"All right, then."

"Be safe," Andreas said again. "Trust in the Holy Spirit. Listen to the voice inside, and you cannot fail."

"And you, brother. Watch out. Don't let that woman control Yakov. Beware of what she says or does."

"Michal?"

Kephas sighed. "Mariamne."

"Oh. Don't you worry about her. She's a nobody."

The brothers laughed.

"Be safe, then."

Mariamne heard the gate slam shut. Kephas was gone. She pressed her palms to her chest with relief. Although she wished him well, her life would be much easier now that she had Yakov's undivided attention.

CHAPTER 15

Jerusalem, Judea, AD 44

A few weeks after Kephas's departure, Tau'ma, Taddai, Shimon, and Barzebedee left for a journey around Samaria and the Decapolis to preach the Good News to their fellow Jews while delicately posing questions about Saul and Barnabas. Yakov had instructed them to return to the compound after three or four new moons, but three harvests later, there was still no news. Yakov tried his best not to worry; they were wise men, and more than capable of avoiding trouble. Besides, hadn't Yeshua once disappeared for eighteen long years, and returned unscathed?

Home at the compound, the previous summer had passed without a single drop of rain, and the plants in their fields had withered. While the disciples struggled to make their stores of food last longer, Yakov hadn't noticed the impending drought. He focused his entire attention on caring for his ailing mother, whose lungs had become infected with an unknown disease. Yakov and the other disciples stayed by her bedside day and night. They placed their hands on her head and abdomen to transmit healing energy into her body, and they fed her herbal potions. But nothing seemed to help.

One morning, Yakov woke to the sound of whimpers. Agonizing moans of pain. He darted up to sit at his mother's side. When he took her hand in his, she smiled. Then she squeezed his hand with the strength of a tiger and whispered, "Let it be, Yakov. Let it be."

Yakov's skin prickled as if an icy wind had swept through the room. They were the first words his mother had spoken in years, and the first time she had recognized him since their move to Jerusalem. "Let what be, Amma?" he asked, but her eyes had already closed and her mind had drifted back into the gloomy space it had occupied ever since Yeshua had passed away.

Yakov's eyes filled with tears. He brought her soft, wrinkled hand to his lips. She coughed and wheezed, as if struggling for air. He lifted her into his arms, rubbed her back, and rocked her like a child. He bathed her in healing energy and sang quietly to her.

Amma's head slumped back, and when Yakov lifted her to face him, her half-opened eyes stared into nothingness.

His mother's spirit had abandoned her body.

"I love you," he said, and he kissed her forehead. Then he leaned his ear to her mouth, aching to hear her admit her affection, as if now, when death had released her, she would utter the words she had never said before.

Yakov cradled her in his arms like a baby and wept. All the courage he had built up over the years, all his hopes of making things right, was gone. Oh, how he had yearned for her love. His tears spilled over his mother's face, and he wiped her wrinkled skin with his calloused fingers. He had spent his entire life trying to make her proud, well aware he had never managed to outshine his older brother. Yeshua, her oldest son, had broken all the rules and caused an irreparable scandal when he ran away to Mesopotamia and left his parents to explain to his devastated fiancée why he could no longer marry her. And yet, Yeshua had remained his mother's greatest love.

Yakov, on the other hand, had strived all his life to embody the perfect son. He had dedicated his youth to apprenticeship in his father's workshop and had shouldered the business after his father passed away. He had even married a girl from a decent family, even though Michal was nowhere near as wealthy as the fiancée Yeshua had left behind. And still, his parents had never voiced a word of appreciation. They had never acknowledged him. As if he didn't matter.

Yakov's heart filled with aching sadness, and he struggled not to wail. Even when Yeshua returned as one of those traveling preachers his father had so despised, his mother had loved the child who had opened her womb more than anything in the world. Yeshua was the jewel of her heart. It had taken Yakov a lifetime to accept it, to forgive her, but now as she lay still in his arms, cold as the waves of Lake Kinneret after a winter storm, he understood why and found peace. Yeshua was the only one of her children who had never truly been hers.

As he kissed her eyelids and gently pressed them shut, Yakov accepted that the lack of love in his own mind, not hers, had created all his suffering. At last, in this moment of sadness and loss, he forgave himself for blaming her, and for judging his mother for an offense she had not committed.

Mariamne, Michal, Yohannah, and the other women anointed his mother's body in oils, covered her with myrrh and aloe, and wrapped her in a linen cloth, to prepare for her burial.

Yakov wept as they laid his mother's body on a platform inside a burial cave, next to Yeshua's ossuary. He didn't want to speak. Instead, he hid behind the others and placed his arm around Michael's soft shoulder.

With tear-filled eyes, his brother Iosa stepped forward. "Birth was not her beginning and death is not the end," he said solemnly to all the disciples who had gathered there for their last farewell. "From today onward, she is free, awakened from the dream that is our lifetime. May she live in peace."

Jerusalem, Judea, AD 45

Early one morning, as Mariamne was on her way to milk the goats, she noticed a man slumped against the stone wall by the open gate. His cloak was tattered and stained with blood. His face was bruised, and his bottom lip split into a raw wound, and one of his eyes swollen shut. Her heart jumped to her throat, and she approached carefully. Was the man still breathing? *Could he be violent?*

Mariamne squatted by his side. Hesitantly, she placed two fingers on his neck to detect a pulse. He jerked, and she almost jumped to her feet. But then he opened one eye and gazed at her with an almost godlike light.

Kephas!

"They released me," he croaked. Then he toppled over, unconscious.

"Michal!" Mariamne cried out. "Come quick. Help me!"

"What now?" Michal answered from inside the house. "Can't you do anything on your own?"

"Hurry! It's Kephas."

In an instant, Michal appeared at her side. With considerable effort, the two women grabbed hold of his hands and feet and dragged Kephas into the house and laid him on a cot.

While Michal scurried to fetch Kephas's wife, Mariamne placed her hands on his chest and drew in God's healing power through the soul's entrance at the crown of her head. The vibrant energy pulsated through her hands into Kephas's heart. Like a dry sponge in water, his body absorbed the healing energy, replenishing every inch with the throbbing gift of life. He was weak, but his spirit had not surrendered: he would survive.

Mariamne barely noticed how Yakov, Michal, and all the other disciples appeared at her side, and how they placed their hands on Kephas, covering him from head to foot. Together, they formed an orb of universal love and blanketed him with divine energy. They united with the creator. With God. They ceased to exist as people, as individuals, and became one. Became nothing. Became all.

The disciples remained in that position until the sun set, until Kephas's life force was replenished and his breathing deepened, strengthened, and finally returned to normal. When Kephas's body released their hands, they knew they could let go.

Later the same evening, after the women had finished cleaning up after supper, Yakov signaled for Mariamne to meet him in his carpentry workshop. He always wanted her there, alone, to listen to his ponderings. Only there did he speak to Mariamne as to a man. Only there could Mariamne be sure she was his closest confidante.

"What do you think happened?" Yakov asked. "Saul's men beat him up?"

"He says the soldiers arrested him."

Yakov picked up a piece of olive wood, viewed it from all angles, then carefully put his knife to it. He stroked its contours, removed layer after layer of excess wood, forming it into a spoon. "Do you believe him?"

"I don't know," she said. "He's still too fragile to talk, but… We've seen bruises and wounds like those before. On Yeshua, the day of his execution."

Yakov's face contorted into a grimace.

He never wanted to speak about Yeshua. Ever. How she wished they could reminisce about him, discuss what happened, and come to terms with their roles in her husband's demise. The guilt. But whenever she approached the subject, Yakov would just make light of it and change the topic.

"If they arrested him, then—for what? For preaching?" Yakov made it sound like a joke, but the flicker of fear in his eyes betrayed him. "He's been gone for years. Anything could have happened. You think this is a sign, a warning?"

"Let's wait until he recovers," Mariamne said. She swept the wood shavings into a heap, collected them onto a thin board, and then discarded them in a pile outside the door. Then she looked back at Yakov. "Let's not make assumptions, shall we?"

Fifteen days passed before Kephas's voice recovered and he felt strong enough to join Mariamne and the others in the courtyard for breakfast. Fifteen days of guessing, of mounting fear.

"It was the Romans," Kephas said. "They arrested me as soon as I entered Jerusalem. On the king's order, is what they told me. But the prison was full of men like me, like *us*. Simple travelers, men of faith, and…" Kephas swallowed as his gaze shifted from Yakov to the flatbread in his hand and back to Yakov. The bread crumbled between his nervous fingers. A flash of pain clouded his eyes. "Barzebedee. He was there, too."

Mariamne almost clapped her hands in delight before she realized what it must mean. "And Tau'ma?"

Kephas shook his head. "I don't know. We lost track of him many moons ago."

"But where is Barzebedee now?"

Kephas's eyes filled with tears. "Gone."

Mariamne gasped.

Yakov squeezed Kephas's shoulder in compassion. "Gone where?"

"Agrippa." Kephas pinched the bridge of his nose and looked at his feet. "He received his portion of the cup, like the Baptizer."

"King Agrippa beheaded him?" Yakov asked. "But that doesn't make any sense." He rubbed his forehead as he gazed out across the valley, over the compound. Then he sighed heavily before he turned back to the others. "It's begun, then, the persecution?"

Mariamne wanted to stand up, embrace Yakov, remove the shadows in his mind. She could feel the terror radiate through his skin. But how could she convince him that his fear was but a sign he didn't trust his own divinity?

"Didn't the king die, go to sleep with his fathers, then?" Michal handed Kephas a new flatbread fresh from the fire to replace the one that had ended up in crumbs on his lap. "Last moon in Caesarea, murdered by the Jews. That's what they say."

"Agrippa. The good Herod." Yakov returned his gaze to the hills. "No Jews would have killed him. Couldn't have. If anything, we supported him."

Michal handed Kephas a cup of fresh milk and made sure he swallowed, watching him like a doting mother.

Mariamne didn't know what to say. Yakov was right: ever since Agrippa had helped dethrone his uncle Antipas and deport him from Galilee, the Jews had favored him. Of all the rulers the Jews had suffered during the last few generations, Agrippa was the least despised. He had even prevented Emperor Caligula from raising his own statue in the holy temple and ordering the Jews to worship him as a god.

"If not Agrippa, then I don't know," Kephas said, his voice still weak, shaking. "Maybe the new king? Is there a new king?"

"Whoever it is must be afraid of rebellion," Yakov guessed.

"They haven't announced the new king of Judea yet." Mariamne said. She looked at Kephas and frowned. "Maybe Emperor Claudius ordered the arrests?"

"Nonsense. Why would an emperor care about us?" Yakov said. "Besides, from what I've heard, his forces are moving west, toward Britannia. No, there's something else going on."

He turned to Kephas. "Tell me, how did you escape?"

"In the middle of the night," Kephas said between mouthfuls of bread, which he chewed with visible pain, his jaw still bruised and swollen. "One of my fellow prisoners woke me. And somehow, the chains on my wrists and ankles had loosened. All I had to do was step away. Simple, like that. He handed me a cloak and a pair of sandals, and we sneaked past the guards, who were fast asleep at their posts. I thought I was dreaming. But we passed the second, then the third guard stations, unnoticed… When we arrived at the gate, it stood wide open, as if someone had cleared our way."

"Yeshua?" Michal said in awe. "It must have been Yeshua."

The stab of pain in Mariamne's heart caught her by surprise, and a sob rose in her throat. Could it have been Yeshua? Was he still here, protecting them?

"And the other prisoner, what happened to him?" Yakov asked, showing no signs of distrust.

"I don't know. Once we had exited the city gate, he disappeared. I never saw him again." Kephas inspected his bruised hands. "I don't know how I'm still alive."

Yakov put his arm around his shoulder and pulled him closer. Kephas grunted in pain. "We mustn't allow fear to paralyze us. Blessed is the one who endures trials. When your faith is tested, it produces endurance. And only from endurance can you mature and become complete, so that in the end you lack nothing."

Mariamne watched her friend with rising concern. Surely Yakov was addressing himself more than Kephas.

Slowly, Kephas regained his strength, and the full story of his travels emerged.

One afternoon, as Kephas, Mariamne, and Yakov rested in a meditation spot on top of the hill overlooking the compound, Kephas gazed up into the white clouds that sailed by above, and said, "You know, he's a wise man, Saul is. He worships Yeshua. And you saw him—he's charismatic. People adore him." Kephas plucked a red poppy and twirled it between his fingers. "We spent many nights talking about Yeshua, about his miracles. Did you know Yeshua fulfilled all Jewish prophecies about the Messiah?" He looked at

Yakov, eager to earn his agreement. "It's remarkable, isn't it? Saul speaks of so many exciting things I never heard of before."

"But Yeshua wasn't the Messiah," Mariamne said, feeling deflated. She looked to Yakov, hoping he would back her up, but Yakov didn't seem to have heard her. He had knelt behind Kephas and, eyes closed, massaged Kephas's shoulders, neck, and scalp. She could tell he was connecting with Kephas on a spirit level, sending healing energy into his mind, to bring him back to his senses.

It didn't stop Kephas from rambling. "Yeshua inspired others to follow his example, didn't he?" Kephas eyes glowed as he absentmindedly tore the petals off the poppy and let them fall to the ground like droplets of blood. "And he was a righteous man. A descendant of King David."

Yakov laughed. "Oh, he would have loved that, for sure—to be a descendant of King David. I remember when Yeshua was little, he thought the world of himself. Lived with his head in the clouds." Yakov chuckled to himself as he pressed his thumbs into Kephas's temples and rubbed them in a circular motion.

"He could have been the Messiah!" Kephas protested. "Maybe. We just didn't know."

"Yeshua? Don't be a fool. He might have been many things to many people, but in all truth, he grew up as a miserable Jewish carpenter in a small Galilean fishing village. If he'd been the Messiah, surely we would have recognized it. Besides, the Messiah is supposed to be a great military leader, someone who will win battles against the Romans." Yakov smirked. "Could you even imagine Yeshua in a battle?"

"In a way, we're all descendants of King David," Kephas said, undisturbed.

"Well, if you put it that way…" Yakov brought his elbows to Kephas's back and rubbed them into Kephas's shoulder blades.

"But Yeshua died," Mariamne said. "God wouldn't have let the Messiah die like that. Crucified."

"Oh, woman! What do *you* know?" Kephas said, and in an instant, his godlike aura gave way to a muddy vibration of someone too attached to the material world and its rewards.

"He was my husband," Mariamne said. She placed her hand on Kephas's shoulder and looked him in the eyes. "Did that minor detail slip your mind?"

She couldn't help but chuckle at the idea of Yeshua being the Messiah. Despite all the wonderful things he had done, ultimately they had killed and tortured him, and nailed him to a cross like a common criminal.

"When the world ends," Kephas added, as if oblivious to the fact that Yakov and Mariamne didn't agree with him, "he'll come back and save us."

"Come back?" Yakov leaned over to face him. "How? You think his bones will grow flesh and hair and eyes?"

"Resurrected," Kephas said, ignoring Yakov's taunts. "Saul says he'll come back in a brand-new body and yes, he will return to us. Because the end of the world is imminent. And on the last day, all of us who have accepted Yeshua as our savior, we'll rise and go to heaven with him. Even the dead will rise from their graves in newly created bodies."

"Kephas, dear friend," Yakov said, and he patted him on the head as if he were a child. "The walk uphill and sitting among us seems to have drained you. Let's go back. You need to rest."

"I don't understand why my news doesn't bring you joy," Kephas said. "We'll all meet him again. Soon. It should please you."

Mariamne met Yakov's gaze. The blows to Kephas's head in prison must have consumed his mind. Had Kephas forgotten how they had returned to Yeshua's grave one year after his passing, unwrapped his remains from the linen shroud, and placed his bones into the ossuary? How could Yeshua possibly return in a body that had long ago decomposed and been reduced to bones?

Or did Kephas refer to reincarnation? Yeshua reborn?

CHAPTER 17

Something about Kephas's story made Yakov restless, and he spent most of the hot and rainless summer alone in the hills, meditating and asking God for advice on how best to confront Saul. Although he was glad his friend had returned, the tidings of how Saul was continuously distorting Yeshua's legacy unnerved him. He should have shoved a stick into the spokes of Saul's cart when he had a chance. Stopped him, somehow. He should have accompanied Saul back to Antioch and should have told everyone the truth about Yeshua. Maybe that would have worked. But then again, Yakov did not have Saul's education or eloquence, nor did he have the Tarsian's impressive charisma. Who would have listened to him?

But shouldn't he at least have tried?

"Don't think about it, Yakov," Mariamne said one afternoon as she followed him into the hills. "Lost time is a meaningless regret. Why don't you redo what you didn't do then?"

"How?"

Mariamne picked a dry straw from the side of the path and chewed on it. "Time's like a dream. We only imagine that time passes day by day. Everything we believe has happened exists in a state of nowhere. We can change the past."

"And bring Yeshua back to life?" Yakov couldn't grasp what she meant to say. How was it possible to redo the past?

"Maybe. If only I knew how, I would. But I do know this: anything that happened in *your* life you can change. The time's always right now, in the present."

Yakov loved her certainty, the way she turned her nose up when she wanted to convince others of all those nonsensical notions that sometimes flowed from her mouth.

"What do you say, then? Ambush Saul and his followers?"

She scrunched her nose. "Violence is never the answer—you know that as well as I do. Let's forget about Saul for now."

"I'm not sure this is a wise plan."

"Let's cure Saul with his own potions. May the best man win."

"And if *he* is the best man?"

Mariamne grinned and planted a quick kiss on his cheek. "*We* are the soldiers of the truth. And despite what Saul may believe, we are the ones who have Yeshua on our side."

But Yakov wasn't convinced. For the first time in his life, he cherished his alone time. He spent entire days walking in the hills, ruminating. At night, he sat alone by the fire and let Michal and Mariamne serve him, not ready to share his deliberations with them. His deepest fears. There must be something he could do. But what? His children were grown. His dear mother had passed. His only responsibility was toward the Assembly.

One evening, Mariamne, Phillipos, and his wife Yohannah, appeared at Yakov's side while he was enjoying his evening meal.

"Look at you! How can you gobble down food when others go hungry?" Mariamne said.

Yakov wiped the olive relish from the corner of his mouth and put his honey cake back on the platter. Who was hungry?

"Hush," Michal demanded. "Honor the sanctity of his evening meal."

Reluctantly, Mariamne, Phillipos, and Yohannah squatted beside her and accepted a vine leaf stuffed with cheese from her hand. They devoured the leaves as if they hadn't eaten for days.

Mariamne's face seemed thinner than ever before. And those dark rings under her eyes, Yakov didn't remember if he'd seen them before.

"You've always preached community, emphasized that we must share all things, like Ebionites," Mariamne said after taking a long sip of water. "And now you have no qualms about accepting food from those whose children's bellies cry empty?"

"Shush, you senseless woman!" Michal said. "Has the women's curse come upon you, that you've lost all respect?"

Yakov stared at Mariamne. "Wait, whose children are starving?"

"You don't know?" She glared at him as if he had gone mad. "In the last two weeks, every disciple who has traveled to the surrounding villages—Joppa, Lydda, Emmaus—all they've had to eat is moldy bread. No family in Judea can share their food. All crops have perished. All fruits and berries have shriveled. The goats, cows, sheep—they're drying up. Not even the landowners can share a simple cup of milk."

Yakov swallowed, overcome by shame.

"But all this food?" he gestured at the piles of goodies before him. "If no one can spare anything, where did all this come from?"

"The Assembly, your community, they're feeding you with their last crumbs. In a day or two, maybe three, our storehouses will be empty. Even the sales of Iosa's and Abram's fabrics have stalled. No one cares about fine clothing anymore. Every pruta goes toward the overpriced grains and produce that are still being sold in the markets. And the last time we looked, even the stalls of the Roman market stood empty."

Yakov's cheeks burned. He pushed his platter away, unable to take another bite. For months, he had lived in his head, blind to the world around him. All he had done was mourn for his mother and tend to his own fears. He had left all the cares of the world to the others.

Yakov glanced down at his belly and pinched the fat that had accumulated at his waist. *How embarrassing.* He had gained weight, had overindulged on rich foods, while all the men, women, and children in the community went hungry. This had to stop. He shot up from his seat, wagging his finger at Michal, warning her to stop eating. With a platter of figs in his hand, he rushed out of his house to share what remained with his brethren.

What he saw was devastating. The soil in the fields had hardened and cracked. The crops had shriveled on their dry stalks and wilted to mere hay. Oxen thin as lambs, sheep lying on their sides in the grass, too weak to stand, and goats with sagging udders drained of milk. Children with swollen bellies stared with protruding eyes at the plate in his hand. They smacked their dry lips, but their mothers held them back, forcing them to respect their elder. Yakov passed one handful of figs after another to the scrawny men and women in his compound, and he told Michal and Mariamne to do the same with the platters of cheeses and breads. How had he not noticed before? Had he not heard the babies crying in the night for a drop of milk? What kind of leader was he?

The little food they had vanished in no time before Yakov remembered his brother's miracle with the two loaves of bread. He should have told them to imagine their stomachs full before he handed out the breads and fruits. Yeshua had fed three dozen with one single loaf. He had asked them to believe the tiny piece of bread would fill them up. And all the disciples had believed him. He recalled how stuffed he had felt, how satisfied. Why had he forgotten about that?

CHAPTER 18

Jerusalem, Judea, AD 46

Month after month passed without rain, and every day, the members of the Assembly grew weaker. One evening, a forum of elders, among them Kephas, Andreas, Bar-Tôlmay, and Phillipos, gathered in the courtyard outside Yakov's house.

"We demand the right to slaughter the sheep!" they cried with voices weakened by hunger. "Our animals are dying. Let us eat them before they go to waste."

Mariamne clutched Yakov's arm to offer him support.

"Have you lost your faith, then?" Yakov kept his voice steady and tried to sound reassuring. But inside him, his heart pounded with fear as he faced the emaciated disciples. Sweat formed on his brow.

The elders watched him with sunken eyes, cautiously deliberating their next move. Andreas, the oldest of them, stepped forward.

"We used to eat fish, mutton. Don't you remember? And we thrived." The men around him nodded. They all remembered. "*You* made us stop. It wasn't our choice."

Yakov sighed. Hunger had blurred their memories.

"No one made you stop," Mariamne said, sweet with compassion. "You all wanted to stop, wanted to be one with Yeshua. Have you forgotten how you longed to embrace his wisdom, be like him?"

"Yeshua ate fish." Bar-Tôlmay, the former plowman from Cana, raised his voice, but when everyone turned to look at him, he lost his resolve and stared at his feet.

Yakov called for everyone to come sit with him by the fire. His heart ached when he saw their misery. What right did he have to deny them nourishment when it was readily available? "Stay with me, my friends. I promise, this too shall pass."

Mariamne leaned forward. "Yeshua allowed you to eat fish, to catch fish and sell it. You're right, he didn't forbid it. But *he* didn't eat fish. I never saw him taste any creature that had once breathed."

Yakov nudged her back. Now was not the time to argue about who was right and who was wrong.

"Eat, if you must, whatever you need. Don't let me hinder you. But if you still have a smidgen of trust in the miracles Yeshua taught, you will stay on the path and we will overcome this ordeal together."

Michal removed a flatbread from the oven with a wooden spatula and gave it to Yakov, who divided it into ten equal pieces, each smaller than an infant's fist.

"Take this," he said, just like his brother had once done, and he placed a chunk of bread into their hands. "It will satisfy you."

Their expressions softened with faith in his words.

"I understand your urge to lessen your hunger. God knows I do. But remember, you only need to address the belief that you are separate from God. Because whoever is one with God lacks nothing."

They listened. Thankfully. Michal had been right to calm them with food.

"This famine is a trial of our faith. Can't you see it's your sense of self, your ego, that is fighting for survival?"

The hollow-eyed people before him bowed their heads and stared at their feet. He could tell they didn't believe him.

"Your hunger stems from a desire to satisfy what you believe you lack. But you can turn it around, be content with what you have. Didn't that shekel-size bread fill you up? Doesn't praying make you happy?"

Yakov looked from one face to another, these wise men and women, whose wrinkled faces glowed with nascent hope in the twilight despite their suffering.

"When you accept that your only problem is your separation from God, from the source, you'll see that anything is possible. You are the creators of your own lives. Imagine your stomachs are full. Believe it! You can lessen everyone's hunger—your children's, your animals', your neighbors'—by connecting with the healing power of God. Miracles do happen."

A few days later, as Yakov went to feed the goats with dried moss, he noticed the number of animals in the enclosure had diminished. Had they passed away from starvation, or had someone slaughtered them for food? He didn't know, and he wouldn't judge. Each one of them was responsible for their own actions, and without faith, hunger could be gruesome.

Surely rain would fall soon. Midwinter was around the corner. One new moon, two, and the crops would sprout again. The world would come back to life. He simply needed to generate enough food for another two or three new moons, and everything would return to normality.

But where would the food come from? The storage rooms stood empty, the handful of ewes and does that used to produce milk had dried up, and the preserves of last year's fruits and vegetables were long gone.

Starving faces followed him wherever he went. Eyes of blame, as if *he* had caused the drought. Yakov climbed the hills behind the compound to get away from it all, to clear his head. How could this happen to them, if nothing real could be threatened and nothing unreal existed? Why was it so hard to provide his brethren with enough nutrition to feed their families?

Had God forsaken him?

Yakov raised his hands to the skies, to beseech the clouds to grant him the rain they so needed. But the single cloud that sailed above was feathery and white, unburdened with rain. He thought of Elijah, the great magus of Israel, who had saved the infidels in Samaria from certain death by bringing them rain after years of drought. He closed his eyes. What would Yeshua have done? He remembered the time when Yeshua and his fishermen had been caught in a violent storm on Lake Kinneret. The wind had swallowed the boat, tossed it from one crest to another, buried it under the waves. Anyone else would have drowned. Any other boat would have capsized and dragged the fishermen to the bottom of the sea. But not this boat. As if by magic, the storm had withered and stilled to a mere whisper. *You just have to believe*, Yeshua had said after they safely returned to the shore. *Believe, and it will come true.*

Could it be that simple? Yakov knelt down on the crusty earth in the middle of the fields that once had yielded both barley and wheat, and onions and cucumbers and every sort of vegetable imaginable. He cupped the dry soil in his hands and let it filter through his fingers. He stared at the sky. Begged. Pleaded. But the sky remained blue and clear. Not a single rain cloud moved into sight.

Yakov's eyes filled with tears, and he banged his fists into the cracked soil.

It was a fool's dream.

He couldn't do it.

Jerusalem, Judea, AD 47

Every day for months, from dawn to dusk, Yakov knelt in prayer in the infertile fields, but the rain refused to fall.

Like a dutiful wife, Michal fed him drops of goat's milk forced from the dried-out does whose kids had starved to death. But whenever Yakov left the house with Mariamne, Michal made a sour face. Yakov waved away her protests. Mariamne was his best friend. She kept him company and stayed by his side all day, praying with him, urging him not to lose faith.

"What have I done wrong, Magdalen?" he asked, his voice colored by bitterness. "Is God punishing me for believing I could follow Yeshua's lead? I'm a nobody."

"God hasn't abandoned you," Mariamne answered, although her faith sometimes wavered and her hope diminished with each passing day. "It's only a test."

"I don't want to die."

"You won't die."

He buried his face in his hands. "I don't want to pursue this life any longer. I can't. Enough already. I tried. And I failed."

Of course it was enough already. But what option did they have? What else could they do? *Be grateful*, she heard a voice in her head say.

"Be grateful," she echoed. "Yeshua always told us to be grateful for what we—"

"Yeshua…" Yakov shook his head with sadness. "Yeshua always knew what to do. I'm not Yeshua."

"Try it. Say thank you."

"For what? For starving? For losing my mind?"

"Say it, Yakov. You're still alive. You have a devoted wife. Disciples. You have a roof over your head. You have me."

Yakov glared at her, then muttered. "Oh well, thank you, Lord."

"You have to mean it, Yakov."

He gazed up into the sky. "Thank you," he said again. "Thank you for keeping me alive. For keeping my brethren alive. Thank you for the drops of milk and the love of my wife and my friends."

He bowed his head, and Mariamne knew he had listened.

Yakov closed his eyes and focused on his heart chakra. As hard as it seemed—impossible, really—he saturated his entire being with gratitude. He connected with God and repeated in his mind, *Thank you, thank you, thank you.*

The surrounding space expanded, and at once he became one with the earth beneath him and the sky above. He united with God and all creatures of the world, and the human beings who suffered with him. He sensed the thirst of the land and the promise of the wind, and he conjured the rain-filled clouds toward him. *Come*, he begged, *release us with rain.* In his mind's eye he invoked ponderous, dusky clouds drifting toward him, enveloping Judea with the pledge of showers. He imagined the scent of the life-giving drops, the touch of wetness on his skin, and visualized the withered roots of all the plants spiraling up to drink of the water they had been denied for so long, until it all became real. It was no longer only a wish in his mind. He relaxed, knowing that heavy drops were falling around him in a pitter-patter, blessing the earth and all beings upon it. A roar of rain, like the first shower after a long dry summer, drumming the earth with its intense chorus of smattering drops, releasing the world from drought. In his mind, he was there, in the heavy rain.

He believed.

But the skies remained clear, with no clouds in sight.

Day after day, week after week, Yakov knelt in the dirt, his hands raised to the sky. Mariamne could feel his pain, his increasing doubts. She yearned to reach out and embrace him, to comfort him. But her place was at his side, not together with him. Michal was his wife, his partner, the one who undressed him at night, covered his body with kisses, and let him dive into her soft embrace. Michal was the one who pampered him with love. All Mariamne could do was stand by and watch him, unable to offer more than an encouraging word or a friendly pat on his shoulder.

By now, all their animals were gone—some dead, others bartered for vegetables or grains. It had been many months since the disciples had eaten anything but roots, insects, and tree bark. No one had the energy to move. They just sat there and stared at the clear sky, wishing for rain that never came.

First the brook had dried out, then the well. Not bathing, not keeping clean, had brought on diseases that were making rounds with the infants and the old and feeble. Even so, Mariamne's faith never wavered. She was convinced they would all survive, everyone who remained. If only she could conjure rain, bring trees and bushes to life, comfort those who had lost their faith. She joined Yakov in his effort, fell to her knees at his side, and buried her face in the dust.

"Anything, Yeshua. I would do anything. Please save us," she pleaded.

A shadow fell over her. When she opened her eyes, she saw a pair of feet at her side. Clean, perfectly manicured toes in pristine sandals. A whiff of citrusy frankincense.

Mariamne gazed up.

"You are praying to the earth now, are you?" The bearded face that grinned benevolently at her was that of a friend.

Saul.

Yakov stared at him, confused in his delirium. What on earth did Saul want now? Had he come to mock their misfortune, bask in his own superiority, deride them with his wealth? But then he noticed Barnabas by the gate, and next to him, three horse-drawn carts laden with produce.

They brought food!

Tears welled in Yakov's eyes. He stood to embrace the man who had come to their aid.

But then the daylight disappeared. Ominous clouds had moved in to blank out the sun. The sky turned black. A ripple of lightning forked across the sky, and then the entire world exploded with rolling thunder. The leaden clouds cracked open and unleashed a torrent of rain.

Yakov met Mariamne's surprised gaze. *It had worked!* He had brought rain. He could do it!

They burst out laughing.

Out of the corner of his eye, Yakov saw how Barnabas and Saul rushed their horses into the barn for shelter, and how all the disciples came out of their huts to stare at the sky in incredulous awe.

Soaked to the bone, Yakov grasped Mariamne's hands, and they danced in the rain, convulsing with laughter.

And then she kissed him.

Surprised, Yakov stepped back.

"I'm sorry," she said, wiping her lips as if she could somehow erase her actions. "I don't know what came over me."

But Yakov just laughed and drew her into his arms. He kissed her over and over again. "We did it, Magdalen," he said. "We conjured rain!"

She brought her hands to his cheeks. "Yeshua saved us," she said.

And just like that, the magic was gone.

"King Abgarus sent me," Saul said a while later when all the disciples had congregated in Yakov's house to share their first meal in months.

Yakov forced himself to take the smallest sips of the milk, to allow his stomach to adjust to nutrients, to food.

Saul looked criminally healthy against the backdrop of skeletal men and women whose eyes bulged from starvation. Yakov chewed carefully on the fresh flatbread that Michal had somehow had the strength to knead and bake for them. He relished the sweet tanginess of the soft goat's cheese with drizzled honey.

Silence hovered among the disciples as they enjoyed the roar of the thunder and the scent of rain that permeated the fresh air with relief. The carts of produce Saul and Barnabas had brought would feed them all, including their neighbors, for months. The toughest of times had come to an end, and they had survived. Their prayers had worked.

"Abgarus, you say?" Yakov felt obliged to speak, to keep up the conversation with the man who had come to their rescue, to whom they now owed their lives. "Isn't that the prophet of Antioch? The husband of that queen…"

"Queen Helen," Mariamne said. "Of Adiabene."

"The same." Saul glanced at her for a moment, before he bit into a stuffed grape leaf. Drops of juice dribble down his chin.

"And he sent us food? To us specifically?" Yakov asked.

"What a gracious man." Kephas gazed at Saul, unabashed admiration plastered across his sunken face.

"An honourable man indeed," Saul continued. "He has taken Yeshua's teachings to heart."

"*You* taught him?" Yakov said.

"No, not I. Abgarus met one of your brothers years ago. Tau'ma, I believe, when your brother traveled through Damascus on his way to the Kushan Empire."

"Tau'ma traveled to the Kushan Empire? He's alive?"

"From what I understand, he's retracing Yeshua's steps to Satavahana," Saul continued.

A warm glow spread inside him, and Yakov sighed with relief. His brother had done well, then.

"A few weeks ago, Lord Abgarus had a vision of horrible famine in Judea," Saul continued. "And he called for me. He requested that my men and I help collect money for food, and that we bring aid to you."

Saul tilted his head with an air of empathy and reached out to pat Yakov's hand, which was resting on his lap.

Yakov surveyed the faces around the room: his extended family, the assembly of brothers and sisters in faith. Their sallow faces had assumed a faint glimmer of life. No matter what fanciful stories Saul may be teaching in Antioch, from today onward they would always owe him their lives.

He brought Saul's hand to his heart. "We thank you kindly for your goodwill. Please stay with us as long as you please. We have plenty of food now to share, and we would welcome your company. Once the rain eases, Kephas will show you where you may pitch your tent."

Yakov waited patiently for Saul's response, wishing Saul would decline the invitation. But how could he even think that way? The man had saved their lives and now, more than ever, he must look upon Saul with love in his heart. Then why did he still find it difficult to overcome his dislike for the man? *Love your neighbor as yourself,* Yeshua had said. *Treat others like you want to be treated.* Saul had traveled a long way to get here. Surely this was a peace offering, a welcome dawn for a new alliance. And Yakov had manifested this situation. He had offered his life to God and had raised his consciousness to a dimension where miracles could arise. He must not let jealousy fog his mind.

Because Saul's visit was just that—a miracle.

Three days later, Mariamne sat resting against the wall of Yakov's house, basking in the sun. She smiled as she breathed in the pure air that followed three days of thunderstorms and reminisced about everything that happened in the last few days. Her stomach bubbled, still unused to digesting the solid meals they had enjoyed since Saul's arrival. Could this charitable gesture truly be an honest attempt to mend their tattered relationship?

All around her, ecstatic children from the nearby villages skipped and raced across muddy fields, alive with fresh hope in their eyes and a jolly spring in their steps. For the first time since Mother Maryam's death, the compound echoed with laughter. Mariamne lifted her face to the sun and closed her eyes. She relaxed, hands resting on her lap, palms facing upward. Tomorrow, Yakov would bring the Assembly to the brook. They would bathe in the cool water and wash away their sorrows, like they used to do. And afterward, she would walk into the hills, find solitude, and meditate. Normalcy would return. Life as it was meant to be lived.

The energy around her shifted and, without opening her eyes, she recognized the aura of the man who had settled down at her side. That faint scent of frankincense—it could only be one man. She exhaled slowly and connected with the divinity inside to eliminate any feelings of mistrust. If every person alive was a drop of God in the limitless ocean of God, so was he.

"You know, Saul," she said, eyes still closed. "Ebionites like us, poor people, we're thankful when God lifts us up. And wealthy men like you should be grateful when God brings you down."

"God has not brought me down. I am glad to have come."

Mariamne joined her palms in front of her heart and bowed her forehead to touch her fingertips, an expression of gratitude Yeshua had taught her.

"We were rich in our poverty." She said and fluttered her eyes open. She filled with infinite love for the man beside her. "Rich in our hearts. Rich because we could share what we had with the others in our community, in the surrounding villages. No one in the Assembly ever went without a meal. But since last year, we've suffered more than anyone could ever have imagined. And knowing true hunger, the kind that makes you want to kill your own children to protect them from starvation, that forces you to feed on worms and ants and fleas, because your survival instinct awakens and you know only one thing: you want to live... That sort of hunger teaches you who you are."

"Who are you, Mariamne Magdalen?"

"I'm like the plant who withered under the blazing heat of the sun, whose blossoms fell off, whose beauty was destroyed."

She expected Saul to protest, to say that she was mistaken, but he didn't. Maybe it was true, then. Perhaps she was no longer beautiful. And she welcomed the blessing of being plain.

"God has changed me, Mariamne. Changed my heart." Saul placed his hand on her shoulder and squeezed it, like a brother.

She shivered under his touch. Did her gauntness bother him? Only the husk remained of the plump, vivacious woman she had once been.

"I heard the calling." He looked solemnly into her eyes. "Yeshua said to me, 'Seek, and the famished will be restored, as if anointed with the finest oil.' But the oil I speak of is not derived from olives or other fruits: it is the mercy of our Father. Only those anointed by God's mercy can be perfect."

"I like that." Mariamne watched him in deep thought and recognized the glimmering brightness that shone from within. His brown eyes sparkled with compassion, and in the stark sunlight he appeared harmless—honest, even. Maybe it was true what he said about Yeshua. Perhaps her husband had truly spoken to Saul. But how could it be true? Yeshua had always spoken of unity, inclusion, and equality. Saul's message was quite the opposite: his Yeshua would save only those who believed in him as the Messiah. Saul's Yeshua would let everyone else burn.

Her head spun. She had to stop focusing on the what-ifs. Despite all that had happened in the past, Saul had returned to them in grace, with kindness, and a cartful of produce that had saved them from certain death. She must forget everything else, be grateful, and love him just the way he was.

"A wise man—or woman," Saul said, "allows truth to nourish him like a river that feeds a tree growing on its banks."

He slid his hand along Mariamne's arm and let it rest at her elbow.

"You're right." Mariamne said as she gently removed his hand from her arm. She lifted her gaze to the peaks of the surrounding hills. "Blessed are the wise who have sought the truth, have found peace within, and are forever unruffled by anyone who tries to trouble them."

CHAPTER 21

A sting of jealousy pinched Yakov's heart as he watched Mariamne and Saul stroll around the compound, side by side, chatting and laughing. A certain glow had returned to her cheeks, and he feared the food was not the only source that lit the light in her eyes and energized her limbs. Against his better judgment, Yakov had counted the days—seven—since Saul and Barnabas had arrived. Every morning, he woke up hoping Saul would announce his hour of departure back to his own disciples and thus he would leave Mariamne alone.

Still, Yakov had to admit Saul had changed. He no longer argued during Yakov's lessons at the temple. He took part in their daily immersion in the brook at dawn. He even meditated with the rest of them. Not once had Saul questioned Yakov's sermons. Instead, he sat quietly among the other disciples, as if he absorbed each word that sprang from Yakov's lips.

"Be grateful," Mariamne said when Yakov commented on the amount of time she spent with Saul. "Look at us: we're all healthy again. We survived. Yeshua must have sent him, don't you think? And Yeshua would not cause us any harm." She brought his hand to her chest. "Heed your own advice, Yakov. Don't fear him. You always say fear binds us to this world. And only forgiveness can set you free."

Yakov squeezed her hand. She was right: everyone deserved a second chance.

*

On the eighth afternoon after Saul's arrival, Yakov stood in front of his brethren at the temple and raised his hands to the sky. "Bless you," he said, addressing God. His voice trembled with emotion. "Thank you for your gifts and for your patience, and for your abundant love. Please accept our gratitude for guiding us and for helping us find peace in our hearts."

Yakov wiped the sweat off his forehead. He couldn't think clearly. Some days he couldn't help but wonder if Saul's peace offering was nothing but an ultimate show of strength. Had the Tarsian bought their trust with his grains and beets and cheeses?

"May I speak?" Saul placed a hand on Yakov's shoulder. A sign of friendship, equality. His white robe gleamed when touched by the sun's rays, unfairly clean compared with the sullied clothes of the poor disciples. And even though Yakov towered above him, Saul always made Yakov feel inferior. Old and worn.

Yakov stretched his back and forced a smile. "Of course."

"I am deeply grateful for your hospitality," Saul said. His perfect teeth glistened. "Our beloved Yeshua called me to your aid, to ease your dire need. Remember, if we ever lack anything, we need only ask God for assistance and He will hear our prayers."

"Are you saying we didn't pray? That we brought the famine upon ourselves?" someone asked.

Yakov searched among the disciples but couldn't tell who had spoken.

"Not at all," Saul continued. "You did believe, and behold what God delivered. He brought me to you."

Yakov found Mariamne's face among the women. She was watching Saul with genuine interest.

"Nothing is more valuable than truth," Saul said. "Neither friendship, nor family, nor power should matter more than truth. Do not hide from those who undermine you. And never allow fear to paralyze you. Be calm, instead. I swear by the living God that I will use all my power to protect you from anyone who threatens you. I will let no one lay a hand upon you."

The temple priests had closed in on them and were watching, listening to the subtle hints of violence. Seventeen years had passed since Yakov had brought Yeshua's disciples to Jerusalem. For nearly two decades, the Assembly had blended in with the rest of the crowd of believers. And here came Saul who, in one instant, placed them right back on the list of suspected agitators and rebels.

"No one's threatening us," Yakov hurried to say. "We live in peace. Our faith teaches us to forgive anyone who has trespassed against us. Only in forgiveness can we find harmony."

He closed his eyes for a moment and conjured love into his heart. "We accept that what we believed someone did against us was nothing but an illusion. And with that, we may forgive all who have offended us." A divine vibration of love enveloped him, and he beamed at the members of the Assembly.

The priests continued walking. They had heard his peaceful sermons before. They did not fear an uprising from this group of faithful Jews.

Yakov's knees sagged with relief. The love of God had filled him and made everything clear: Saul posed no threat to the disciples. He was not a wicked man. But his beliefs were of a different fabric, and he didn't belong here.

The sooner Saul realized that, the sooner he would leave.

"May I walk you back?"

Saul caught Mariamne's hand as she exited the temple through the Nicanor Gate. The guardsmen snickered at them, as if insinuating they were lovers.

But she wasn't in love. Or was she? Ever since Saul had arrived, he had been nothing but patient and generous. He had not pushed himself on her again, only conversed with her while she was cooking, cleaning, or mending clothes. He always took great care not to disturb her.

At first, she had tried to keep her distance, well aware that she could never reconcile his faith with hers. But in her heart, she could not deny that her pulse quickened when she looked upon his intelligent eyes and those smooth lips. And he was calm and present, like Yeshua. And kind. When her hands were busy working, Saul would peel an apple, cut it into bite-sized pieces, and delicately place them in her mouth.

Her hand remained in his warm grasp, and she relished the comfort of a man's touch, even though she should have pulled her hand away by now.

"Yakov is waiting for me," she said, and she shaded her eyes with her free hand to see how far Yakov had gone. "We always walk back together."

"He left with the others. I told him not to wait for you. He does have a wife at home."

That sting of nausea again, a whisper in the depths of her soul. Something was not right. The man who was holding her hand, who tempted her heart, was not trustworthy.

"Well, let's hurry home, then." She pulled her hand away and increased her pace. "I must help Michal with the evening meal."

Saul caught her hand in a resolute grip.

She winced with pain.

"Michal can make do without you," he said. "We must enjoy this fine spring day."

Mariamne scanned the path that ran up the side of the Mount of Olives, but the others were nowhere to be seen. How could she have stayed so far behind? Had she subconsciously stalled and bided her time, waited for Saul? What did she want with him? She didn't even know.

"I brought some nuts and figs," Saul said. "Perhaps we can pause in this fine meadow? Behold these beautiful almond trees, so fresh in bloom."

"No, not there." She blinked away the tears that always sprang up when she passed through the fields of Gethsemane. To others, this peaceful garden may have appeared as if made for lovers, but to

Mariamne the very essence of its earth sang with death. This was where Yeshua had been arrested, where they had last kissed.

Her mind wandered back to that night. She recalled how their friend Yudah, accompanied by Roman soldiers, had approached Yeshua, all according to Yeshua's own command. How the soldiers had dragged Yeshua away. And then, how the other disciples had attacked Yudah, beaten and kicked him, until he fled, bloodied and bruised. Where was Yudah now? Was he still alive?

"Whereto has your beautiful mind wandered?" Saul pulled her into his arms, his mouth mere inches from hers.

She tried to push him away. She didn't want to give him hope. She didn't want to view him as a man, a potential lover. Tears burned behind her eyelids. *Yeshua, I miss you so.*

Saul looked at her, stunned. "Have I misspoken?"

"There's a brook by the hills, close to the path that leads back to the compound," Mariamne said and she wriggled herself free. "We can rest there while we cool our feet in the water."

Saul's grin showed apparent relief.

Mariamne hurried up the hill, trying to reject the guilt that still haunted her after all these years. She had let Yeshua down. Betrayed him when he most needed her. And while everyone else blamed Yudah, she was the one who had denied him a fresh start in Alexandria, or that land in the far east, Kapila-something. Yeshua would still be alive had she agreed to leave with him. And now what? Had he sent Saul as his replacement?

The bubbling brook soothed her tired feet as she massaged her toes and arches.

Saul sat by her side, their thighs touching. A familiar sting of desire vibrated through her, and she closed her eyes. His warm breath tickled her neck. If only she could let go, live in the moment without worrying about the consequences. His mouth was so close to hers, she could barely restrain herself. She longed to turn her face toward his and let their lips meet, but she couldn't. The closeness of his body filled her with yearning, but nothing he did could remove that shadow of fear.

"Do you love me, sweet Mariamne?"

She laughed. Of course she didn't. But why else was she here? Why else would she permit him to jeopardize her reputation? A widow should never be alone with an unmarried man.

"No?" Saul's eyes lit up.

"No!" She said, but a warm glow spread across her cheeks, and she knew he wouldn't believe her.

When Saul placed his arm around her waist, she didn't object. She should get up now and walk away, but she didn't want to. She wanted him to remove her robe and her tunic and cover her body with his, let his tongue slide over her breasts and suck on her nipples, touch the wetness that pulsated between her thighs, penetrate her.

She shivered. She had to get up. This was wrong.

"But I do love you, Magdalen, you are quite aware." His eyes bore into hers. "I have always loved you. That's why I returned, to save you."

"Yeshua sent you," Mariamne said. Her voice sounded hoarse. But she had to speak Yeshua's name out loud, make it real. She shouldn't be here. She should push Saul away.

"Yeshua is gone." Saul tucked a stray lock of hair behind her ear. When she didn't object, he pushed her headscarf back and let it fall to her shoulders. Gently, he combed his fingers through her dark curls. "But I am still here."

He guided her face toward him, and she closed her eyes. Her lips ached with the desire to kiss him, and for one moment, she let go. His supple lips pressed against hers, and when she opened her mouth to taste him, his tongue met hers. The hunger with which he kissed her was taunting. His coarse beard tickled and scratched her chin as he pressed his tongue deeper, leaning over her, forcing her onto the ground. She pushed back and straightened her spine, allowing him leeway only over her face, her mouth. Like a fumbling adolescent, he bluntly grabbed her breast before she could object. And when she did, he let his hand rest on the small of her back.

Oh, how lovely were those kisses! And how she yearned to spread her legs and invite him in. But when his hand sought its way between her knees and slowly made its way up under her tunic, between her thighs, she sobered up. With a jerk, she pulled herself away.

"Please, my love, please…" Saul's voice was husky with desire. He reached for her hand, but she withdrew it. She scrambled to her feet and stepped away from him.

"I'm sorry," she said as she smoothed out her tunic and adjusted her robe.

What had she done? How could she have been so foolish?

"My love, please!" Saul rose to his feet and reached out to invite her back into his arms. "Let me kiss your worries away."

Mariamne stepped back. "I can't."

Saul enveloped her in a snug embrace. "I know you want this, Magdalen. I will marry you, take care of you. I'll make all your dreams come true. And imagine, together we will be invincible. We will conquer the Roman Empire with our new faith. I know what words to use, what stories to tell. I understand how they think, how to make them believe. But I need you by my side."

"I'm sorry, I can't." Why hadn't she seen him like this before? Manipulative. Only eager to satisfy his own interests, to gain power over others.

"You can!" Saul embraced her even more tightly, and although she wriggled, she couldn't free herself. "I know you want me. You need me."

He kissed her cheeks, her eyelids, the tip of her nose. "Why don't you let go of all this nonsense about being poor and sharing everything? I can offer you the world. You will never go hungry again."

A wail rose in Mariamne's throat, but she would not cry. Not in front of him. Why had she allowed his tender words and gentle manner seduce her? He hadn't returned to help them; he had come to rescue her and carry her away as a prize.

"No one else can ever love you like I do."

She pulled herself away, pushed him back to arm's-length distance.

"I don't need a man's love. Don't you understand? I don't have to seek happiness outside of myself. I *am* love. *You* are love. We all are. But as long as we search for happiness elsewhere, we'll always be disappointed."

"My banner over you is pure love, you know it is. I did all this for you." Saul reached out his hand to her, but Mariamne ignored it. "Yeshua sent me. He implored me to save you."

"And what if you're wrong?" she asked. "Delusional? Wouldn't you rather be happy than right?"

"Stop it, my love." Saul embraced her from behind and snuggled his face into the crevice of her neck.

Mariamne let him hold her for a moment before she turned to face him. "One day you'll understand. And you'll be grateful I told you this now, so you won't have to spend your life hunting for happiness."

"Mariamne. Magdalen. Listen to me. Can't you hear what I am telling you?" Saul took her hands in his and pulled her toward him. "I love you. I will care for you until the end of time. No matter what happens, I will be there for you. You do not have to dwell in poverty. I will grant you a carefree life. Come with me."

"No, Saul, I belong here."

"I will offer you anything your heart desires. We will live in luxury. My people in Antioch adore me, and they will give up everything they own for me. They adore the gospel of Yeshua that I share: the story about his resurrection after three days, how he rose to heaven. It's a familiar story they have heard before. Like their Adonis, Dionysus, even Osiris." Saul's eyes shone as he spoke of his followers. "And they offer me money; I practically roll in denarii, drachma, and shekels. I would dress you in the most exquisite garments, silks. You would look like the queen you are…"

Mariamne watched as her suitor ran out of air. She couldn't help but feel sorry for him.

"You have a good heart, Saul, I truly believe that. But I've made a pledge to the Assembly, and I'm meant to stay here. We live in Yeshua's spirit, according to his teachings. We may not be bathing in silver, as you say, but we share all income between us equally. Yeshua said that if you give all you have to the poor, you will find a treasure in heaven. And however grateful I am to you, and always will be, for saving our lives, my heaven is here among my equals. I don't need fancy clothes. I have no desire to make others adore me. I need to live in love."

"You can be poor with me, can you not? And as for love, I have cartloads of love for you."

The light in his eyes, the passion, had waned. His words no longer carried the same conviction.

She smiled sadly.

"You don't love me?" he asked.

She shook her head.

Saul stared at her, incredulous. Then he started pacing back and forth, kicking up the dust with his sandals. "Barnabas," he said. "I should have listened to Barnabas."

"Saul, I'm truly sorry. I am."

He stopped and glared at her, the look of love replaced by ire. "Barnabas always said you were a whore, like all women. And here I believed you were a saint for having married Yeshua. But you are nothing but a filthy harlot who opens her legs to any man who casts his eyes upon you."

For a moment, Mariamne thought he would spit at her. Instead, he picked up the package of fruits he had brought for a snack and threw it at her. "Eat, you hideous termagant. We would not want you to starve, would we?"

Mariamne shuddered as she watched him walk away. She had permitted him to seduce her with his eloquence, his charm. She had tried to view him as an equal, a seed of God. But her rejection had triggered a lovelessness in him, and before her very eyes he had fallen out of grace, out of oneness with God.

Yeshua had sent him to save their lives and to test her faith.

That was all.

Yakov thrust the hoe into the hardened soil with all his might, again and again, to prepare the field for planting. His arms ached from the effort. Frustrated, he ran his finger over the edge to make sure the blade was still sharp. It was. He had to accept that only his body had weakened.

"Barnabas!"

Yakov looked up and saw Saul storm into the compound. Alone.

A chill ran through the air. Something was wrong, very wrong. Where was Mariamne?

Yakov put the hoe down and followed Saul to his tent. Red-faced with fury, Saul stuffed his belongings into a sack and bound it with a coarse rope. Tight.

"You're not leaving us so soon?" Yakov said with kindness, trying to subdue the bubble of hope that rose through his chest. "Michal's preparing a delicious lentil stew with carrots for supper…"

Saul didn't even dignify Yakov with a glance. Instead, he walked around the outside of his tent and pulled up the stakes that held the sidewalls in place. "Delicious stew?" he asked. "Tell me, does it contain any meat? Chicken? Lamb?"

"Of course not."

"Then it's nothing but food for rabbits. Who eats that slop?"

Yakov frowned. What had Mariamne done to arouse his anger? "Yeshua said—"

"What do *you* know about what Yeshua said?" Saul smirked. "You know nothing. You have no notion about his divinity. You and your lot: such imbeciles. You dwell in poverty. You believe yourselves superior to one and all. But you are not worthy. You struggle for the sake of struggling. You do not even understand what Yeshua taught you. He died for your sins so you would not have to suffer. He wanted you to *enjoy* life!"

Saul lifted the heavy bundle onto his back. "Barnabas," he shouted. "We are leaving!"

Barnabas came running and immediately started disassembling the tent.

"We give thanks for your hospitality," Barnabas said, somewhat confused. "And please, remember our charity—"

Saul leaned over and whispered something in Barnabas's ear, then called out: "Kephas, will you bring our carts and horses!"

"Don't tell me you're leaving?" Kephas asked.

Saul rested his hand on his shoulder. "I trust we will see you soon? Please come visit us again in Antioch."

Yakov bowed his head and closed his eyes. He pressed his palms together in front of his heart and begged for the light of peace to fill him, to release the jealousy and anger that had taken root within him. From now on, he must view Saul and Barnabas as equals, as men of God, and be grateful for this lesson of universal love.

"We must forgive him, Yakov," Mariamne said when she finally returned to the compound at sunset, well after Saul and Barnabas had left. Untouched and unharmed.

Yakov's soul sang with relief. A part of him had feared she would return in tatters, her betrayal visible to the naked eye, like the roses on her cheeks that appeared whenever Saul looked at her. But she entered the compound that evening with her head held high and without a single grass stain on her tunic. She had not let the Tarsian have her.

Mariamne squatted next to Michal and took the bowl of sliced carrots and onions from her hands. She removed the lid of the spice jar and added pinches of ground cumin into the mix.

Yakov grinned as he settled to rest by the fire. No drama this time. He was tired of dealing with his jealous wife, who still, after all these years, barely accepted the beautiful Mariamne as a member of their household.

"Love can hold no grievances," Mariamne said. "We must let Saul go with love." She chopped up sprigs of parsley on a wooden plank and added the fresh herbs to the vegetables.

"I know that."

"He's not to blame. What bothers you exists only in your mind."

She was right. Why couldn't he forgive Saul, like he could any other man who crossed him? What was it about Saul that made Yakov forget all he had learned?

"If you can't forgive him," Mariamne said, "your anger will linger as a token of your failure to unite with God."

Michal rolled her eyes.

Yakov looked down at his clasped hands. Saul was wise and rich and accomplished, everything Yakov was not. He was educated and charming and eloquent, and he had caught Mariamne's eye in a way that had sent darts of resentment through Yakov's core. In those instances, he had forgotten she was his brother's widow and his closest friend. More than anything, he should want Mariamne to be happy. But Saul was not the right man for her. He spoke with a forked tongue. She deserved a better man.

Yakov folded a piece of flatbread with his right hand and used it to scoop up the lentil stew from the platter they all shared. Michal watched his every move until he took a bite and gasped with satisfaction. "Mmm, delicious. Michal, you've outdone yourself."

Cooing like a dove, Michal squatted next to him and indulged in the meal. The peace Yakov had longed for during Saul's and Barnabas's visit had returned, and now they could all eat in tranquility.

"But tell me, what happened?" Yakov asked Mariamne later. "What caused Saul's anger to wax so hot?"

"Nothing you need to bother your mind about," Mariamne said. "Your speech at the temple gave him another heart, that's all. He realized he needed to return home to his own people, and that his mission here had come to an end."

"Mission? What mission?" Michal asked.

"He brought us food and made sure we made it through the crisis. And we'll always be grateful to him."

"I told you!" Michal stared pointedly at her husband. "He's a man of honor."

Yakov chewed slowly. Then he turned to his wife and said, "Indeed, yakiri, that is all that matters."

Mariamne loved hearing Yakov whistle again, well aware how worried he had been that she would leave with Saul as his bride. But how could she? Yakov was her best friend. She could never abandon him, whatever Michal might wish.

Nevertheless, in the days to come, her thoughts wandered back to that kiss. The passionate embrace. The fire that had ignited in her loins and released juices that saturated her body. In that moment, she had desired Saul as much as he craved her. But if she had given in, let him bow down upon her to satisfy her momentary lust, she would have felt sullied. Filthy. And used.

She had no interest in a lifelong romantic companionship. Not with Saul. Not with anyone. Besides, she suspected Saul had wanted her mostly because of his desire to replace Yeshua. He had convinced himself that Mariamne was predestined to be his wife. But she didn't love Saul. And when he called her "harlot" and "termagant," whatever that meant, his true self showed. A man who could treat women with such disrespect deserved nothing more than a lover for sale. But she mourned for him. He seemed lost and lonely. If only he had listened to Yakov, he might have found the peace of God.

Mariamne's heart ached. Never again would she take a chance with a man. She was old already, almost barren. From now on she must focus on the teachings—nothing else. She would dedicate her life to help others awaken.

"The troublesome times are over," Yakov called out to the group who had assembled in the courtyard in front of his house a few days later. "We survived the famine, praise God!"

The men and women watched him in sad agreement. They had gone through hell in the past year—faith would not be easy to restore.

"Blessed be our brothers Saul and Barnabas," he continued. "We must never forget how their generosity saved our lives." He surveyed the faces that looked up at him. "And please, I'm aware how much you have endured, and I wish I could have done more to ease the suffering, to shorten your—" His voice cracked.

"You should have let us eat the animals!" someone shouted from the back. "My son would still be alive if you had allowed us to slaughter the chickens."

"Your son's time had come. His illness could not have been avoided." Yakov sounded more confident than he felt. "I'm sorry if this strikes you as harsh, but we must remember not to judge anyone: no one is to blame but the weather."

"God hates us! God punished us."

Yakov shaded his eyes to see who had spoken, but no one dared look at him. "God loves us! We live in purity, in selflessness. In equality and peace. We fulfill his most important command: we worship no other God besides the one and only Lord of the Jews. And we love each other, our neighbors, as ourselves. Why on earth would God hate us?"

A murmur went through the crowd. Words dissecting what Yakov had just said.

Kephas rose to stand before him. "Don't you remember this phrase, Yakov: 'I gave you cleanliness in all your cities, and filled your lack of bread, yet you did not return to me'?"

Yakov nodded. "The psalms of Amos."

Kephas continued, "And this: 'I withheld the rain from you for many moons before the harvest. I sent rain to one place, but not a drop to another, so the fields on which it did not rain would dry out. Yet you did not return to me.'"

Yakov sighed. "Kephas, that's got nothing to do with us. Droughts happen to the best of people. We have done nothing wrong. We live in God, we never renounced him. And we received rain. I brought you rain."

Kephas straightened his back. "Yet you scrunch up your nose at the foods Saul brought us. You satisfied your hunger, and then you threw him out."

"I didn't… He chose to leave. I had nothing to do with it."

"And you?" Kephas turned to Mariamne. "You accept none of the blame, either?"

Mariamne shook her head slowly, but red roses of shame colored her cheeks.

"Leave her out of this," Levi said and stepped in front of her, as if to shield her from Kephas's ire.

Yakov tried to still his beating heart. "Have ears, Kephas. Listen to your brothers. Let love purify your heart of fearful thoughts."

Kephas's cheeks turned ruddy. He grabbed Yakov by the shoulders and turned him to face the disciples. "Can't you see? Look at these shriveled faces before you. They left their pleasant lives in Galilee to live in poverty with you. In Judea, of all places. We're fishermen and farmers; we don't know how to outwit priests and kings and governors. And we're not used to feed our families with parched grass. Surely we're no sheep." Kephas paused and coughed into the crook of his elbow. "You can't replace Yeshua, you know. I cannot fathom why anyone ever imagined you could. You never bring us any novel ideas or new parables. You've lost us."

Yakov trembled with humiliation. Was it true? Had he failed them? His heart raced as he held his palms out to the men and women before him, his extended family, his closest friends. "Is that what you think?"

A few of the women were quietly crying, the men stared at their laps. No one dared meet his gaze.

"Is this truly what you believe? That I have brought you nothing but misery?"

Silence.

Yakov's chest tightened as if his heart was about to burst. He had spent half a lifetime serving this community. He had done everything in his power to keep them happy and healthy. Had they forgotten how they had all prospered before the famine?

"Saul is right, you know," Kephas said, now calmer. "Yeshua was the son of God, and nothing any of us can do can live up to his legacy." He patted Yakov's shoulder. "You did your best, I will agree to that. But now we need to look to the future. Follow someone who knows Yeshua better. We can't dwell in his memory; we must live in his spirit."

Yakov's stomach hurt with such force he thought he would gag. He grabbed onto Kephas's arm to steady himself.

"Listen to yourselves," Mariamne said. "You're not held hostage here. You can leave anytime you choose. But have you forgotten that all your eyes view before you will one day decompose and return to dust, to nothingness? That's why Yakov always says only good deeds matter. Whatever you decide to do—stay or leave—let that peace remain within you, whatever horrors life throws at you. Because only love is real."

Mariamne's presence, the power of her words, radiated compassion. He should have let her take charge a long time ago. Unlike other women, she was wise and strong and soothing, and Yeshua's spirit lived on within her.

"Mariamne is right," he said once his heartbeat had returned to a normal pace. "If you aren't happy here, you may leave. No one forces you to stay. But if you do leave, Yeshua's words will die with you. Despite what Saul may believe, and what Kephas said, *we* are the only ones who knew Yeshua. We understood his message. Only together can we make sure his words survive and that he did not die in vain."

Kephas looked from Yakov to Mariamne, then down at his hands. "I have to pursue what I believe will bring the most success. And Saul's gospel... I'm sorry, but it's probably what Yeshua would have wished."

Yakov's eyes filled with tears. "Yeshua was my brother. I knew him. I loved him."

Kephas shrugged. "I knew him, too." He turned away from them, hesitated for a moment, and, backing away slowly, separated himself from the group.

Saul had won him over.

• CHAPTER 23 •

Jerusalem, Judea, AD 48

Yakov wrapped his hands in his linen scarf to shield them from the winds that raged unusually hard for late spring. He had to carry on. The Assembly depended on him. He had only one job in life: to guide his companions in daily prayer. Then why did he feel such a reluctance to go to the temple today? On most afternoons, every step toward the holy abode of God filled him with increasingly abundant energy, as if he were carried on the wings of angels. Today, however, he would have preferred to stay at home, cover himself with a heavy blanket, and dream the day away in bed with a cup of hot milk.

Had he grown tired of teaching? Impossible. Deep inside, he understood the cause of his reluctance: today was the first day of Passover. The anniversary of Yeshua's death.

"Look at the legionnaires," Mariamne whispered in his ear when they entered the temple courtyard. She moved her chin at the Roman soldiers stationed on the roofs over the porticos.

"This is Rome's way of avoiding chaos?" Yakov couldn't believe his eyes. "Who do they wish to impress with those shiny swords?"

Ever since Ventidius Cumanus, the new governor, had risen to power a few weeks earlier, the temple had resembled a war zone. Gone was the peaceful sanctuary for prayer and stillness.

"You think it's because of that preacher they killed, the man they called Theudas?" Mariamne asked.

"Who knows? Maybe those are just rumors they spread to frighten us into submission. Who can tell what's true and what are lies these days?"

But everyone knew the Romans' patience had reached its limit. They feared an uprising, now more than ever, as the provinces filled with pretentious field preachers who portrayed themselves as the long-promised, warmongering Messiah. One of them, a peaceful preacher called Theudas, had simply been in the wrong place at the wrong time. The Roman soldiers had attacked him by the Jordan River where Theudas was emulating Moses by attempting to part the waters to allow his followers to pass through. For this, they had ridiculed Theudas and ultimately beheaded him. They had made an example of him, a warning to all others.

Today, the temple courtyard was swarming with faithful Jews who had traveled to Jerusalem from all over the world to take part in the festivities. Worshippers occupied every inch of space. When Yakov noticed that a group of Silician Jews had occupied their usual spot in Solomon's Portico, he led his Assembly past the money changers to a farther corner of the courtyard, next to the Women's Court. They nestled close together to keep warm and covered their noses with their scarves to avoid inhaling the smoke from the burning incense and sacrificial fires. But there was nowhere else to go. This would have to do for today.

"Look around you," Yakov said as he planted himself cross-legged on his mat. "See those soldiers, their hands on the shafts of their daggers, ready for attack? The high priest has sacrificed the house of Yahweh, like those wretched lambs that scream in terror as they are pulled to their deaths. The Romans may mock and disrespect us, but one day, God will release us from all bondage. Those poor souls." He gestured at the Roman soldiers who stood guard on the roofs. "One day, we'll all be released from the bitterness of this world, and so will those soldiers. We will all unite with God."

The soldiers surely couldn't hear him, but they gawked at the men and women of the Assembly.

"A wise man won't hesitate to ask a young child about the secrets of life," Yakov said. He studied the wind-kissed faces around him. "Others, however, will grow old and wither, because they'll always remain separate from God."

"How can we become wiser, then?" a young widow asked. "Should we fast, perhaps?"

Yakov pulled his mantle closer. A Passover afternoon should not be this cold.

"You already observe a perfect diet. You pray every day. You have dedicated your lives to becoming perfect. But have you learned to love one and all?"

"Because we are all God?" Yudah Tzaer asked.

Yakov nodded. "Because we're all one with God."

The soldiers on the roof platforms seemed restless. They paced from one position to another, then back again, surveying the crowd, shouting commands, acting agitated and nervous. The air vibrated with screaming matches between impoverished travelers and greedy merchants who tried to push their flawed animals on unsuspecting foreigners. In one corner, a brawl broke out between a long-bearded Asian pilgrim and a local Jew. They wrestled each other to the ground, knocking over a cage of doves, which cracked open and sent a dozen birds into startled freedom. Immediately, soldiers surrounded the pilgrim, stabbed him in the leg, and dragged the bleeding man away as he shouted obscenities in a language few visitors understood.

Yakov shuddered. Yeshua had also caused a riot here once, a lifetime ago. His brother had run amok among the merchants, shoved their tables to the ground, and screamed out his anger like a madman. Before that day, Yakov had never heard Yeshua raise his voice. Just one random, impulsive act of rage in his life. And then—death. Would the Asian pilgrim meet the same fate? Or would they banish him from Jerusalem and discard him outside the city wall? Who knew what kind of punishment a man like Ventidius Cumanus would inflict? According to the rumors, he was even more ruthless than his predecessor. But sometimes the most ferocious lion had the gentlest heart.

Once the soldiers had returned to their positions on the roofs and everyone seemed to have settled back to normal, Yakov continued his sermon. Surely the crowd would calm down now that they had seen what awaited those who caused trouble.

"Whatever you do, find it in your heart not to judge them," he glanced up at the soldiers. "The Romans and their legionnaires may appear menacing, but they're only testing our commitment to peace."

A rumble shook the plaza. Yakov looked up.

An earthquake?

The entire place quivered with uneasiness. Yakov stretched his neck to get a better view. Something was wrong. Too many people crowded this walled-in space. He thought of the seven gates around the courtyard. If anything happened, which one was closest? Where should they run?

"Let's bow our heads and recall the story of Passover," Yakov continued. He tried to keep his voice calm while observed his surroundings for any movements. "When God punished the Aegyptians for enslaving the Jews by killing their firstborn sons, he made a commitment to spare the Jews."

Yakov's heart throbbed. What could possibly go wrong? Was he overreacting?

"Can anyone tell me how?" He looked to the children around him and hoped one of the youngest would respond.

"God 'passed over' their homes. He didn't kill any of our babies," a little girl said, chewing the strands of her hair.

Yakov caressed her cheek. "Yes, that's so, my little wise one. But when the Pharaoh found out God had spared the Jewish children, he became so angry, he practically chased the Israelites out of his kingdom."

His smile waned. The Passover events had happened more than a thousand years ago, and they were still in the same situation. The only difference was that now they were slaves of the Romans instead of the pharaohs. He combed his fingers through his hair. He had to find a positive note.

"These childlike men," Yakov said, and he glanced up at the soldiers standing guard on the roofs. "They live their lives in a false world of horror and confusion, as if they are asleep and haunted by nightmares."

"They don't appear to be asleep," Mariamne said. "They're taunting us."

A shiver crept up Yakov's spine, and he jerked his head to free himself of the memory that had blasted its way to the forefront of his mind. The Roman soldiers had mocked Yeshua as they drove those rusty nails through his wrists and feet. Like animals. Predators. How could he ever release them from blame? Yet Yeshua had forgiven them.

"Those who are trapped in the middle of these confusing dreams see nothing," Yakov continued. "They don't even understand that their entire lives are nothing but illusions."

He stood up and pretended to stretch his legs as he scanned the courtyard for any impending threats. "Others cast off ignorance as if it were slumber when they wake up to reality."

Not far from them, a scrawny adolescent picked up a pebble and hurled it with full force at a legionnaire, missing the soldier's brow by a mere inch.

Before anyone could react, the soldier jumped off the roof, grabbed the boy by the nape of his neck, and punched his face. The boy wailed as he wiped his bloody nose. But to everyone's surprise, the soldier simply shoved the boy to the ground and raised a warning finger at him before letting him go. Those who had gathered around to watch drew a breath of relief as the soldier returned to his position on the roof. And soon enough, everything seemed to return to normal.

But something had changed.

"Get up," Yakov whispered, loud enough for all the disciples to hear. "Let's walk, slowly, toward the exit. Don't make a scene."

"Are you serious?" Andreas said and rolled his eyes. "You're afraid of a gaggle of boys dressed as soldiers?"

"Move. Slowly. Pretend to be chatting. Smiling. We have to get out of here."

Some men muttered in agreement with Andreas. Others stared from Yakov to Andreas and back, unable to take a stand.

Mariamne sidled up to Yakov. "What's wrong?"

"Nothing, I hope. It's just that…"

Yakov looked up in time to see a soldier turn his back to the pilgrims and bend down. Then he pulled up his skirt and lowered his loincloth. With his bare buttocks in the air, he shouted, "Come lick my testiculis, you filthy peasants!"

Yakov's heart stopped beating. All he heard was his own voice yell, "Run!"

As if in a trance, he pushed the disciples toward the nearest gate. Stumbling over each other, they scrambled with rushed steps until they came to a stop.

A soldier blocked their exit.

"Excuse me," Yakov said in perfect Greek. "Will you let us pass?"

The soldier sneered.

Behind them, a ruckus had erupted: pilgrims and locals in fistfights with the soldiers.

They had to get out. Now.

"Please," Mariamne begged. "I can tell you're a compassionate man, a family man…"

The soldier smirked.

Yakov looked back. All the soldiers had jumped off the roof and were swinging their swords across the crowd, hitting whatever they could reach, slashing into legs and arms, animals and children.

"Take these." Yudah Tzaer held out his palm with five Tyrian silver shekels. It was more money than Yakov had ever seen. A fortune.

The soldier looked at the money, then back at Yudah Tzaer. His face colored with greed, and he grinned. With a finger to his lips, he lowered his sword and stepped aside, to allow Yakov, Mariamne, and their companions narrow passage to slip through the gate.

Once outside, they dashed down the stairs, as fast as their legs could run, and fled toward the hills of Gethsemane. Behind them, screams of terror echoed between the temple walls, cries of death. And then, as they climbed the hills, panting with despair: absolute silence.

"Is everyone with us?" Mariamne said, catching her breath. "No one left behind?"

Yakov counted the men and women who crouched together, gasping in shock. They were all there. Safe. He had reacted in time. He slumped onto his knees, too exhausted to move another inch, and covered his face with his hands.

"Where did you get the money?" Mariamne asked Yudah Tzaer.

"Promise not to scorn me?"

Yakov stared at his nephew, dumbfounded. Yudah Tzaer had saved their lives. Whatever miracle had brought him the minor fortune and guided him to bring it to the temple today, Yakov was grateful.

"You're my son. I could never—"

"From Saul."

Yakov's head spun. Why would Saul give Yudah Tzaer money?

"He told me to come and see him. Follow him."

"And you agreed?" Mariamne looked horrified.

"It's a lot of money."

Yakov couldn't believe the words that had come out of his nephew's mouth. Once again, he owed Saul his life?

"Will you go?" he asked.

"No, Uncle, I would never go." He kissed his mother's forehead. "I was just playing his own game. Against him."

Yakov sighed with relief. They didn't owe Saul anything. Yudah Tzaer had saved them. Only a son of Yeshua would be that wise.

Later that night, as all the disciples cozied up by a bonfire singing songs of lament about the flight from Aegyptos, they heard someone bang on the gate of the compound.

Mariamne watched warily as Yakov rose to see who it could be. She hoped it was one of their own, one of the disciples who had returned from their pilgrimage.

Instead, a stranger with deep slashes across his face, in a robe stained with blood, stood at the gate. "I beg your refuge, kind friends," he croaked as his eyes, sparked with terror, darted back toward the road.

Yakov stepped aside to allow him entrance and quickly bolted the gate behind him. After Andreas and Yudah Tzaer helped the man sit down by the bonfire, Mariamne brought a vat of fresh water and clean rags. Together with Michal, the women washed his wounds.

"You were there. I saw you," the man said to Yakov in faltering Aramaic. "Aren't you the Ebionite teacher, the one they call Yakov the Just?"

Yakov cringed at the nickname the temple priests had awarded him. He didn't deserve the epithet. Still, the man had the right to know he had arrived at a safe place. "I am," he answered at last. "And who may you be?"

"My name is Shemuel bar Azai. I'm a carpet weaver, all the way from Provincia, in Gallia Narbonensis."

"You followed us here?" Yakov asked. "Are you a Roman citizen?"

"No! I'm a Jew, like you."

"Then how did you find us?"

Shemuel's eyes darkened with sorrow. "I ran, as far as my legs would carry me. I didn't know where to go, where I could be safe.

Then I heard your singing. You're Jews…" His voice shivered. "I mean no harm."

Mariamne gently placed one hand on his forehead to channel healing and peace into his mind. This man posed no threat. He couldn't even have fought the weakest of their men in the state he was in.

"I saw you there," Shemuel said again to Yakov. "I heard you preach. How did you get out?"

Everyone's eyes went to Yudah Tzaer.

"We left early," Mariamne blurted before anyone revealed something that might place them in danger. Even though it appeared unlikely, this man could be a Roman spy. "And you, why don't you tell us what happened after we left?"

Shemuel stroked his beard, then flinched when his hand grazed his wounds. Mariamne noticed his little finger had been amputated. Cut off for stealing?

"A soldier exposed his bare… privates to all the pilgrims. Imagine! What kind of man stoops to that level? In front of women and children, no less. On Passover!"

All the disciples lowered their heads at the thought.

"One of us, a Jewish man, climbed up on the roof and pulled down the half-naked soldier," Shemuel continued. "And before we knew it, a riot erupted. A brawl. Not one person stepped back—every one of us fought. You saw how many people there were at the temple. Thousands. Tens of thousands, perhaps. I fought, too, I'm ashamed to say. I couldn't help it. I'm a man of peace, but all the anger and frustration of living under the rule of those infidels… It boiled to the surface. For a moment, I even believed we would win. That we had recaptured the temple, our own territory. That the moment had come when our lives would finally change." He paused. "But then the killing started."

"Killing?" Yakov echoed.

A paralyzing pain spread through Mariamne's chest.

"The courtyard filled with soldiers," Shemuel said. "That governor of yours, Cumanus, must have seen the turmoil from his tower. Before we could blink, hundreds of legionnaires had joined the temple guardsmen in battle against us. Everyone ran for the exits, but the gates were all blocked. We were caught in a trap. Nowhere to escape. I have never seen so many people die before me." Shemuel's voice broke, and Michal handed him a cup of water. He drank slowly, as if gathering his strength to continue.

"All those people you saw in the temple today," Shemuel said, "they're gone. Butchered. Trampled to death."

"And you?" Yudah Tzaer asked. "How did you escape?"

Shemuel's eyes shadowed with shame.

"I lay onto the ground and pulled my headscarf over my face. I pretended to be dead. I lay there, immobile among the corpses, until the sun set and at last the soldiers left. Some of the gates are locked from the inside. I slid the bolt open and sneaked away as quietly as I could."

Mariamne's entire being filled with despair. A few moons ago, they had all hoped the new governor would bring much-needed change to Jerusalem. Peace, even.

"I bless you for your kindness," Shemuel said, "for your hospitality. And if your path ever takes you to Gallia…"

Yudah Tzaer stood, abruptly. He ran his fingers through his long brown hair, eyes narrowed, his lips twisted into tight resolution. "I need to go."

Mariamne watched her son, dazed by a sudden chill not caused by the fierce vernal winds.

"It's too dangerous," Yakov interrupted. "The world outside is not safe. We must remain here in hiding for now."

"I can't just stay here and wait to die." Yudah Tzaer turned to his mother. "I need to go out, preach. Do something."

"Listen to your mother." Yakov patted his nephew's shoulder. "We must stay here quietly, like we used to. Pray to God, ask for peace."

"What happened to all your courage?" Yudah Tzaer looked Yakov up and down. "And your faith that nothing real can be threatened?"

Yakov hung his head, defeated.

"Can you stand up to others only when you're embalmed in safety?" Yudah Tzaer continued. "Now is the time to go out there. We must fight for what's right."

"You could be killed," Mariamne said, her heart twisting into knots. She couldn't lose him. Not Yudah Tzaer. Not now.

"Don't worry. My father will look after me."

Mariamne closed her eyes to stem the tide of tears.

"Let him go," Yakov said bitterly. "He's as foolhardy as Yeshua always was. Nothing you do or say will deter him."

She glared at him. But her son was ready to gird up his loins and leave. She had no right to make him stay.

CHAPTER 24

Jerusalem, Judea, AD 49

Spring turned to summer, and fall turned to winter, without a word from Yudah Tzaer. Another spring came, followed by yet another summer. Every morning, Mariamne awoke with a single prayer: infinite love and gratitude for Yudah Tzaer's return. And every evening, she sent a word of thanks to Yeshua for keeping her son safe another day. Despite her conviction that Yudah Tzaer was wise enough to always act in the safest manner, she feared he would take up with the wrong crowd who could persuade him to capitulate in his beliefs. Or that he would fall prey to the Romans, whose assaults on innocent pilgrims were on the rise.

One fine summer day, Mariamne was sitting in the cool shade of the compound wall. With a basket on her lap, she picked through the summer's lentils and cleaned them of twigs and stones. The air stood still and thick and layered her skin with moisture. Beside her, Michal leaned over a round hand-stone. With arms as hefty as a grown man's thighs, she used the strength of her entire body to grind grains of barley by rubbing them against a flat bottom stone. So strong. So determined. And immensely proud when she gathered the perfect flour into a bowl. She wiped her forehead with one hand and dried it on her sweat-stained tunic. Then she placed two more palmfuls of barley between the stones and started grinding again. Once in a while she leered at Mariamne, who no longer had the strength for such physically challenging work. Mariamne smiled back. Over the years, she had learned to shower her sister-in-law with love, expecting no affection in return.

"Ladies." Yakov peeked out through the door. "Is the midday meal ready?"

"Oh no, yakiri," Michal said, "not yet."

"What's taking you so long? I'm famished. Do you need the hand of an able man?" He winked at his wife.

Michal shooed him away, giggling like a maiden. "You go on, rest your weary head. Leave the cooking to us women." She chuckled to herself as she returned her focus to the grinding stone. "Men, they think they can do it all. Manage an entire compound, take care of the animals, and still help the poor women with the food."

Mariamne bit her tongue. She guided the prayer of the holy bath at dawn. She fed the animals, cooked breakfast, cleaned their house, oversaw the craftsmen and shepherds to make sure no one needed her assistance, and prepared the midday meal. She attended the daily sermon, made supper, fed the animals again, and crashed into bed well after midnight. She did it all without a word of complaint, because this life was all she had ever wanted. She was living her dream. Why should it matter if no one else acknowledged her?

She scooped water into the clay pot that hung from a tripod over the fire. Then she added the lentils, garlic, cumin, cloves, salt, bay leaves, and a drop of goat's milk to the stew and covered the pot with a wooden lid. While Michal kept busy grinding the barley and daydreaming of her husband, Mariamne sat down to cut some cucumbers and carrots into cubes that she would mix with a splash of olive oil and lemon juice.

"Bread?" Mariamne asked, rousing Michal from her daydreams. "Shouldn't we have bread with our meal?"

"Can't you see I'm not nearly finished? A whole sack of barley I've ground while you have been sitting there doing nothing. And are those lentils even clean?" Michal peered into the bowl of lentils that Mariamne had cleaned earlier. "Or will I have to chew on stones and break my teeth like the other day?"

"Not at all. You keep grinding your grains, and I'll make the bread," Mariamne said. She removed the dough from its linen bundle where it had been rising and sniffed its fresh scent. "Mmm. Yakov sure loves his bread."

"Give it to me!" Michal grabbed the dough from her hands. "I told you I would do it."

"Oh? I thought you were busy with the barley."

Mariamne tried not to let Michal's outburst bother her and sat down to chop some onions and leeks. Before Mariamne moved into their house, Michal had believed that she was happily married. As the years passed, however, she must have realized that she and Yakov had nothing in common but their sons and daughters. And now that the children had grown up, all Michal had left was a husband who spent most of his time in Mariamne's company.

Yakov stepped into the courtyard, yawned from his nap, and stretched his arms up in the air. "It smells delicious. What is it, barley stew?"

"Lentil." Mariamne looked up from her vegetables. "Michal is making the bread."

"Wheat bread, yakiri." Michal held the basket up under his nose to show off her perfect rounds of flatbreads.

"Mmm" Yakov said, and Michal basked in her husband's praise.

Soon the courtyard filled with guests from the compound and from neighboring villages, all seated around large communal platters of food. Every meal was an open invitation, and often dozens of guests would share in their prayer of gratitude and enjoy their supper together. Miraculously, there was always enough for everyone.

As they dipped their last pieces of bread in the stew, two road-worn men stepped into the courtyard.

When Mariamne recognized them, she almost choked.

Yudah Tzaer and Taddai.

"My child!" She dropped everything and rushed to cover her son with kisses. "My dearest child!"

Michal, Yakov, and Taddai's wife, Rebekah, rushed to envelope Taddai in a tight embrace.

But Yudah Tzaer remained stiff in Mariamne's arms.

"What is it? What's wrong, my child?" She pushed him to arm's length to study his face.

Her son's eyes brewed with fear. Deep lines of worry layered his forehead as he grasped his mother's hands and kissed them.

"Look here!" Taddai said and rummaged through his sack. He brought out a papyrus scroll.

Yakov grabbed it from his hand and unfurled it. He studied the letters with a furrowed brow, then pushed it back to his son. "What does it say?"

"We had it read to us." Taddai's eyes shifted from his father, to his mother, to Mariamne.

"It's about Father," Yudah Tzaer added.

"Yeshua?" Mariamne said.

Yudah Tzaer nodded. "It says my father's the only one who can save us when the world comes to an end."

Yakov rubbed his temples in confusion. "Who wrote this rubbish?"

"It's signed by Paulus, Silas, and Timothy."

"Who?"

Yudah Tzaer's gaze dimmed with pain. "It's Saul, Uncle. Paulus is Saul. Saul wrote this letter."

Distraught, Yakov called for the Assembly to gather, and asked Levi, the only one among them who could decipher letters, to read the scroll out loud.

"'To the people of Thessalonia, who belong to the Father and the Lord Yeshua Christos, may grace and peace be yours,'" Levi read. "'Our brothers in Yeshua Christos, who turned away from idols, and awaited God's Son to descend from heaven: his own son, whom he raised from death and who will rescue us from God's imminent wrath.'"

"Wait a moment," Yakov said. "This letter isn't about your father. It's about another Yeshua. Someone called Christos."

"In Greek," Taddai explained, "*Christos* means 'the Anointed One.' The Messiah. They're calling Yeshua the Messiah."

"That bastard of a drunken goat!" Yakov turned to Mariamne. "I told him not to spread any more lies. Didn't he promise to respect us?"

Mariamne urged Levi to continue.

"'We have not appealed to you with impure motives,'" Levi read on. "'We follow God's commands and he has judged us worthy of his gospel. We have not sought praise from anyone, not even the brothers of the Lord.'"

Yakov tensed with anger. "Of course they didn't get praise from us. He's a liar and a crook. What did he expect?"

"'Because we do not seek to please people,'" Levi continued reading, "'we aim only to please God. But we acknowledge that you have suffered, like the brethren of Christos in Judea, who are persecuted by the same Jews who killed Lord Yeshua, and who also persecuted us.'"

The disciples looked at one another, stunned.

"The Jews didn't kill Yeshua."

"The nerve. To come here and make up stories."

"The snake!"

"What else do you know, Yudah Tzaer? Taddai?" Yakov asked.

"He doesn't live in Antioch any longer," Yudah Tzaer said. "He travels around the empire and speaks to the poorest of people, those who are so tired of the Roman rule and so hungry for a word of hope, they'd believe anything. Saul establishes places of worship everywhere he goes, and they call them *ecclesias*. Churches. Like synagogues, but not open to everyone. They allow you to participate only if you swear that this Christos was the *only* son of God. Then they pour water on the believers' heads and say, 'Now you are alive in Yeshua Christos.'"

Yakov scoffed. "Alive in Yeshua Christos. Imagine that."

"It's working, Father," Taddai interrupted. "Saul promotes his churches like exclusive societies. The hungry, the desperate, they're begging to join him. They believe he's got all the answers, that he will share his wealth."

"He'll make up any lies to get followers," Yudah Tzaer continued. "His throat is like an open sepulcher—he'll say whatever appeals to them. And as a token, they give him all the money they own."

"Saul lives off of these poor people," Taddai added. "Saul says Yeshua specifically chose him and Barnabas to do the work of God."

"Oh, I see, like Moses?" Mariamne said.

Everyone laughed.

"They travel all around the world," Yudah Tzaer continued. "To Seleucia, even to Cyprus. They go to synagogues and markets. They deceive anyone who will listen."

"They're not afraid of the Romans, then?" Phillipos said.

"They have no reason to be."

"The zealots, though, they're everywhere," Taddai interjected. "They stir up trouble and fight anyone who poses a threat to them."

His wife, Rebekah, took his hand, brought it to her lips, and kissed it. "Were you ever afraid?"

"Nowhere is safe any longer. Soldiers will stop you and search you at every crossroad, looking for weapons. As far as I know, there were anti-Roman factions in all settlements we passed through. To be honest, I can't tell you how many brawls I've seen between Jews and Romans. Sometimes I think I'm lucky to be alive."

"But we don't carry daggers," Yudah Tzaer said. "We travel in peace, and we greet both Romans and zealots with respect…"

Yakov scratched his head. How had he been so foolish, to allow these inexperienced men to travel into the jaws of danger? Was Yeshua's message worth the sacrifice?

"Did you see them?" Mariamne asked. "Saul and Barnabas?"

Taddai shook his head.

"Me, neither," Yudah Tzaer said. "But I followed them for a while, stayed a day behind. I wanted to know what they were up to, what they were saying. But in Paphos, on Cyprus, where I stayed for a few days to offer healing to the locals, a band of Saul's followers confronted me."

Mariamne pulled her headscarf over her face in shock.

"At first they were kind," Yudah Tzaer continued. "They didn't know who I was, and they wanted me to join their cause. But I refused. I told them I'm a bearer of The Way, my father Yeshua's true message. I explained how Saul spreads lies about my father, and that he was definitely not the only son of God."

"Good," Yakov said. "Well done."

"They didn't like that. So they spread rumors about me, accused me of being a sorcerer and a false prophet, full of all kinds of deceit and trickery. They even warned the locals about me."

Mariamne put her arm around Yudah Tzaer's shoulders. "Then what happened?" she asked, her voice as soft as cream. "Did you see them again?"

"I pretended to leave Cyprus to escape my tormentors, although in truth I continued to trace Saul's and Barnabas's footsteps. But they moved quickly from place to place. And with all the money they had collected, they didn't need to spare any costs, while I… I had to beg my way around."

The rays of the harsh afternoon sun burned the top of their heads. When Yakov saw that everyone's tunics were soaked with sweat, they raised a sheet above the courtyard to offer some shade. Michal and Mariamne filled a skin with water and let it make the rounds among the disciples. Once they had all cooled off, Yudah Tzaer continued:

"A village in Pisidia had invited Saul to speak, and that's where they went next. You know how Saul is—charming, seductive…" Yudah Tzaer glanced at his mother before he continued. "The common rabble likes him. The pagans. And the Romans, too, they don't mind worshipping yet another god and adding this Christos to their list of deities. I wish I had better tidings, but we need to understand what we're fighting. Saul's gospel is made up of legends and magic, all the things poor people want. And when they learn that they don't have to make an effort to be saved, simply worship this Christos to purchase their passage to heaven, they ask no questions. They don't need to become better men or change their lives. They don't have to be good and generous and helpful to others."

"Did he mean God's Kingdom—*that* heaven?" someone asked.

"Yes, that's what they promise people. Anyone who accepts this Yeshua Christos into their hearts will go to heaven. All others will be cast into the netherworld of Sheol. Saul says God fulfilled his promise to his people by bringing them his own son, the savior Yeshua Christos."

"I can believe some of that," Mariamne said. "At least I can believe God sent Yeshua to teach us his message of love."

"But Mother, that's not what Saul says," Yudah Tzaer objected. "He tells this story about Yochanan the Baptizer, that the Baptizer took one look at my father and told his followers that, 'This man who stands before us is the one we've all been waiting for. He's the Messiah. I'm not even worthy to wear his sandals.' Something to that effect."

Yakov laughed. "Oh, goodness, of all the joy upon Yeshua's head! I mean, truly. Yeshua would have loved that someone thought he was the Messiah. And cousin Yochanan, of all people? I remember when Yeshua returned from his first pilgrimage to Jerusalem as a child. He was so broken. All this time, he had imagined how he would go to the temple and that once he was there, God would reach out and touch him because he was extraordinarily gifted. Instead, his uncle Zekharyah ridiculed him and said a carpenter's son is nothing but a craftsman and can never be a priest. He told Yeshua he was a nobody."

Yakov chuckled. It was still funny.

"This isn't a laughing matter," Mariamne scolded.

"It's the truth! And Yeshua would have laughed, too. As much in love as he was with himself when he first left home, he returned as a grown man with a healthy sense of humor. And for Yochanan to say he was too lowly to wear Yeshua's sandals, that's just too much."

"What else?"

The crowd was getting impatient. Yakov signalled to Yudah Tzaer to continue.

"He says the Jews didn't recognize Yeshua as the Messiah, and that's why they killed him."

"First Saul said he's a Jew," Phillipos muttered, "and then he says Jews killed Yeshua? Can he make up his mind?"

"Saul says the Jews demanded that Pilatus kill Yeshua," Taddai added. "And then, listen to this: when Yeshua died, God raised him from the dead and then Yeshua walked around, whole again in a shining new earthly body, and visited all his Galilean friends and family."

"Isn't that what Kephas told us once?" Yakov asked. "He believed Yeshua would return to us in a new body or something?"

Andreas shrugged and looked at Mariamne. "And you? Don't I remember you saying that you had spoken to Yeshua after he died? That night in Kephas's house in Capernaum."

Yakov glared at Andreas. *Did he need to bring that up now?* Mariamne had been in shock. She had probably dreamed about Yeshua. But whatever she had claimed that night sounded exactly like something Yeshua would have said. And he had believed her.

"I did," Mariamne rose, as she had then, to face her accuser. "Yeshua spoke to me. But he came in spirit, never in the flesh."

Andreas laughed. "That's what you say now."

Yakov put his arm around Taddai and squeezed his shoulder. "Go on, son. Is there more?"

"Saul tells people my grandmother was a virgin all her life."

"Mother Maryam?" Mariamne said with a smirk.

"And my father, then?" Yakov said. "He didn't exist? I sprang from plain air? And what about all our brothers and sisters?"

"They believe God is Yeshua's father. And that your mother had no other children."

All the disciples looked at each other. Laughter spread around the courtyard.

"He forgot about Yakov already?" Mariamne asked. "And Tau'ma and Iosa and Salome…"

"He doesn't care. It's what works. Then he says that everyone's sins will be forgiven. All they have to do is believe in this Yeshua Christos."

"Without good deeds?" Yakov said. "You steal your neighbor's mule, but the next day you're forgiven, so you can steal another one, then another one, again and again?"

"According to Saul, the law of Christos has replaced the law of Moses. And the Torah has become irrelevant."

"I shouldn't have invited him in." Yakov slammed his cup against the ground so hard the dust soared. "He could have used someone else's name, someone else's story. We gave his imaginary deity life. We provided a name, a history. Now he's using it against us. Against Yeshua."

"But that's not true," Mariamne said. "Remember, he had already heard about Yeshua when he first visited. He sought us out, because he was already entranced by Yeshua. You're not to blame."

"I shouldn't have trusted him."

"You did what was right," Mariamne said.

"Uncle, the man's drunk with conceit." Yudah Tzaer slouched down next to Yakov. "Nothing you could have done would've changed that."

"The question is—where do we go from here?" Phillipos stood and stretched his legs. "How can we stop him? Or can we?"

"We'll continue what we do best, to spread Yeshua's teachings, no matter what Saul says or does." Yakov clenched his fists. "We *will* win this fight. The righteous always win."

"Saul is winning, Uncle."

Yakov stared at his nephew. He couldn't be right. Impossible. Saul had fallen prey to his ego, whereas the Assembly members were still true to God.

"There must be something we can do," Mariamne said.

"Can't we talk to him?" Phillipos spoke up. "Perhaps if we lay down some rules, we can coexist. Like we always planned to do."

"He won't agree to anything. He hates us."

The crowd fell silent in deep thought.

Michal fetched the broom as if she needed to keep busy. Everyone lifted their feet to allow her to sweep under and around them.

"We must appeal to his ego," Taddai said. "Pretend to accept him as one of us. That's what he always wanted, even if he'd never admit it. We'll let him believe we accept him into our midst, speak to him like equals."

"He'll only take advantage of us again," Mariamne said.

Yakov could sense her uncertainty, her unwillingness to let Saul return, seduce her again with his handsome face, his eloquence, his promises. Did she fear she wouldn't be able to resist him next time?

"All right. We'll devise a foolproof plan," Yakov said. "Look how many wise men there are among us."

"And women," Mariamne added.

Yakov laughed and patted her shoulder. "And women. In the end, we're all one, and therefore so is he. It's decided, then?" He searched the faces of his fellow disciples to make sure they were all in agreement. Then he turned to Levi. "Tomorrow, right at dawn, Michal will hand you a basket of eggs. You'll purchase a scroll of papyrus, two feet long, and bring a feather and ink. We'll draw up an invitation and send it first thing tomorrow morning."

And there they were: Saul, Barnabas, and Kephas entered the gate of the compound, as if no time had passed. Kephas's wife rushed to greet her husband, shrieking with delight as she knelt by his feet and brought his hands to her lips. The other disciples approached the travelers with caution, but when they noticed Kephas, they rushed to kiss his cheeks and pat him on the back. In their eyes, Kephas was still one of them.

"Welcome back to our humble compound," Yakov said and spread his arms wide. "May your stay here be long and restful."

Moments later, as they settled down to share a meal after their long journey, Mariamne casually peeked at Saul over her shoulder. Despite his short stature, he always appeared taller than other men. And more handsome, with his bright brown eyes, white teeth, and perfectly trimmed beard. She had to look, if just once, to ingest his noble face, delicate hands, and immaculately clean feet. And then, she promised herself, she would never view him as a man again. She even smiled a little, with mixed feelings, when she saw he was limping. Rumors had it that the citizens of Iconium had chased Barnabas out of town with stones raining over them.

"Vicious little things, those Pisidians," Saul said, and he took his seat closest to the meal platter, as if he didn't remember how he had fled from the compound with his tail between his legs only two years earlier.

"It's been difficult, then, your work?" Yakov asked, gesturing to Saul to help himself to the grilled lamb that the disciples had bought and prepared especially for him, as a token of peace.

"Not at all. Success paved our path, you'd be glad to know. The good Barnabas and I traveled along the coast of the Great Sea and informed the locals about your brother Yeshua. We have assisted oh so many in turning from their sinful idols and accepting Yahweh in their hearts."

"Is that so? And you haven't suffered under the Romans during your travels?"

"No, no." Barnabas said. "No problem with Romans."

"Aha?" Yakov scratched his beard. "Because we've received tidings that Emperor Claudius expelled all Jews from Rome."

"Have you, now?" Saul said. "I had not heard. And we certainly have not been affected."

"In that case, we are most pleased for you,"

Saul leaned forward nonchalantly and scooped up roasted barley with his right hand. With the other, he picked up a large cut of lamb. The smell of meat made Mariamne gag, but she pulled her headscarf over her face and pinched her nose closed. She had to stay silent. Any outburst from her could make Saul defensive and jeopardize their quest for an agreement.

"After Iconium we passed through Lystra, where I healed a lame man with mere faith." Saul nodded at Yakov with a boisterous twist to his mouth. "I did not even touch the man. I merely asked him to accept Yeshua Christos into his heart and believe. Before I could act further, the man jumped up from his mat and danced around like a lusty child."

"Yeshua Christos?" Yakov feigned ignorance. "Who is this Yeshua Christos?"

Mariamne held her breath in apprehension.

Saul combed his fingers through his hair. "My friend, have I not told you?" He placed one hand on Yakov's thigh. "When Yeshua appeared to me in all his glory, he called me his successor: the heir of the Messiah." Saul's eyes glittered. "Out of all men, God chose *me*. And although Kephas here has confessed that your brother, during the time he dwelled among you, was a good and simple man, he has now become the Messiah. The Christos."

"But—" Yakov interrupted, only to be silenced by Barnabas.

"Saul speaks truth. We baptize men in whole world. In name Christos. They are new now. New men."

Mariamne snickered behind her veil.

Kephas shot her an angry look.

"Sometimes people don't look so joyously upon you, though?" Yakov's voice oozed with sympathy. "I notice you're limping."

"Sometimes. Rarely." Saul pinched a strand of his beard and looked at it pensively. "But yes, some people frown at first when we preach against their faith, before they understand that we can save their souls. Mostly, however, people adore us. They worship the ground we tread on, bless their poor souls."

"And after Lystra, you returned to Antioch, where you received our letter?" Yudah Tzaer asked, making himself known for the first time.

"After some time, we did. After stopping by Derbe, Lystra, and Iconium again, where we strengthened the beliefs of our followers, and encouraged them to stay true to their faith. We passed through Perga and Attalia in Pamphylia before we sailed back to Antioch."

Saul searched Yudah Tzaer's face, as if he hadn't recognized him until now. "How have you fared, my son?"

"I'm in good spirits, Master Saul."

Mariamne laughed at how her son had placed a palpable distance between himself and the man who had once tried to buy his allegiance.

"You must visit the church in Antioch," Saul said, nodding at Yudah Tzaer. "In fact, you should all come. I have established churches all over the world and have appointed elders to manage the income and conduct the prayers until we—" With his forefinger, he drew a uniting circle in the air between himself, Kephas, and Barnabas. "Until we return."

"After Antioch you came straight here, to us?" Mariamne asked, to get the focus off her son.

Saul ignored her. "We stayed in Antioch for some time. In fact, the wording of your letter confused us." Saul withdrew a rolled up, worn papyrus from his sack and unfurled it. "This is from you? 'From the elders in Jerusalem, to the brethren in Antioch, Syria, and Cilicia: Greetings.' We honestly did not understand the meaning of your letter, of your invitation, until the good Kephas congregated with some of your traveling brethren."

"Our brethren?" Yakov looked at Kephas. "You've seen Tau'ma and Shimon? How are they—"

"Other men." Kephas raised his palms in dismissal. "Pilgrims who may have learned from Tau'ma or Shimon, or even heard our message in the temple, or…"

"And I must say, your men have behaved contemptuously," Saul continued. "They have hounded our faithful believers and told them they can't be saved unless they are circumcised under the law of Moses."

Saul's eyes bore into Yakov's, demanding an answer.

"You can't be *saved* by circumcision," Yakov said.

"Precisely! That is what I always tell my faithful ones." Saul looked pleased.

"It's a covenant with God," Yakov added.

"Perhaps, but it cannot save you! Am I correct?"

"Oh yes. You can only be *saved*, as you call it, by uniting with God."

Saul almost bounced off his seat with excitement. "We are in agreement, then. You can only be saved by believing that Yeshua Christos is your Savior, and that he died for your sins, and was resurrected on—"

"No! What?" Yakov stifled a laugh.

"What sins?" Phillipos asked.

"Yeshua Christos died for our sins," Saul said. "And after three days, his body rose from the grave, and he walked the earth in his renewed flesh before God called him home to heaven. The day the world ends, any day now, he will return on a cloud and bring home those who have been saved in his name. He will call us to join him in heaven, and we will live in God's kingdom for all time."

Phillipos hugged his knees and rested his chin on his fist. "You must be speaking about someone else. Our teacher's name was Yeshua bar Yosef. Some people called him the Nazarene, but never Christos. And he died. We buried his bones here in Jerusalem. He didn't rise from his grave. And he most surely didn't die for anyone's sins."

"He didn't even believe in sin," Mariamne added. "Besides, no one can save us but ourselves. No one can, and no one may. We alone must walk the path."

Saul pretended not to hear her.

Yakov straightened his face to hide his relief. The smoldering fire between Mariamne and Saul had finally died.

"Let's come to a consensus," Yakov said to Saul and Kephas the next day, as the three men walked up a hill behind the compound. Because Saul was limping, he needed monumental effort to make it to the top. Mariamne sauntered a few steps behind the men. They took a seat at a holy outlook spot that served as a temporary place of worship until the unrest around the temple died down.

"I know we may not agree on everything, but in general we're not that different, are we?" Yakov said.

"You invited us here." Saul glanced at Mariamne over his shoulder, before he returned his focus to Yakov. "I did not have to heed your call. I came because I sensed you needed my advice."

Yakov listened with compassion.

"You appear displaced, and it causes me grief," Saul continued. "You have lost your way again, like the time when we came to your aid during the great drought."

"Deep inside, we want the same thing," Yakov said. "But there's something that always confuses me about you. What sparks your need to fabricate stories and pretend you know something we don't?"

Saul laughed and patted Yakov's back. "Look at you: a kind and righteous man. Your brother chose wisely when he appointed you as his successor for the Assembly. But alas, he had not yet made my acquaintance. Now that Yeshua has requested that I complete his mission, I would like you to accept my best wishes."

Mariamne elbowed her way in between the men and faced Saul. "Will you listen for *one* moment? Why do you need to speak all the time? Don't you understand that the wisdom of the man before you rises much higher than yours?"

Saul smirked as if amused that a woman was speaking her mind. But Mariamne wouldn't be dismissed that easily. "Yeshua chose Yakov because there was no other choice. Not you. Not me. Not even Kephas."

"I didn't say anything," Kephas said. "Why are you looking at me?"

Yakov took Kephas's hand. "Speak your mind, old friend. Or has a lizard eaten your tongue?"

Kephas pulled his hand away. "I know what you think. Yes, I came here with Saul and Barnabas. But I've missed you."

Saul's smile faded, as if his secret weapon had turned against him.

"I've held strong," Kephas said, and used his hand to smooth out the dried earth on the ground beside him. "I've kept the law of Moses. I've dined apart from the gentiles. And I have always, regardless of what you may have heard, insisted on circumcision as a rule. I've upheld the law and everything Yeshua taught me."

Saul laughed. "He speaks the truth. Kephas, forever faithful to the Jewish tenet—at least whenever others are watching. And especially since your brethren arrived to meddle with us. Before that, he gladly dined with anyone. And, I must confess, once your men understood that we may become whole in God's eyes only through our faith in

Yeshua Christos, they turned into innocent sheep. They realized my truth was the only truth."

Kephas looked so uncomfortable in his own skin that Yakov had to squeeze his friend's shoulder for comfort.

Saul continued, even louder than before: "We please God by our union with Christos. I have been put to death together with Christos on the same cross. It is no longer I who live, but Christos who lives within me. And I refuse to reject the grace of God! That's why we must condemn the law of the Jews. Because if someone could please God through the law of Moses, it would mean Yeshua Christos died for nothing!"

"The difference between Yeshua and you," Yakov said, "is that Yeshua's every thought and action stemmed from unconditional love. Once we approach all people we meet with love, we become one with God. Because we are all sons of God. We are all love."

"Yeshua Christos was the one and only Son of God," Saul said. "That is the truth, not whatever rubbish you just proclaimed."

Yakov gazed across the valley. This wasn't working. How could he make Saul understand that Yeshua was a teacher, not a god? That his lessons were more valuable than his person?

Mariamne squatted next to Saul and looked into his eyes, without fear. "We need to work together. Yeshua's message, the Good News, that's what's important. If we can keep his message alive, Yeshua didn't die for nothing."

"The Good News?" Saul raised his eyebrows. "Have you closed your ears to all the words I have spoken? I communicate with Yeshua Christos every moment, every day. He guides my every step, every action."

"Is that so?" Mariamne tilted her head and gazed at Saul from under her eyelashes, making herself look irresistible.

What would Saul do now? Would he listen to her?

"If that's the case, what is he saying right now?" she asked sweetly.

Saul chortled, his gaze lost among the clouds. "If he had met me before he died, he would have chosen me as your leader. He *did* choose me. Of this I hold no doubt."

A heavy raindrop spluttered on the top of Yakov's head, and he looked up. The sky had filled with ominous clouds. He shuddered. "Saul, please listen to me. We should strive toward a common goal, help each other. Yeshua wants me to carry his torch. He has faith in me."

"I'm glad you came," Mariamne said.

Saul refused to look at her.

"We all are. Truly. Let's make this a new beginning. We can grow from here, like fresh buds in springtime."

The raindrops were falling faster. More densely. Yakov scoured the sky for signs of what to expect: persistent rain or passing gloom?

"Why does it always rain when I visit?" Saul complained and pulled his headscarf over his forehead.

"It's not raining that hard," Kephas said. "Listen, Yakov, you've got to see Saul's point of view, too. Hear him speak. To tell you the truth, sometimes when Saul speaks, I think Yeshua is back, as if he speaks through him."

Saul grinned.

Yakov looked at Saul and shook his head. "Perhaps the light of God does show through you at times. Like it shows through any of us. But would you please listen? We can work together, as one."

"He's right," Mariamne said.

Yakov exhaled as a sense of peace enveloped him. *Dearest Mariamne, always on my side.* "We can," he said. "If only you would try to see things from our point of view."

The rain splattered harder and harder.

Saul stood and wiped the wet mud from his mantle. "It is impossible to think with a clear head in this downpour. Let us return to your shack, I mean your house. I understand that you truly believe God loves you, and what you do is enough. But if God loved you, he would hear your prayers, like he did Elijah's. Can't you see? You are more like King Ahab. You have placed your faith in a false god."

They barely made it under cover before the rain turned torrential. Michal made space for everyone inside the barn, shooing the poor goats and donkeys out into the courtyard.

Although Yakov had laughed at Saul's comment about the prophet Elijah and King Ahab, it had crept under his skin. According to legend, the king of Israel had married a princess of Tyre and had allowed her to worship the pagan gods Baal and Astarte in his own castle. When Yahweh discovered this sin, he became outraged and cursed Ahab's kingdom with a terrible drought that resulted in years of famine. Then he sent his prophet Elijah to explain that worshipping false gods had brought the famine to his people and to teach King Ahab how he could set things right. But instead of listening to Elijah's advice, King Ahab challenged Elijah to a competition to determine which was the most powerful god: Yahweh or Baal. The king called on Baal to bring rain, but nothing happened. But when Elijah called on Yahweh, a thunderstorm immediately erupted and a flood of rain soaked the dried-out country. King Ahab admitted his defeat, but in the end Elijah killed him, anyway.

No doubt Saul considered himself superior to Yakov. But didn't he understand he was the one who was making a false god out of Yeshua, like Ahab had made of Baal? Not the other way around.

"Maybe you're both right," Kephas said when they had regrouped in the dark enclosure that reeked of animal excrement, listening to the rain drumming against the clay-covered straw roof. "It's time to make peace. Forget our disagreements."

Yakov looked expectantly from Kephas to Saul.

Mariamne leaned forward and spoke directly to Saul: "We understand that in your world, among the people you encounter, circumcision is not important. That the gentiles have other customs, other ways of proving their allegiance to God. But you've traveled all the way from Antioch to Judea for a reason. Are you willing to form an alliance with us or not?"

Saul shifted in his seat. He turned his back to Mariamne and addressed Yakov. "If you still, after all I have tried to explain, consider circumcision important and cannot fathom that faith in our Lord, our savior, will suffice, then you are men of trifling power. You still believe that when a woman has given birth to a son, she shall be unclean for seven days. And on the eighth day the flesh of a male child's foreskin must be cut?"

Yakov drew a deep breath and tried to quiet his beating heart. A wave of nausea swept over him. "It's a Jewish tradition."

Saul crinkled his nose. "Correct me if I am mistaken, but don't the sacred scriptures, the scrolls of Shemot, suggest that a lowly slave, if circumcised, may join your Passover meal, whereas a wealthy traveler whose foreskin remains intact should never be invited? Then how can you insist all men are of equal value?"

"Why are you so opposed to circumcision?" Yakov prodded. "It's a simple act of acknowledging God. A proof of commitment that you are serious in your devotion to God."

Saul grinned, but Yakov could tell he had made a point.

"And why can't *you* accept that Yeshua Christos commanded me to bring his gospel to gentiles who do not care about circumcision? Honestly, I struggle to understand your strictness concerning the matter. Why would God care if all those holy men in the Far East, those with whom you claim Yeshua studied, were circumcised?"

Yakov's cheeks flushed with anger. This man would not negotiate. He picked up a stick and stabbed the tip into the soft clay floor, breaking it into chunks of dirt.

"Surely grown men shouldn't have to endure the snip," Kephas said. "Adults."

"Ouch!" Saul laughed and grabbed his groin to emphasize how painful the procedure would be.

But the pain should not be the issue. A day or two of discomfort was an insignificant price to pay to show allegiance to God.

"Can we all agree," Mariamne said, louder this time, "that we'll be stronger if we unite? If only we accept each other's views, however absurd these fantasies may seem, we could reach more people and spread Yeshua's word farther. There's no need to fight each other." She leaned forward and placed her hand on Saul's knee. "Did Yeshua require that all men be cut? No, but the world is a different place now. More dangerous. We live under a constant threat."

Saul grabbed her wrist and shoved it back into her own lap. "What I speak of is not a fantasy."

"Why not let Saul and Barnabas communicate their gospel to gentiles?" Kephas suggested. "Isn't the message, the Good News, what's important?"

The Good News. That's what this was all about. Yeshua had given his life for this peaceful, uniting message of oneness.

"Kephas's words make sense," Mariamne said. She patted the floor next to her to urge Yakov to sit down.

Yakov swallowed. The look on her face, those immense eyes, full of love and admiration for him. She was right. It was time to let this go. If Saul preached only to gentiles, and left the Assembly to teach all the Jews in Judea, Samaria, Galilee, and the Decapolis, how much damage could he cause?

"All right." Yakov stretched his hand out to Saul. "Let's agree on this; circumcision is unnecessary for non-Jews. But don't break the yoke of faith: from now on you will preach only to gentiles, and you won't speak of Yeshua as a god."

Saul looked at his outstretched hand.

"Saul?" Kephas said, eager to have them come to a consensus.

Without turning to look at Kephas, Saul grasped Yakov's forearm, and Yakov grabbed his. With a firm grip, they nodded to each other as a sign of agreement.

Yakov sighed with relief. At last, their struggles had come to an end. From now on, life would be easier. "Blessed is your mother, who brought your goodwill to this world, Saul."

"It's Paulus, actually," Saul said, and let go of Yakov's arm. "My correct name is Paulus. I thought you knew."

"Kephas, don't do this," Yakov pleaded as they watched Kephas and his wife roll their tunics and mantles into bundles and stuff them into their traveling sacks. A rising wave of failure washed over him and blinded him with angst. How could Kephas still choose Saul over him, especially now that their power struggle had ended?

"It's Rosh Chodesh soon," Levi added. "Let your wife celebrate the new moon with her sisters before you leave us."

Yakov had tried for days—even begged—but whatever he said blew over Kephas's head like bubbles from a swirling brook. His words sailed away into the wind and popped into nothingness without any effect on his friend.

"Saul's promised to let me lead one of his churches in Syria, Yakov. How can I say no? And I'll remain your trusted source," Kephas said, unconvincingly. "Let me go—let me preach the Good News like we used to do. I'll keep an eye on Saul, make sure he tells the truth about Yeshua and the Kingdom of God."

"You still bleed with envy." Levi said. "That's why you're leaving."

Kephas's wife pulled her headscarf over her head to cover her flustered face.

"You think I'm envious? Of whom?"

Levi scoffed. Kephas's reason to leave had nothing to do with keeping Saul on the straight and tapered path. Kephas, who had once been a successful fisherman, now found it difficult to settle into anonymity. He still longed for people to admire him. And what better way than by telling strangers he had once been the confidant of the Messiah?

But Yakov still loved Kephas like a brother, and the anger soon dissipated into sorrow. There was nothing anyone could do. Kephas was a free man. He had the right to leave and start anew in a land up north.

They walked Kephas and his wife to the crossroad and watched them disappear into the Judean hills.

"Come." Mariamne grasped Yakov's hand. "Let's think this over."

Yakov shivered at the warmth of her skin when her hand enveloped his. But surely Mariamne meant to confer no intimacy.

They climbed to the peak of a hill pockmarked with hundreds of rock-hewn tombs overlooking the Kidron Valley.

"The times have changed," she said as she folded her linen scarf and placed it on the ground as a clean seat for the two of them. "We must make alternative plans, decide how we can bring peace to this unknown world."

Yakov avoided her eyes. He knew too well how easy it would be to lose himself in those seductive wells of her soul. "I believed we'd won, but with Kephas leaving... We have already faced defeat."

"I will never give up." She gently pressed his hand to her lips. "And you're wrong. We're winning. We *have* won."

Jerusalem, Judea, AD 52

Another three years passed without a word from Saul or Kephas or Barnabas. Now that they had come to an agreement, life seemed easier, more full of hope. In the safety of their compound, Mariamne and Yakov could pretend their life remained unburdened by threats from Romans and rebels, and all that mattered was that their message was spreading from mouth to mouth, farther and farther from Judea, like a word on a wing.

Every day, Mariamne hiked up the steep path to the meditation rock on top of the hill overlooking their compound. Today was no different. In the distance, fluffy clouds moved toward her, blowing in from the faraway ocean. Springtime was finally here, with its delicate green leaves, tiny flower buds that sprang open, and new seedlings that stretched up through the cracked dry earth. Rain would come soon with days of fresh winds, ending the annual drought and allowing her to rest and enjoy the warm licks of the sun.

And like any other day, she found Yakov already sitting there, in a deep trance. She cleared her throat. When Yakov opened his eyes, she flashed him a smile. He was older now, more weary. She must have aged too, but she couldn't see it and didn't feel it. Her body was as eager as before, although she had let no man touch her since she rejected Saul all those years ago. She had not remarried and had not allowed herself a moment of carnal relief, except for the ecstasy her fingers brought her at night beneath her heavy blanket.

"A shekel for your thoughts," she said and stroked a strand of hair from his eyes.

I love you, she hoped he would say. She longed to melt into his arms and taste his sweet lips, press her body against his.

But instead of succumbing to his desires, he froze at her touch.

"You're still worried about the zealots?" she asked. The war between good and evil had escalated into a war between evil and evil. In their quest to cast out the Romans from Judea, the zealots were killing innocent people and thus inadvertently placing all others in the path of danger.

"Taddai came upon another letter. From Thessalonica."

"Rome?"

Yakov chortled. "Your sense of geography is terrible. It's in Macedonia. But the scroll is tattered and worn, so who knows when it was written. Perhaps years ago, long before Saul's last visit."

Mariamne's eyes widened, but Yakov just shrugged.

"And? What does it say?"

Yakov lifted her chin with his finger, and she raised her mouth to meet his. But when she opened her eyes, his eyes brimmed with worry, not love.

"It's Saul. Paulus. He didn't abide by any of the rules we agreed upon. He tells his followers *we* are the ones who displease God. That we're hostile to everyone but our own people."

"I told you not to worry about him," she said. "Leave him to score points with the pagans and the ignorants."

"It's more than that. Paulus claims the Assembly of Jerusalem has sinned against God and that we have brought the cup of God's fury down upon ourselves."

Mariamne frowned. But she knew that whatever Paulus did, there was no need for concern. "These people, they're far away. Macedonia, isn't that what you told me? They'll never come here, we'll never meet them. Who cares what they believe?"

"I care!" Yakov said. "Saul's mocking us. He's laughing at our expense."

"He's a tentmaker, Yakov. He doesn't need manners."

"And these people who adore him? I can't understand why."

"Maybe they don't." Mariamne squeezed his shoulder with compassion. "Maybe it's all in his imagination."

But a seed of doubt had sprouted in her mind.

"'The Lord has spoken,'" Levi read out loud from the scroll that Taddai had intercepted. A crowd of disciples had gathered before him in Yakov's courtyard.

"'The day of the Lord will arrive as a thief in the night,'" he continued reading. "'The archangel's voice will shout out a command, and when God's trumpet blares, the Lord will descend from above. The deceased followers of Yeshua Christos will rise from their graves, and the Lord will gather us all up into the clouds to meet God. From then on, we will always remain beside our Lord.'"

Levi paused, confused. "What lord?"

"What else does it say?" Yakov asked.

"'Once everything is calm and quiet,'" Levi continued, his gaze pinned on the papyrus scroll in his hands, "'destruction will hit the earth. Fire and fury, without warning, resembling the birthing pains of a woman in labor.'"

Mariamne smirked. The childless Saul knew nothing about giving birth.

"'But you, my Thessalonian brothers in Christos, will not dwell in darkness,'" Levi read. "'Awake and sober, we belong to the light. God did not choose us to suffer his anger, but to possess salvation through our Lord Yeshua Christos.'"

Mariamne broke out laughing. She watched Yakov chew on his thumb to contain himself, but the chuckles exploded from his mouth, and soon they all giggled.

"Yeshua would've been furious," Phillipos said. "Save some and let others burn? What kind of god has Paulus created?"

Mariamne tried to stifle her grin. "Yeshua would have laughed, too. Don't you remember? Rage always amused him. He never became defensive."

Levi cleared his voice and read, "'Make it your aim to be good to all the people you meet.'"

"He should talk," Mariamne said.

"'Lift your souls to God at all times,'" Levi continued. "'Be joyful in your union with Yeshua Christos.'"

"So, is this Yeshua Christos a god?" Phillipos asked. "What happened to 'Thou shalt have no other gods before me'?"

Yakov chuckled, but his eyes teemed with sadness.

"Levi read, 'By the authority of the Lord, I proclaim this letter to all believers. May the grace of our Lord Yeshua Christos be with you.'"

The crowd fell silent as Levi rolled up the papyrus scroll.

Mariamne felt defeated. All the effort of inviting Saul and Barnabas to Jerusalem, of negotiating and coming to an agreement, had been for nothing. Saul was traveling farther, speaking to more people, delivering an increasingly fantastical gospel. How much longer could they keep Yeshua's original message alive?

"We've got to do something," Bar-Tôlmay said.

Yakov scratched his back. "Let's spend a moment every day praying for his happiness. *May he be blessed, may he be joyful, may love surround him.* And perhaps one day we'll find that either he has changed—or we no longer care."

"And what else?" Mariamne urged. "We need to take action."

"Mother's right," Yudah Tzaer said. "We have to do something. Who is willing to travel?"

"What about Ventidius Cumanus? Won't he try to stop us?" Phillipos asked.

A glimpse of fear flashed in Yakov's eyes before he recovered his gravitas. "Who is Cumanus, anyway? He's guided by the gods of greed. If we proceed with love, with faith in our success, we cannot fail." He looked at his fellow disciples. "Who is ready to fight back?"

They all raised their hands. Every man, woman, and child among them wanted to accept the challenge, go out on the road, and preach Yeshua's true words to the people of Judea, Samaria, Galilee, and far beyond. They heeded the call of centuries of oppression and grasped at this opportunity to make a difference in the world outside Judea.

But a grim shadow eclipsed Mariamne's heart.

Were they sending their brethren to their death?

"Look at you," Yakov called out to the excited crowd before him a few days later as they rested on the slopes of the Mount of Olives among trees in full bloom. They were close enough to the temple to absorb its divine energy, still safely out of reach of the legionnaires stationed outside the gates of the Holy City. "I see your passion for our cause. But remember to always remain students, forever learning." When he detected their disappointed faces, he added, "Oh, don't fret, you're all wonderful teachers. But you must revel in your ignorance, because only students are allowed to make mistakes. And we all do. Often. Even our Yeshua. Although he was perfect most of the time, he wasn't perfect *all* the time."

The men and women of the Assembly shifted in their seats, impatient. Yakov scrambled to find the right words and insert some notes of positivity. They had to do this right, or their message would dissipate, like the petals of the delicate olive flowers that fell like gentle snowflakes to the ground at the softest breeze. "Don't despair, my dearest friends. Much like we place a bit in the mouth of a mule to make it obey our commands, or use a small rudder to steer a boat through a storm, our tongues can bring powerful changes to the lives of others."

Everyone's tongues moved in their mouths to test their power, and Yakov laughed. An immense sense of relief washed over him. He could do this. He was born to do this.

"Remember that great fire last year?" he continued. "The one that consumed village after village before it died down. It was set ablaze by the tiniest flame! Our tongues are like that fire. One tongue can do a world of good, but if we're not careful, it can also spread wickedness throughout our beings like poisoned blood. Trust that you will all be safe, because a spring cannot bring forth both sweet and bitter waters. A fig tree cannot bear olives, and a grapevine cannot bear figs. Nor can a salty sea make sweet drinking water."

All eyes were on him, confused. He had to be clearer. He reached out and drank from the waterskin, then wiped his face with the back of his hand. He shifted in his seat to ease the dull ache in his lower back from sitting still too long. "Many years ago, on a day not unlike this, my brother Yeshua gathered a small group of us around him. Mariamne and I, and also Kephas and Tau'ma, and our old friend Yudah... Andreas, you were there, too."

Andreas nodded, with a faint expression of reminiscence.

Oh, how young and innocent they had been then. How naïve. And still, how well they had taught. Surely the young men and women who had grown up in the Assembly were even better fit for missionary work. Yakov's heart swelled with love as he looked from one disciple to the next. "Yeshua always said that the teacher and learner are one. When we teach, we demonstrate what we know, and at the same time we listen to our own words. We diminish our self-doubt. Remain present, in the moment, and dwell in that holy instant. Recognize God in everyone around you and listen to what their souls are telling you. Teach others to begin their day with a cleansing bath and a prayer, and to open their hearts and become one with all. Now, who still thinks they are ready to teach?"

Days turned into weeks, and spring turned into summer while Yakov and Mariamne trained all the apostles who had volunteered to travel far and wide to spread the Good News around the world while a few stayed behind to keep the compound functioning. More women than men had to remain, because the women were better at farming, at animal keeping, at cooking and cleaning. The compound also needed a carpenter, a weaver, and a couple of strong guardsmen, as well as the tailors Iosa and Abram, whose fine garments brought in more money than all the other sales combined. Both Yakov and Mariamne would remain to care for Michal, who had fallen ill. But Andreas had applied to travel, as had Yudah Tzaer, and all three of Yakov's sons.

"I'm going to look for Shimon," Taddai said one day. "I know he's still out there preaching, and I'd like to go find him."

"It might not be a wise plan." Yakov patted Taddai's shoulder in an effort to impose his fatherly power upon his grown son. "Remember what a short fuse Shimon has. He might get you into trouble."

"Father, have you forgotten that I already traveled with him? He has a temper, yes, but he's also good and kind and fair. And he's wise. I'll go find him, continue his work wherever he is. Surely a man of his age will need a younger companion."

Yakov looked at Taddai, suddenly astonished at the fine wrinkles at the corners of his son's eyes and the odd gray strands in his beard. His son was no longer a child. Of course he could only do good, could only strengthen whatever Shimon had built. "But how will you find him?"

Taddai laughed. "Don't you remember how passionate he was? How people would stop and listen to him because of his powerful voice?"

"I remember, always yelling."

"Not yelling, shouting with excitement. There's no one like him."

"You want to go south, then?"

"No, to Persia. I heard he has settled there."

"Persia? That's too far. A young man should not travel alone through the deserts."

"Uncle Yeshua traveled alone throughout the entire world."

"The world was different in those days. Safer." Yakov folded his arms across his chest, hoping to gather strength. But instead he felt deflated, empty. He had no power over Taddai, nor did he have the right to hold him back. "And what about Rebekah? Your children?"

Taddai lifted his chin to gaze straight at his father. The wind tousled his long hair.

Yakov's eyes did not yield. But Taddai would not budge. He had already made up his mind, although the sadness in his eyes revealed that the decision had not come easily.

"I will let her know tonight," Taddai said.

Yakov's heart ached at the thought of losing his son. "You'll do what you have to do. Just remember, we all have the same purpose; we are all children of God."

"I know, Abba."

"Don't convince yourself you're special and others are not. All God's children are special. And none of God's children is special."

Taddai placed his arm around his father and squeezed his shoulder. "I *know*. You've told me a hundred times before."

"Please return unscathed. Promise?"

Taddai kissed the top of his father's head.

As Yakov watched him walk away, he sensed with all the certainty of his entire being that once his son left, he would never return.

Mariamne wished she could reach out and embrace Yakov. Tell him that everything would be all right. But ever since Michal had fallen ill and become bedridden, he had become even less approachable. Apart from conducting the prayer during the early morning baths, Yakov rarely left his wife's side. It seemed he no longer had any time—or need—for Mariamne.

One night, long after everyone had slipped off to sleep, Mariamne woke and found Yakov sitting alone in the courtyard, cross-legged, with his palms resting on his lap, contemplating the stars above. He startled as she sat down at his side, close enough for their thighs to touch.

"My son is leaving, too." She wanted him to know she understood his pain.

Yakov simply sat there, motionless, without acknowledging her presence.

"I know you feel responsible for every one of us. But you didn't make their decisions. They volunteered."

Mariamne placed her hand gently on his thigh. Yakov flinched, but he didn't move away.

"I spoke to Bar-Tôlmay," she said. "He'll join Taddai on his travels east. The two of them will do well together."

A tear ran down Yakov's face. He wiped it away, then pushed her hand off his thigh. "Bar-Tôlmay is old."

"Not older than you. And he's a faithful man. Wise and honest. Taddai will be safer traveling with him than alone."

Yakov scrambled to his feet and brushed the dust from his robe. "Is it worth it?"

Mariamne looked at him, confused.

"What we're doing. Is protecting our message from Paulus's lies so important it's worth the risk of sending our men to their demise?"

Mariamne rose and embraced him like a child. She didn't care if anyone saw them. She was long past caring what others thought.

Yakov wriggled himself free. He walked to the gate, his gaze still focused on the stars, as if hoping they would provide the assurance he needed. "It's not right. This isn't right."

"They all volunteered."

"They stepped forward only because I asked them to. They believe in me. And they shouldn't."

"Don't say that."

"It's true. I'm asking them to save a message, to risk their lives for something that might not matter in the end."

"You're only doing what Yeshua did. They believe, as he did, as we do, that if we can teach others oneness with God, they will find peace. Freedom. Salvation, even."

"What if it doesn't matter?"

"Don't be silly. Nothing else matters. We have to bring enlightenment to as many as we can reach. Yeshua died for this."

"He died for himself."

Mariamne shivered, as if a frosty wind had permeated her soul. "Don't," she said quietly, but the same thought had crossed her mind more than once. Yeshua had died because he refused to give up. He possessed an almost criminal faith in God. He believed that if you awakened to the truth, you'd become one with God while still alive, and you would not have to be reborn again. Reaching Nirvana was the meaning of life, he said, adamant that all people needed to learn this, that the knowledge would eradicate any troubles, wars, and all suffering. But their worries had not dissipated. Twenty years later, they were still struggling to convince others of the truth in Yeshua's words. Maybe they had been wrong; maybe returning to Jerusalem had been a misguided move. Perhaps they should have gone out on pilgrimages from day one, like Paulus had. Instead, they had been crouching here like crippled ducks, waiting for a hunter to find them and shoot them down.

"We've got to do this, Yakov. It's bigger than you or me. It's more important than any of us. God depends on us to save the world. And they will all be safe. Yeshua will protect them."

"I hope you're right, Mariamne. I dearly hope so."

A few days later, Mariamne, Yakov, and the other disciples went to the temple for the first time since the uprising. They ventured through the checkpoints, passed the Roman soldiers standing guard at the crossroads, and hiked across the valley and up the temple stairs for a last sermon before the apostles set out on their journeys. The atmosphere at the holy temple had changed. God's abode, which had once been a sacred, almost ethereal place, was now chaotic and crude and loud, full of gentiles and beggars. The only spot where you could find serenity these days was at the far end of Solomon's Portico, where, when you closed your eyes, you could still feel heaven seep through your skin and fill your entire being with pure love. And once you became one with the crowd, it was worth the stress of arriving and leaving.

"The time has come for us to face the world in peace," Yakov said after everyone had settled around him in the shade. "We must always rise above our troubles. Don't fear those who attack you. Those who act in violence are nothing but sad and lonely men. They're terrified of the world. You, however, know how to access the stillness of God inside, whatever happens on the outside. We've survived the most frightful circumstances. Now we can endure anything. Always respond with affection, never with anger or trembling. Only love can win."

Mariamne closed her eyes and drank in his words. Last night Yakov had appeared overwhelmed with doubt. This morning he had awakened with fresh resolve, convinced their plan was the right course of action. Still, she knew him well enough to know what caused him the most anxiety was the risk of failing those who trusted him. He was a decent man. The best of them all.

"When you face the power of darkness," Yakov continued, "don't be afraid and think your time has come. Fear empowers the darkness. Instead, seek for the place of refuge in your souls, the all-knowing, the domicile of God, where no threats or enemies exist."

Yakov had closed his eyes and was speaking from his heart. Mariamne relaxed and devoured his words.

Bar-Tôlmay cleared his throat. "When I listen to you, Yakov—I mean, when you speak—who is it who speaks, and who listens?"

Yakov laughed, as if he had been expecting the question. "One who speaks also listens. You know that, don't you? Just like the one who sees also opens the eyes and ears of others."

Mariamne let love flow from her chest, and like a ray of the sun, she reached out to Yakov and enveloped his heart.

"All what you seek," Yakov said, "you can find within. The voice inside you has all the power of the spirit, because it is spirit. Always remember that."

Back at the compound, Michal's health withered with each passing day. What had started as a simple cold slowly spread to her lungs and then throughout her entire body and ultimately rendered her debilitated. Whatever Yakov did, however he tried to cure her with herbs and potions and healing hands, her soul seemed to have surrendered to its final passage.

Yakov took Michal's feeble hand in his. "Live for me," he said. "Survive for me, yakiri. I can't go on without you."

Michal's eyelids fluttered but failed to open. Yakov wiped her forehead with a damp cloth, doing whatever he could to bring her comfort in her last hours. Oh, how he regretted ignoring Michal all those nights when she had turned her back to him in bed because he had come back home late after a long walk in the hills with Mariamne. He should have made his wife feel loved and desired. Instead, he had grunted his annoyance with the jealousy that devoured her. Sadly, Michal had to become sick and fade away before Yakov realized his mistake. The fool he had been!

"Do you love me?" Michal said, her voice barely audible.

"Of course."

Michal's parched lips moved as if to say something, but no sound escaped.

Yakov crouched down and leaned closer to her mouth to hear better.

"And Mariamne?" she asked. Breathed.

A hurricane of guilt rose through his core and swallowed him whole. His cheeks burned. "No," he lied. "She's a friend, that's all. Always was. Please believe me."

Out of the corner of his eye, he saw Mariamne move into the shadow by the door. She had heard him. But right at this moment, he didn't care.

"Live for me!" His voice cracked with despair. Tears filled his eyes, and he let them fall freely, aware that his wife was drifting into oblivion, into nothingness.

This time, Michal's lips remained still. Her facial muscles relaxed like a field that settles after a breeze has rippled through it, and the lines of her forehead smoothed.

"Don't go!" Yakov pleaded as her body went limp. He lifted her into his arms, to coax her back to life, but the moan that passed her lips carried her last gust of life.

His gaze moved up to the ceiling where, for a moment, a flicker of light danced in circles before it dissolved into thin air.

And his wife's body turned cold in his arms.

The sun had barely risen above the mountain ridge when Yakov staggered out into the courtyard. All around, his best men and women were filling their traveling sacks with their most essential belongings. Even his sons, unaware that their mother had passed, were preparing for the most important journey of their lives. For a moment, Yakov wondered if he should share the sad news, but he didn't want to burden them. Their grief would be for naught. They could never bring their mother back.

"Come gather around me," Yakov called out, struggling to keep his voice stable.

With their hair still wet from their ritual bath, the apostles left their packs on the ground and entered the courtyard where Mariamne and Yohannah had kindled the fire and were baking flatbreads for the travelers to take on their journey.

Mariamne's striking eyes pleaded for Yakov's attention, but he couldn't bother with her right now.

Instead, he pulled Taddai to his chest and kissed his grown son's forehead.

"The true Kingdom of God lives within you," he said to his son and to everyone around him. "Never forget that your good deeds are as important as your faith."

Mariamne and Yohannah walked in between the apostles and handed out pieces of bread drizzled with honey and topped with cheese and olives. Whenever Yakov's gaze accidentally met Mariamne's, he turned his face away.

"Remove any traces of anger, suspicion, and jealousy from your minds," he preached. "Don't let negative thoughts taint you. Fill your hearts with love today. Gladness is the only way to clear your mind and make you free."

Phillipos placed his arm around his wife, Yohannah, and drew her close for an intimate kiss. Yakov shuddered with a sting of envy at the affection they shared. Kindred souls. The two had met when Yohannah had first joined Yeshua's disciples as an affluent widow who had brought the group considerable funds. Soon afterward, passion blossomed, and they had exchanged their marital vows. And now Phillipos was leaving her to preach in faraway lands, Syria and Cilicia, perhaps even farther away in Cappadocia and Pisidia. How on earth had Phillipos persuaded his wife to let him go?

Yakov quavered with fatigue, but he forced himself to stay focused. Had he slept at all? He wasn't sure. Michal had passed in the dead of night, and he had lain there with her frail body in his arms, immersing her in all the love he had failed to offer while she was alive.

"Let me tell you a story," he continued. He rubbed his eyes to stay awake. "When God created the world, he collected water in a jug, and the Word appeared from it." He stifled a yawn. "The Word rose high into the sky, above the stars. And God said to the Word, 'Go, and send a message to the people of this world, so they may not be in want from generation to generation.'" Yakov paused and absorbed a jolt of energy through the crown of his head. "The Word sent fountains of milk and honey and oil and fine fruit to the beings on earth. He sent delicious spices and healing herbs to make sure none ever had to fall ill."

The impending travelers bowed their heads in recognition.

"You all carry the Word within you, my friends. You're the ones who will ensure that the world will not be in want in future generations. Everything depends on you."

"We will not disappoint you," Levi said. He had decided to travel with nothing but the sandals on his feet and the mantle on his back, like Yeshua had taught them long ago. And, because of his age, a walking stick.

"Never give up," Yakov said at last. "Remember, you'll never walk alone. I'm always with you, always there, as you walk on through the wind and the rain. And so is Yeshua." His heart wanted to scream out, warn them about what they might encounter on the road. Instead, he bowed his head and joined his palms in front of his chest in reverence to the light within each of the apostles. And when they saw this, they rose and picked up their traveling sacks, and one by one they embraced him before they sauntered out the compound gate and disappeared down the road.

CHAPTER 28

Jerusalem, Judea, AD 54

A year passed without a word from any of the apostles on the road. But at the compound, life continued as usual for the few people who remained. One late summer day, as Mariamne and Yohannah stood in the shallow brook washing the Assembly members' clothes, Mariamne's thoughts wandered to Yakov. Michal's death should have brought them closer, but ever since his wife passed, Yakov had chosen solitude as a penance. Mariamne had expected his need to be alone to pass, and she had believed he would soon return to her side. But an entire year had gone by and Yakov was still keeping his distance. He wouldn't even look at her.

She missed him.

"Do you think we have enough apples and figs to keep us through winter?" Mariamne asked Yohannah. The women had been friends for a long time, but it wasn't until Yohannah's husband, Phillipos, left and Yakov turned his back on Mariamne that they truly bonded.

"We always have enough. If only you believe."

Mariamne smiled. Yohannah lived Yeshua's words every day of every moon. The perfect disciple.

"You think they'll return soon?" Mariamne regretted the words as soon as they escaped her mouth. Phillipos should have taken Yohannah along on his pilgrimage. Instead, he had mumbled some excuse about the roads not being safe for women. However,

Yohannah suspected he had grown tired of her and sought the freedom found only among the company of men.

"Shouldn't we worry more about sowing the barley in time than harvesting the fruits?" Yohannah hung a clean tunic to dry on the branches of a chestnut tree. Then she picked up another tunic from the pile of unwashed clothes. "We need rain. When was the last time we went through an entire month of Heshvan without rain?"

"We didn't harvest a lot of wheat in the spring, either," Mariamne said thoughtfully. "You're right: I need to believe more."

"That's all we can do." Yohannah laughed and shrugged. Then she bent down to rub the linen fabric in the cool water. "Two women left behind, washing our tunics like lunatics until our knuckles bleed. Because what's left but to believe?"

Mariamne didn't understand what Yohannah found so amusing. But she was right: the only thing that brightened their days was remembering Yeshua's words. Crumbs of heaven. "Do you ever doubt, though?"

Yohannah wavered for a moment, for a twinkle of time. But then her face lit up. "Not at all. I believe because I was there, with Yeshua. He could calm a stormy lake with his mind. And Yakov can bring rain. You've seen it."

I've seen it, and still I dwell in doubt from time to time. I'm not worthy of being his disciple.

"Yakov will bring us rain again," Yohannah continued. "Talk to him, won't you? I know how close you are."

Were. We were close, Mariamne wanted to say. But how could she explain to Yohannah how she longed to love her brother-in-law in a way not suitable for friends? As a man. For all she knew, Yakov had noticed her desire, and he still rejected her.

"Yes, that's what I'll do," Mariamne said instead, and she continued to scrub her garments in silence until the sun disappeared behind the hills and the babbling stream turned frigid.

*

"Rain?" Yakov asked between mouthfuls of carrot stew. He did not even look up at the woman who had served him. "Why, are you worried about the harvest?"

He scooped up another fistful of stew with his bread, opened his mouth, and chewed, deep in thought.

"It's the end of Heshvan."

"Tomorrow," Yakov said with confidence. He stretched his neck to gaze out the window. "That's when it'll rain. See those black clouds over there? That's rain."

Mariamne felt defeated. How could they live in the same house, share their meals, and not even look at each other? She had lost count of the nights she had lain awake, yearning for his touch, for his kisses, her limbs burning with lust, and yet she had not mustered the courage to sneak into his room and cuddle up in his bed. What if he pushed her away? She wouldn't survive his rejection. She would prefer living in harmony like siblings. Like a brother and sister whose eyes never met.

"The olive harvest was plentiful. And the sugarcane," Yakov said, and he burped quietly into his fist. "So many lambs, too. We had more lambs born this summer than ever before. We'll be swimming in wool next spring."

At least he was talking to her. They were making progress. Slow and steady. Maybe all she needed was to believe, like Yohannah had said.

"We won't starve, that's for sure," she responded. She lowered her head and handed him a bowl of water to wash his hands after the meal. Clean, wash, and cook. That was all he wanted from her. Like a servant. Or even a slave. But if she were a slave, at least he could have taken advantage of her body, relieved himself. She would have welcomed this affection, however crude. But she was neither a slave nor a servant. She was his brother's widow, his sister-in-law, the mother of his nephew.

Yakov dried his hands on his mantle, picked up his walking staff, and stepped into the courtyard. Without a single word. He climbed the hills to their meditation spot. If only she could join him. Instead, she stayed behind and washed the clay platter and pots, swept the floor, and made his bed. She rubbed lavender blossoms on his sheets to give them a fresh scent and touched her lips at the place of the pillow where he would place his head. Hoping he would feel her love. And that one day he would return to her.

Yakov limped up the steep path. He steadied himself on the rustic staff made of olive wood that his younger brother had sent him from Capernaum. Many years ago, Yakov could have carved an exquisite staff with the most intricate design, but after years of neglect, he had lost his touch. He missed that sometimes, the focus on placing the carving knife at the perfect angle, and then disappearing into a trance of oneness with the wood and the knife that shaped it into flowers, leaves, animals… He could have carved a better staff than this before he turned five. But his brother had crafted this walking stick with love, and that meant more than anything.

He stopped halfway up the slope to rub his aching knee. The years had taken a toll on him. His legs had lost their strength and flexibility. Stiff and sore, they made each step an effort. But he cherished his time alone in the hills. Only there could he surrender his worries about the traveling apostles and ease the anguish about keeping the remaining disciples safe, clothed, and fed. Damn Mariamne for bringing up the lack of rain. What was he to do? Did she think he hadn't realized it? Many years had passed since the great famine, but every year brought its own struggles, and the fear of starvation never left him.

He longed for the past, his effortless life as a carpenter in Capernaum. In his youth, his focus had been on making doors and benches and tables, and sometimes even those fancy Roman high seats they called chairs. He had stayed out of trouble, fed his family, and enjoyed a trouble-free existence. No storms had darkened his skies until Yeshua returned from his travels with his wild ideas. And like a mad monkey, Yakov had left his wife and children to join his brother on a thankless quest around Lake Kinneret. Then he had made the same mistake again with the move to Jerusalem. What had he been thinking?

But he knew why he had made those decisions. The Assembly had saved hundreds of people from a life in misery. They had brightened the hearts of the poor and brought hope to people in despair. They had healed thousands from fatal diseases. Everyone but Michal. Tears sprang to his eyes. He hadn't managed to cure his own wife.

And why hadn't Mariamne even tried?

Oh, Mariamne. She embodied the memories of all the mistakes he had made. And she played a prominent part in all his decisions. Perhaps Michal had been right about her. The seductress, the woman all men desired, the one who spread her legs to anyone who wanted her. *No.* Yakov shook his head. That was unfair. Mariamne had turned Paulus away. And she had turned Yakov away, too, any time he had lost himself in a moment of weakness. As close as they were, their friendship had never evolved beyond amicable embraces.

Then why did he feel so guilty?

Yakov unrolled his prayer mat on the ground, in the same location where he and Mariamne had meditated together every evening of every year, except on nights of heavy rain. The grass underneath had turned yellow, and the ground had worn bare. They had prayed there, side by side, for decades until Michal passed. Just the two of them, always together. Although thirteen new moons had traveled across the sky since Michal died, Yakov still wasn't ready to include Mariamne in his life again. Perhaps he would never be ready.

He pulled a blanket over his shoulders to keep warm. Then he closed his eyes and rested his hands on his lap, palms facing up. He inhaled the light of heaven and released all the stress, all the worries, and connected with God.

Long after sunset, when he returned to the house, he had to push his fingers into his ears to filter out the soft snores from Mariamne's quarters. Relieved that she was asleep and wouldn't confront him with those probing eyes, he slumped onto his bed, undressed, and pulled the sheet over his head. A stirring between his legs reminded him of how lonely he had been. No man should have to live without a wife. As he stroked himself, his thoughts meandered back to the lovely Mariamne. Once his closest ally, always his brother's widow. The unique and wonderful woman who had caused him to neglect his own wife. With a firm grip, he fondled himself faster and faster until he moaned with pleasure and released all the passion he had subdued. Wiping his mattress dry with a cloth, his cheeks burned with shame. He couldn't remain like that, alone and frustrated. He should take a wife, or perhaps a servant. Someone ugly, someone he wouldn't love. Someone to share his bed and warm him through the cold and dreary winter.

Tomorrow he would go into town and seek a maiden, someone young, untouched, and malleable. Yet someone whose face would never let him forget the promise of devotion he had made to his wife. Someone he would never love.

CHAPTER 29

Jerusalem, Judea, AD 55

A sheen of sweat covered Mariamne's brow. Her arms throbbed as she raised the sickle and let the sharp blade slash down across the stalks. During spring harvest, all the women in the compound came together to gather the white barley before the grains fell off and disappeared back into the earth. A fortnight of rain had left the soil soft and soggy. Gone was the memory of last summer's drought. Chunks of mud stuck to the soles of her bare feet and made every step cumbersome as she filled her basket with crops. The few remaining men claimed to be too tired or too busy with "more important" tasks like guarding the gate, tending to the animals, or replacing the rotten wood in the fence around the enclosed pastures.

She wiped her brow and glanced toward her house, where Yakov was still asleep. Or possibly making love to the servant he had hired last fall, a poor girl with one blind eye and a hook of a nose so strong you could hang a clothesline upon it. Truth be told, the girl was barely more than a slave, but as the Assembly's rules did not permit owning slaves—*everyone is equal*—Yakov had introduced her as a house servant. Mariamne scoffed. A maid who was terrible at cooking and cleaning, who only reluctantly helped with any chores around the house, but who willingly lay naked in bed all night long and offered her limber body to a ravenous old man who could no longer feel love.

Mariamne couldn't wrap her mind around it. Yakov could have married her instead. *Should* have married her, now that they were both widowed and free. Instead, he had rushed to Jerusalem like a runaway camel, bribed some destitute mother to give him her innocent but unweddable daughter as a servant to satisfy his carnal needs. What would happen if the girl became pregnant with his child? God only knew.

The good news in all this misery, Mariamne had to admit, was that Yakov kept their trysts secret. The other Assembly members believed Yakov had hired the girl to assist Mariamne with housekeeping now that Michal had passed. No one suspected what happened behind closed doors. And if they had known? Would they still have called him Yakov the Just? Mariamne moaned with frustration. She raised the sickle high above her head and, with a vengeance, sliced the stalks as if the force could bring balm to her bleeding heart. They all adored Yakov, much like they once had revered Yeshua: like a prophet, a wise man who could do no wrong. Even if they caught Yakov naked in bed with the servant, they would not believe it. They would think he had slipped and accidentally fallen upon the naked girl. Or that she had forced him to do it, the poor old man. Mariamne laughed bitterly and wiped a tear that had escaped her eye. What would Yeshua have done in her situation? He would have walked away. He would have accepted the rejection and moved on. Perhaps that's what she needed to do, too.

Mariamne carried the heavy basket, overflowing with barley, to the storehouse where the children of the compound sat in a circle on the mud floor. They separated the barley heads from the stalks and removed the chaff. Another group of children placed the barley in a wooden mortar filled with water and gently pounded the grains with a pestle to remove most of the bran. Then they scattered the grains on a blanket outside to dry in the sun. After a few days, they could easily remove the remaining bran by rubbing the dried grains between two hands.

Mariamne squatted in the shade, with her back against the storehouse wall, delirious from the heat. The sun had barely reached its midpoint in the sky. Her arms ached from all the pulling, cutting, and carrying she had done since dawn. Half a day remained before she could lie down to rest. And tomorrow, the same routine would start all over again. Was it worth the effort? Should she give up? Perhaps it was time to return to Magdala, to her aging parents, and live the rest of her days in peace and comfort.

A soft wind caressed her cheeks. She scratched her neck and moved her headscarf out of her eyes. The other women toiled in the fields without a single complaint. The children labored as hard as any adult and completed their chores with laughter and joy, filling the day with jokes and games. Even the men who tended to the animals, wove the cloth, sheared the sheep, and carried basketfuls of goods for sale in the market never uttered one word of regret. Then why couldn't she be happy?

Yakov ambled groggily out of bed and gestured for Talitha to bring him the vat of water for washing. As he wiped himself clean, he studied the naked girl who was kneeling by his feet with her head lowered in submission. Her tangled hair brushed the floor. Such an unblemished young body, such perky, delicate breasts, firm thighs, and smooth skin. His eyes were drawn to the moist, furry triangle between her legs, and he held back a desire to lift her onto his lap and make love to her again. Outside, he could hear the sounds of the Assembly members working, and he felt ashamed for tending to his lust inside the cool house while the others slaved away in the midday sun.

"Talitha, bring me my tunic and mantle," he demanded, forcing the girl up from the floor. "And get dressed. The workers are hungry."

The girl rose, her head still hanging low. She shuffled across the room to bring him the sand-colored tunic that hung on a nail by the window where Yakov had placed it overnight to freshen in the breeze. Her high, round buttocks bounced with her every step, and he had to look away to not become aroused again. Talitha, he called her: *Little Girl*. She must have mentioned her name when they first met, but he couldn't remember what it was. And he couldn't care less. He didn't want to know her, didn't want to know anything about her.

Talitha watched him get dressed without lending a hand to help, and for a moment it bothered him that she simply stood there, as naked as God had made her. She didn't offer an opinion or desire, never uttered a word of protest. Did she even think at all?

"Get dressed!" he ordered again. "Food, remember?"

He could hear the irritation in his voice and regretted it. The girl was not to blame. But if she never learned to cook and clean, how long could he keep up this charade? How long until the others realized the girl was incapable of any domestic duties besides spreading her legs and making love like a passionate beast?

He threaded his mantle over his head, tied it at the waist, and left Talitha behind as he entered the courtyard. The bright sun forced him to squint as he gazed upon the dozens of strong-willed, wise women who labored hard to bring in the crops of barley before they rotted. Proper women, many of them handpicked by Yeshua as the most ready for enlightenment.

Yakov cupped his hands in front of his mouth and blew between his thumb joints, letting out a hollow cuckoo sound. Immediately, everyone came to a stop and turned to look at him.

"Come, come," he called. "Time for a prayer before we stuff ourselves with our midday meal."

He glanced behind him and saw Talitha standing idle in the doorway.

"Go on," he prodded. "Food!"

His voice rang softer this time. The girl hung her head and shuffled to the kitchen. Yakov wondered what lousy meal she would cook this time, but he had other things on his mind besides worrying about how the food tasted. As long as their meal was filling and nourishing, nothing else mattered.

*

"Listen, I know we all work hard, and that the sun is harsh," Yakov said to the Assembly members seated around him in the shady part of the courtyard. "Do you ever ask yourselves if it's worth it, toiling day and night to stay alive?"

The women and men listened, grateful for a moment of rest. They absorbed his words and sipped from the waterskin that was passed around. Yakov's heart filled with affection. They still trusted him, believed in him.

"You're magnificent people, the very best." Yakov glanced back at the fire pit, where Mariamne sat, cross-legged, peeling onions. Talitha was squatting next to her, cutting squash into halves and de-seeding them. Yakov looked from the plain adolescent girl to the radiant woman and back at the girl again before he was overcome with shame. How had he allowed himself to become like this?

He brought his attention back to the Assembly.

"When black clouds cover the skies, when everything appears a struggle, we must pause. Allow ourselves to feel oneness with God. Be grateful for all we have. Because only dissatisfaction can cause terror and fear."

Yakov closed his eyes. Why couldn't he reach that light inside? Where was the connection—where had it gone? He focused on each of his chakras, one after another, like Yeshua had once advised him, starting with the deep red root chakra at the bottom of his spine, followed by the orange sacral chakra two thumbs below his navel, the center of reproduction that vibrated with life. He breathed light into the bright yellow chakra of intuition right below his rib cage, and he continued to the emerald heart chakra in the center of his chest. His heart felt dull and dark and closed, and no matter how hard he tried, the chakra wouldn't open.

He thought of Michal. Of his mother. Of Yeshua. The people he loved the most. He thought of his father, his children, and his brother Tau'ma. And without meaning to, he thought of Mariamne. Just a gasp of a moment, and light seeped into his heart, little by little, until a ray of unconditional love flared up within him, and he was ready to move on to the next center of energy, the vividly aquamarine chakra in the depth of his throat. The indigo-colored third eye chakra between his eyebrows, opened up easily, and after he reached the violet crown chakra on top of his head, he connected all the chakras to allow the kundalini power to race up his spine and through his limbs. Vibrant, loving light filled his entire being. And although aware the crowd around him was waiting, he took the time he needed before he opened his eyes again to continue his sermon.

"Sometimes we doubt our own wholeness: our holiness. And we suffer. Only when we truly unite with God, and live in the present moment, will we find happiness again."

Heads nodded, bodies swayed. His moment of connection had affected them all, and he sensed a peace among them that he had not known in a long time.

"Remember how Yeshua enlightened us when we still lived in darkness? He showed us the way to the light. He became our guide, provided a safe harbor where we could lay our heads and rest. And like he guided us, you will guide others, who in turn will guide others until all people in the entire world have found enlightenment."

Yakov gazed at the faces around him. Some of them might remember Yeshua uttering the same words a long time ago.

"If God calls you, go to meet him, because you are called to do his will. You know where you came from and where you are going, like a drunkard will wake up sober in the morning and regain control of himself."

Yeshua, Yakov thought. *What would have become of him had he lived longer? Would he have returned to Mesopotamia? Escaped to Alexandria?* Yakov glanced at Mariamne. Yeshua had adored his wife, and she had adored him. Yakov jerked his head to free himself of the impending sense of envy.

Instead, he said, "Let us lift our souls and pray."

Everyone bowed their heads and pressed their palms together in front of their hearts.

"Holy Father," Yakov began, "Father of the light, hear us—"

Bang!

He opened one eye. What was that?

Bang. Bang, bang. Bang!

Bang!

The gate. Someone was banging on the gate.

One of the guards rushed to open it.

A shabby man entered, his hair matted with dirt, his beard unkempt, and his mantle in tatters.

"Uncle," he said, his voice shrouded in grief, and he threw his arms around Yakov.

Yakov pushed the young man back to view him at arm's length. The dark brown eyes seemed familiar. Could this haggard being be…?

"Yudah Tzaer!" Mariamne sprang up to embrace her son.

"I'm sorry," Yudah Tzaer said. "Phillipos… He's dead."

Yakov watched them as in a dream.

A nightmare.

Phillipos? It couldn't be true. Mustn't be true.

Then he saw Yohannah staring at Yudah Tzaer, her face paralyzed with shock.

Phillipos's wife.

Mariamne held him tight and Yudah Tzaer collapsed in his mother's arms like a small child. Her son! Oh, how he had changed. His face had become hard and worn. His eyes had lost their innocence.

"Bring him a drink of water," Yakov called out. He helped Yudah Tzaer to sit by his side.

Talitha came traipsing like a puppy and handed Yakov a cup of water. The silly girl didn't even have enough common sense to hand the cup directly to Yudah Tzaer.

Yakov rested his hand behind Yudah Tzaer's neck and brought the cup to his nephew's lips to help him drink. The water drizzled down the corners of his mouth.

"Phillipos?" Yohannah collapsed at Yudah Tzaer's feet, her face contorted in pain. "Are you sure?"

Yudah Tzaer rubbed his forehead with both hands. He opened his mouth to say something, but his chapped lips didn't form any words. Instead, he stared at his feet.

Mariamne drew her son closer and buried his head in her chest. She looked at Yohannah and tried to find the right words, but nothing came to mind.

"You're mistaken," Yakov said, shaking his head. "It must've been someone else. Another man."

Yudah Tzaer shook his head.

"You have no doubt at all?" Yakov prodded. "Did you see him close? Can't it have been another pilgrim, someone who resembled him?"

Yudah Tzaer shrank into a tiny knot, hugging his knees as if to protect himself from evil. He rocked from side to side.

A horrid wail rose from Yohannah's throat as she collapsed to the ground. She clawed her nails into the earth and screamed. Yakov rose to aid her, but she shot up and shoved him away. Then she rushed out of the courtyard. Her wails echoed between the hills where the fruit trees had just sprung into bloom, like an ironic message of hope from God.

Mariamne watched her in despair. She longed to help, but she couldn't let go of her son. He needed her, too.

"What happened?" Mariamne asked once he had calmed down. "And how can you be so sure?"

"Would I have run all the way from Phrygia if I harbored any doubts? Would I have begged rides with ships and caravans across the continents on a rumor? Would I?"

"He really is dead?" Yakov stared at his nephew. It was more a statement than a question.

"How?" Mariamne searched Yudah Tzaer's eyes as they filled with tears again.

He wiped them away, leaving a sooty smear across his face. "They killed him."

"Who? Emperor Claudius?"

Yudah Tzaer stared at her in confusion. "No, Mother, don't you know he died?"

"Who?"

"Claudius. His wife poisoned him."

In the background, Talitha swayed back and forth, back and forth, and for a moment Mariamne felt sorry for the girl. It wasn't Talitha's fault that Yakov had brought her to the Assembly only to treat her like a slave. He had not allowed her to become part of their family. How could Talitha ever understand what was going on, why everyone was so upset? She knew nothing about Yeshua or his Good News. She had never met Yudah Tzaer or Phillipos or any of the other apostles who had left two years earlier. She could not possibly understand why they were all crying.

"Who killed Phillipos, then?" Yakov asked. "Paulus? Was it Paulus who killed him?"

Yudah Tzaer looked at his uncle as if he were speaking a foreign language. "Paulus? Why would he bother?"

"You're saying Paulus is no longer a threat?"

"Paulus is drunk with power. He's formed churches everywhere—in Pisidia, Galatia, all across Asia Minor, even Achaia. We all visit his churches and tell them the truth about Yeshua, what he taught, what he believed... We're in a war of faith with him, but despite his arrogance, he's not a murderer."

"Who, then?" Mariamne swiped a strand of hair from her son's eyes. "Who would want to hurt a humble pilgrim like Phillipos?"

"The Romans?" a little boy said, lips trembling.

They had all heard how the Romans persecuted field preachers and their followers, including those who worshipped Paulus's god, Yeshua Christos. The Romans couldn't possibly know—and wouldn't even care—that the Assembly followed an entirely different Yeshua.

Just then, Yohannah sauntered back into the courtyard, eyes swollen. Without a word, she settled by Mariamne's side, into her friend's embrace.

Yudah Tzaer took another sip of water and closed his eyes, as if to gather courage. "Phillipos's success became his curse. I never knew my father, but I'm sure he would have been proud. Word reached me about Phillipos's miraculous healings, his profound sermons as far away as Palmyra. And I had to see for myself. I caught up with him a few months ago in Hierapolis." Yudah Tzaer smiled sadly at the memory. "What a magnificent sight! There he was, preaching in front of hundreds of Phrygians. Even the wife of the Roman governor! They were all enthralled by his message."

Yohannah let out a whimper. Mariamne's heart wanted to break. She rubbed her friend's back and said softly, "I know, I know." For what else could she do?

Yakov motioned for Yudah Tzaer to continue.

"You see, Phillipos had gained an immense following in Scythia and Phrygia. While in Hierapolis, he met the wife of a Roman governor, and she became a great believer. Phillipos trained her to teach Yeshua's word among the Phrygian elite. But one afternoon, a few days after I arrived, her husband came upon them in a forest glen, heads close together, whispering."

Yohannah sniffled.

"No, don't misunderstand me, Yohannah. They were not alone; dozens of others were with them. But the governor became enraged with jealousy and threatened to kill them both. The very next morning, they arrested Phillipos. Jailed him…"

Yudah Tzaer quietly wiped a tear that was running down his cheek.

"And then what happened?" Yakov asked, his voice hoarse with pain. "He fled? Tell me you helped him escape."

"It's too much. I can't…"

"Enough, Yudah," Mariamne said and hugged Yohannah closer. "We've heard enough."

"No." Yohannah said quietly. "I need to… I just need to know."

Everyone turned to look at her as she sat up straighter and wiped her eyes. "We have to know."

Yudah Tzaer looked at Yakov, then at Mariamne.

"Go on, my child," Mariamne said, her mouth dry and her heart racing.

"For several days, I hid in a shack outside the fort where they kept Phillipos prisoner, and I waited for him. I thought the governor would come to his senses and realize he's an honest man. He had done nothing wrong. I truly believed they would let him go…"

Yudah Tzaer's voice trembled with remorse. Mariamne grasped his hand and kissed it. Her boy, her courageous boy.

"I bribed the jailers to bring him food," Yudah Tzaer said, quietly. "For several days I went back to the fort, every morning and every night, until one day they told me not to come anymore. The governor had sentenced him to death."

Yohannah wailed and slumped to the ground.

"Death," Mariamne repeated. She didn't want to believe what she had heard. She reached for Yohannah, but her friend slapped her hand away. No one could reach her in her depth of sorrow.

Yakov buried his face in his hands. "This is what I feared. I should never have let him go."

Mariamne longed to relieve the guilt that was tearing Yakov apart, but she couldn't move away from her son, and from Yohannah. "How?" she asked, at last.

"They tortured him. Whipped him until his back was nothing but a raw flesh wound. And then they…"

Mariamne pulled the convulsing Yohannah into her arms and hugged her close. "Tell us, child," she said to Yudah Tzaer. "You're not to blame."

"They hung him on a cross. They left him to die, bleeding, on a filthy cross…"

Yakov gulped, eyes wide with terror. "I should never have—" His words drowned in his throat, and he burst into sobs.

"And all the while he was hanging there," Yudah Tzaer continued, "before he lost consciousness, he preached about the Kingdom of God, about Yeshua, and said we are all one with God. That there is no death."

The whole courtyard swirled around her, and Mariamne had to place one hand on the ground to steady herself, to keep from toppling over. They had crucified Phillipos, just like Yeshua. Her stomach turned, and before she could help it, she fainted.

The summer brought nothing but leaden clouds and a constant drizzle. If the sun flickered for a moment, it quickly went into hiding again, only to appear sleepily five days later. The birds rarely sang, and the absence of buzzing bees contributed to the grayness that seemed to hover over Judea. Even the blossoms of the apricot and plum trees withered from a lack of nourishing light.

Ever since they had received notice about Phillipos's death, the remaining members of the compound had voiced their worries, their reluctance to pursue the cause. Over two decades had passed since the disciples had moved to Jerusalem to continue preaching the Good News, and what did they have to show for it? Near-starvation and death. Yakov had heard the murmurings from the other huts late at night: they all sounded resigned, ready to give up.

He wanted to call the apostles back home to safety. But how? He didn't even know where they had gone.

He needed time to think. He hiked up the hill and settled at the vantage point overlooking the sleeping compound. Phillipos's death had paralyzed them all. He should have listened to the voice in his head. The one that had warned him not to send the disciples out into the world to preach Yeshua's words of salvation through oneness with God. What for? Staying alive was what mattered, and he had been foolish enough to think that faith and the goodness of their hearts was enough to keep them safe. Were the apostles even aware of the increasing threat to their lives? If the Romans hated the Jews here in Judea, Yakov could only imagine how imperiled any Jews must be in the territories closer to the capital.

He rubbed his temples to ease the tension headache that was building from worrying about the disciples night and day. Most of the apostles had traveled toward Rome, where they had pledged to win ground back from Paulus. But to no avail, it seemed, despite what Yudah Tzaer had said. Now and then, foreign pilgrims would approach Yakov at the temple and hand him letters that the apostles had intercepted on the road. Letters that Paulus had written to his followers in different corners of the world.

Yakov's stomach growled. He vaguely remembered he hadn't eaten in the last few days. But how could he eat, when his brethren were placing themselves in the path of death because of his nonsensical plans? If only Paulus had listened. Why did the man have to be so stubborn? So selfish?

Yakov spat in frustration. How could people be fooled into believing in a Romanesque god who would "save them" purely by belief in him? They might as well have remained in worship of Apollo or Mithras. Then again, if they had, Paulus couldn't have portrayed himself as the only man who held divine knowledge. Because according to Paulus, only he could communicate with Yeshua Christos. Oh, how blind they were!

Far below, the compound stirred in the morning light. The women stepped out of their huts, stretched, and placed earthen jars on their heads to go fetch water from the brook. The men lit bonfires. Some youngsters entered the pasture to milk the cows that were already moaning with pain from overflowing udders.

He should start moving. The hour had come for their ritual bath at dawn. And then? The temple? Yakov shivered. The Romans had ruined the once sacred temple with their armed guardsmen and checkpoints. Still, the disciples all wanted to go. Yakov brought his palms together and tried to breathe love and gratitude into his heart. He had to stay strong. They all trusted him.

Yakov the Just. What a joke.

*

"I've decided to return to Magdala," Mariamne said a few days later, and she smiled, as if her words would mean nothing to him.

Yakov stared at her.

"Now?" He regretted the question as soon as it left his mouth. What a dumb thing to say. "But you can't go. It's too dangerous." Another foolish phrase. His stomach turned into a knot. He couldn't breathe. If she left him, where would he get the energy to continue?

Mariamne chuckled without joy. "It's safer than here." She picked through the wool in the sack on her lap, cleaning it of insects and dirt.

Her nimble fingers combed through the waxy hairs and then wiped the filth on the skirt of her tunic. Yakov wanted to grab her. Shake her. How could she sit there, complacent, as if nothing mattered?

"You can't go. Your son got married only days ago. Yudah Tzaer needs you. His wife needs you."

The sadness in her eyes almost killed him. What had he done? Why had he hired a maiden to satisfy his carnal desires when all his heart desired was to hold Mariamne and never let her go?

"Tomorrow morning. Yudah Tzaer will accompany me there, but afterward he will return. He won't leave you. Ever."

And you will? Yakov wanted to say. But his tongue stayed glued to his teeth. A taste of blood, of metal, filled his mouth. He coughed and turned away, hiding his tear-filled eyes in his sleeve.

He had lost her. There was nothing he could do.

He stormed out of the house. In the darkness, at the top of the hill, he screamed with frustration. How could he have imagined he could replace Yeshua? Step into his sandals and continue his brother's work? All he had ever wanted was to inspire people and awaken them. Show them that God's Kingdom was alive inside them. But what had he accomplished?

Nothing.

Mariamne stayed at a safe distance behind Yakov as he rushed up the hill, aware that he needed to be alone. She let him cry his heart out before she approached him. But when she sat down at his side and put her arm around his shoulder, Yakov shook himself free.

"I will be safe," she said. "Yeshua will protect me. Like he will protect you."

Yakov stared at her. "Yeshua? He never protected us."

Never? Marianne hugged her knees. "How can you say that? Don't you remember how Yeshua agreed to die to save us when he had brought too much attention to our group? He left us only so we could continue his work."

"That's what you think. You knew him for two years. You never knew him the way I did. All my life, since I was a child, all I ever heard about was how wise my brother was. Such a selfless soul. Divine. He could do nothing wrong."

"Your parents were proud of him. I'm sure they were proud of you, too. Your mother loved you so much. She even came here to Jerusalem to live with you."

"As if she had a choice. I was never good enough for my father, for my mother."

"You're good enough for me. For all of us in the Assembly." Marianne took his hand in hers.

"Oh well, thank you." Yakov rolled his eyes. "Good enough. That's all I've ever aspired to." He yanked his hand away. Then he slid onto his back and stared into the sky.

"Please don't be like that," she said.

"Like what? Sarcastic?"

She tried to take his hand back into hers again, but he pushed her away.

"My parents adored Yeshua. He could do nothing wrong. I was almost happy when he ran away when we were little. Finally, I thought, I could be the oldest son, the one they took such pride in. The one who would marry well and inherit my father's workshop."

"And you did. You inherited everything."

"I hoped that, once Yeshua had left, and we hadn't heard from him for a year, they would forget about him and focus on me. That I could step right into his place and that my parents would go out of their way to choose the best wife for me."

"And they did," Mariamne said. "Michal was lovely."

Yakov raised one eyebrow. "Lovely? Is that what you reckoned?"

He was provoking her.

"She was a faithful wife and cared for you until her last days."

"My father brought dozens of maidens to meet with Yeshua, and that arrogant mamzer, he rejected them all. One after another. This one is too thin. That one has funny eyes. 'I just don't feel it,' he would say."

Mariamne had never heard Yakov speak like this before. He loved Yeshua. And Yeshua loved Yakov. They had been the best of friends.

"When it was my turn, after my first trip to the temple for Passover, they brought Michal over and I had no say in whether I wanted to marry her."

"She was good to you, Yakov. She gave you three sons."

A single tear rolled down Yakov's cheek, and he wiped it away with the back of his hand. "I wanted to leave, too. I wanted to run away from the chains of marriage and seek adventure in Mesopotamia, like my brother had. But more than anything, I wanted my parents to be proud of me. So I stayed. I married Michal. I became the best carpenter in all of Galilee. I took care of my mother when Abba passed away."

"She loved you for it." Mariamne slipped down next to him and kissed his balding head. "Your mother adored you."

"They never stopped speaking about Yeshua. What a noble son he was. So wise and wonderful. He had caused them so much pain and such embarrassment when he left before the wedding and my parents had to break up his betrothal. And yet, once a month or two had passed, they spoke of Yeshua as the perfect son again."

"*You* were the perfect son."

"I hated him." Yakov raised himself up on his forearm and stared at Mariamne. "Did you know that? I hated him. I wished he'd die."

"You loved him. I know you did."

Yakov stared at her as if he despised her, too. Then he sighed and rubbed the furrowed point between his eyebrows. "Maybe. But I hated him more."

Mariamne rubbed his cheek. "He loved you more than anything. Even more than me."

"And then he came back," Yakov said as if he hadn't heard her. "One day he was there in all his glory, dirty as a vagabond, with a scraggly beard and long, filthy hair. And as much as I hated seeing the amazement in Mother's eyes, I was happy, too."

"You loved him."

"And everything went back to the way it had been when we were children. Yeshua was the son who could do nothing wrong. My mother let him go out and preach all over Galilee like one of those crazy wandering preachers my father had abhorred."

An icy wind rippled through Mariamne's core. She had never seen Yakov worked up like this.

"And what did I do? I followed him."

"Your brother was an admirable man. We all wanted to be like him."

A heavy raindrop spluttered onto her head. Then another.

Yakov looked up into the sky as a torrent of rain broke.

"Saul is right," he said, with the rain streaming down his face, soaking him. "I'm useless. I lack the wisdom or knowledge to lead anyone."

"You're not useless, Yakov."

"Why don't you leave, go back to Magdala where you belong?" Yakov said, and he stormed down the hill.

Mariamne fell onto her knees, covered her face with her hands, and she wept.

He didn't want her to stay.

CHAPTER 31

Two days later, Mariamne sang softly to herself as she and Yudah Tzaer strode along a sun-scorched Samarian road on their way to Magdala. She hadn't traveled farther than the temple in many years, but after the first day of walking, joy had filled her heart and a spring had returned to her step. Perhaps she wasn't that old after all. She had simply been sitting still for too long. And maybe, just maybe, leaving Jerusalem and Yakov and all the memories behind had revived her.

The moment she and Yudah Tzaer left Judea, the heat returned and summer appeared in its true image: intense and scalding. The earth sang with life: purple anemones, blue bellflowers, and red poppies peeked through the high grass. Golden butterflies seared through the air on newly sprung wings. Grapes, apples, and peaches ripened on the trees.

All along the way, through the hills of northern Judea into Samaria and crossing the Jordan Valley to Galilee, legionnaires stood guard at every crossroad. They searched and interrogated all travelers who passed.

Mariamne couldn't help but notice how her son shrank and lowered his head each time they approached a checkpoint, as if to make himself invisible. But she told him to stand tall. He had nothing to fear. He was only a young man escorting his mother home. Nothing more.

"I saw him again," Yudah Tzaer said one morning as they crossed the Jordan River in a place where the water ran shallow. "I meant to tell you."

"Who? Your father?"

Yudah Tzaer laughed. "My father? No, silly."

Mariamne rose to her tiptoes and kissed his cheek. Of course—why should Yudah Tzaer see his father? He never appeared to anyone but her, and even then only in her dreams. With every passing year, those dreams had become less frequent. She assumed Yeshua's spirit had moved on.

"I saw Paulus."

Mariamne's heart froze. "Where?"

"A while ago, even before Phillipos left for Hierapolis, I passed a town called Ephesus. I had heard of this new church Paulus had built. I sneaked in, undiscovered, and stayed in the back. I wanted to know what he was telling people these days."

"Did you tell Yakov about this?"

Yudah Tzaer shook his head.

"You should have told him." She stopped to remove an irritating stone from her sandal. "Yakov needs to know these things."

"Mother, you know as well as I do that Uncle has lost his passion. He's surrendered his sword. I don't think he can face Paulus any longer."

"That's simple talk." Mariamne glared at him. But something in her son's words rang true.

They walked a while in silence.

"Apparently Paulus encountered a group of the Baptizer's disciples in Ephesus," Yudah Tzaer continued, "and somehow he persuaded them to let him baptize them again. This time, in the name of Christos."

Mariamne frowned. It sounded like something Paulus would do.

"He sprinkled the Baptizer's followers with water and placed his hands on their heads and said, 'I baptize you in the name of Christos.' Then he kissed them on the mouth."

"Men and women alike?"

"Yes! And sometimes the strangest thing happened: the newly baptized started blabbering ecstatically. Incoherent words, as if possessed by demons. They wobbled and rattled and prattled until they fell exhausted to the ground."

Mariamne searched her son's face. "And he never saw you?"

"I stayed in the back. Watched him. One day I asked one of his followers how the same people could be 'baptized' again and again anytime a newcomer arrived." Yudah Tzaer chuckled. "But he had no answer. They all knew it was a lie, but they wouldn't hear it. The blabbering was just for show."

"I see." Mariamne's stomach ached with anxiety. How could his followers be so blindly supportive that they believed Paulus even though he was lying?

"He frightens them. Warns them about the end of the world," Yudah Tzaer continued. "That's how he hooks them. If they don't accept Yeshua Christos as their savior, they will all go to hell."

"But only the truly wicked will stay in Gehinnom for all time," she said, frowning. "All others will pass through."

"He gives them bread and wine, and he tells his followers that the bread is Yeshua Christos's body and the wine is his blood. Then he makes them eat and drink it."

Mariamne's face crinkled in disgust. "They drink his blood?"

Yudah Tzaer grasped Mariamne's hand and kissed it. "Mother, don't worry about him."

"How can I not worry? He's distorting the message your father died to protect, that Phillipos died for. And who knows how many others?"

"He amuses me, Mother. I heard Paulus complain about how his followers have no strength in their faith. In fact, they welcome our apostles, although we speak about a different Yeshua. They must sense that ours is the true message of God."

Mariamne laughed. A different Yeshua indeed: the *real* Yeshua.

"I've seen how Paulus shakes with fury when he speaks about how our apostles convince his followers to believe in a different gospel."

Yudah Tzaer gazed into the distance, lost in his thoughts. "And soon after I left, I heard the people of Ephesus drove Paulus away. His new faith interfered too much with their worship of the goddess Artemis."

"Good."

"I guess."

"This Artemis, she's a Roman goddess?" Mariamne asked.

"Greek, actually. A goddess of chastity. It should have suited Paulus, don't you think? He who preaches about celibacy, as if it were God's command."

"But it's illegal. Celibacy. He doesn't care about that?"

Yudah Tzaer scoffed.

"Then he never married?" Mariamne said.

"No, he despises women."

Mariamne straightened her back and shielded her eyes from the sun with her hand. The road lay sparkling hot before them, endless. She squatted down to rest and fanned her face with her headscarf. "He didn't use to hate women," she said as she massaged her swollen ankles. "But his life was never easy. He always wanted to be like Yeshua."

"But he never knew him?"

"No, Paulus never met your father."

Mariamne and Yudah Tzaer sauntered slowly, steadily along the paved road the Romans had built along the shores of Lake Kinneret, the one that led all the way from Aegyptos through Jerusalem and Magdala, through Capernaum to Damascus, and far beyond to the Parthian Empire and Macedonia. They paused for a moment in Tiberias, a bustling city built in honor of the Emperor Tiberius only three decades ago. But now the whitewashed walls had yellowed, and the streets had cracked from neglect. Ever since the new governor, Agrippa II, had moved his residence to Caesarea Maritima on the coast of the Great Sea many years ago, the Romans had seen no need to preserve this town.

In Emmaus, on the western shore of the lake, Mariamne and Yudah Tzaer refreshed themselves in the healing waters of the natural hot springs. Afterward, as Mariamne sat on a boulder above the pools and let her tunic dry in the blazing sun, she heard the sound of stomping. Hundreds of soldiers marched by on the hillside road.

"Come look," she called in the lowest voice possible. The sheer size of the group made her shiver in fear.

Yudah Tzaer hauled himself up from the bath and sped up the slippery stairs. He almost crashed into her. His face was struck with panic as he peeked through a hole in the wall and watched the never-ending line of legionnaires march by. "They're coming for us."

"Just stay calm." She covered him with her dry mantle. "Let's pretend nothing's bothering us."

But her heart ached; the memories of Phillipos's execution still traumatized him. She should never have brought him along.

Luckily, the soldiers didn't stop. Didn't even come closer. Instead, they kept marching straight ahead toward Tiberius, without as much as a glimpse in the direction of Mariamne and her son.

"They're not looking for us," she assured him, and she caressed his wet hair. "It must be about something else."

"But there are so many of them."

Mariamne sharpened her ears. They were shouting, "Hail, hail" something. But it didn't sound like "Hail, Agrippa," she was quite sure of that. And not "Hail, Claudius," either. It sounded like "Hail, Nero," but who was Nero?

None of the other bathers seemed disturbed by the noise. Gentiles, Mariamne reckoned. And why would they care? This was not their land. Why would they worry about Roman occupants as long as they had nice baths to relax in and theaters for entertainment?

"Come, dear," Mariamne said. She kissed Yudah Tzaer's cheek. "Let's continue. You'll dry as we're walking. It's not much farther now."

At the peak of the next hill, the lakeside town of Magdala Nunayya sprawled out before them: fertile fields and those familiar towers that gave the town its name. Mariamne sniffed the air. The wind carried a comforting scent of dried fish.

A smile spread across her face. *Home.*

"Look!" She pointed at a cluster of houses on the far end of the lake, a few miles beyond the towers of Magdala. "See the village there? That's where your father grew up."

Yudah Tzaer perked up. "Capernaum?"

"Yes. Can you believe your father lived only a stone's throw away, and yet he had to travel around half the world before he found me."

Magdala hadn't lost an ounce of its loveliness: the rose gardens, the rhododendrons and the fig trees heavy with ripe fruit.

Mariamne clutched Yudah Tzaer's hand to her heart as they walked down the familiar alley to her father's house at the back of a dead-end street. Were her parents still alive? Would someone have sent word if they had passed? She banged as hard as she could on the door. If her parents were at the back of the garden, they would not hear.

She banged and banged until shuffles on the other side of the door made her heart jump with excitement.

The door opened with a creak.

"Yes?" a youthful woman asked.

Mariamne's heart sank. Her parents had passed, then?

But behind the woman, a bearded man approached. Worn and tired, the man gazed at her, confused.

There was no mistaking those oceanic eyes.

"Abba, it's me!" Mariamne said. Tears swallowed her voice. She pushed right past the woman and threw her arms around her father. When he returned her embrace, she burst into sobs. Oh, how she had missed him!

"Yudah Tzaer, come here," she said when she finally pulled herself away.

"Your son?" Her father's face broke into a wide grin.

"Yes, my son. Yeshua's son."

Her father beamed at his grandson. "Come in. I've been waiting for you."

"And she?" Mariamne gestured at the woman who stood by, watching them with fascination.

"This is Re'ut. I hired her to care for your mother when she fell ill. She helps me around the house."

"And Mother?"

Her father hung his head and shrugged.

Mariamne embraced her father again as tears flooded her eyes. At least he was still here. She vowed to spend the rest of her life caring for him.

CHAPTER 32

Jerusalem, Judea, AD 57

For Yakov, the next two years passed in a fog. One meaningless day after another, with the same chores, the same meals, the same sermons, without a single break. He peered out of his doorway and sighed in frustration. It was snowing. That darned snow kept falling, covering the compound with a soft blanket of white flakes, as if to remind him of the purity of life he was meant to preserve. He blew his nose and smoothed one hand over his sunken belly. The reserves of lentils and barley from last year's miserable harvest were running low, and the rations of food diminished with every passing day. Even the little money they made from selling Abram and Iosa's fabrics had dissipated. How long would his fellow Assembly members accept his shortcomings? Why did it never get easier? What did God want from him?

He drew his mantle closer around him and rubbed his arms for warmth. How many disciples would submit to an icy bath on a morning like this? Most of them would make excuses of old age or some ailment they had miraculously suffered only last night. But how could he blame them? A meditation by the cozy fire could work just as well.

Yakov crossed his arms across his chest and squeezed his shoulders until they cracked. The furrows on his forehead had deepened. He rarely felt the urge to laugh. He was lonely, despite Yohannah's company. She had abruptly dismissed Talitha and moved into his house soon after Mariamne left. But if Yohannah had hoped a spark of love would ignite between them, she would have to hope in vain. As far as Yakov was concerned, he was done with women.

"Master, your hot milk." Yohannah snuggled up next to him. She teased him with the nickname Master, unaware that her words tore open a wound of always being compared with his brother.

Yakov accepted the warm cup and touched her cheek in a clumsy attempt at a caress. She was not to blame. She didn't know better.

"The winter's rough this year, Master."

"Spring will be here soon enough."

"And we're running low on firewood." She put her arm around him, but he wormed himself free. Gently, inconspicuously. Then he pulled his blanket more tightly around himself.

"Did you hear the latest news?" he said, eager to change the subject. "Paulus arrived by ship in Caesarea not long ago."

"Is he on his way to Judea, then?"

Yakov wiped the milk from his beard and handed the mug back to Yohannah. "If he comes, he comes. I'm going down to the brook for the morning bath. Go see who else will join me."

Yohannah blushed, lips moist with saliva. When she leaned over, as if to offer a kiss, Yakov rose and smoothed the wrinkles of his mantle.

"You're kind to me, Yohannah," he said. "I couldn't have wished for a better sister."

After the frigid bath, the women welcomed the men back to the compound with steaming carrot soup and a blazing fire. The men huddled together and sipped their soup as they warmed their bodies to a healthy temperature. Yakov wondered how to best communicate his suggestion that they should resume their prayers at the temple. In the event of Paulus's return, he'd better rekindle his relationship with the priests. Enough of hiding from the Romans; they had to secure their bonds with any allies that remained.

"I've got news to share," Yakov said when they had finished eating. "You remember Saul? Paulus?"

Everyone looked up, their faces tinted with apprehension.

Yakov drew a deep breath before he continued. "I can't say I've heard this from a reliable source, so perhaps there's no cause to worry. But there's talk about a certain wealthy Cilician preacher who travels with a large entourage on his way to Jerusalem. Of course, these days, words fly like autumn leaves when shaking the trunk of an apple tree. It may mean nothing. All the same, I wanted you to be aware, in case his path crosses ours. We must prepare to face him with goodwill and tolerance. And stay calm."

"Calm?" Yohannah said. "How can you say that, after all the trouble he's caused?"

When Yakov patted her shoulder, she relaxed beneath his touch.

"Remember the story about the traveler who was attacked by robbers and left to die on the side of the road?" he said. "First, a Sadducee priest passed by and ignored him. A Levite also turned a blind eye. Only a lowly Samaritan took pity on the dying man, brought him to an inn, and gave the traveler his last denarius. He left without expecting a word of gratitude. He did this from the goodness of his heart, aware that God rewards all good deeds in one way or another."

No one dared say anything. They all pretended to tie the strings of their sandals, or adjust their moth-eaten mantles over their threadbare tunics.

"We are the good Samaritans," Yakov said. "We're the ones who turn the other cheek and treat all men and women as a brother. Like a flame in God's menorah. Everyone, including Paulus."

That same afternoon, all the remaining disciples trekked across the hills in solemnity toward the temple. There should be no reason they couldn't come to an agreement with Paulus, Yakov thought. Surely the man must have learned from his mistakes. At least an essence of Yeshua's message of love must have trickled into his heart.

Their message of oneness with God must have made more sense than the story about a pseudo-Grecian Messiah he was weaving.

Yakov and the disciples had to suffer through multiple Roman checkpoints before they could finally seek shelter from the bone-shattering winds in Solomon's Portico. And instantly, the breeze stilled to a quiet dance, as if their mere presence heightened the vibration of the temple courtyard. Yakov's heart hummed with gladness. It was true, then, that they brought peace wherever they went.

As soon as Yakov stood up to speak, dozens of curious strangers approached to hear what the eminent teacher, Yakov the Just, spoke of on this freezing day of Shebat.

He waved them closer, calling one and all to share the space and create a hub of communal body heat.

"Will you all attest that you are wise?" He searched the eyes of one person after another, making sure they felt included.

Nods and smiles all around. The disciples were confident in their knowledge. Yohannah leaned forward, like Mariamne had taught her, because women still had to persist to be acknowledged.

Yakov scratched his beard pensively. "Excellent. And you've proved yourselves through good deeds and worthy lives. Humble lives. But even the wisest of men sometimes struggles with jealousy or bitterness. If you ever do, will you come see me?"

Again, they nodded. They all trusted him.

"You mustn't fear confessing any doubts you may have. Although we all know our friend Paulus hides behind an aura of wisdom, we have a choice in how we approach him. Or any relationship in our lives: we can either bless—or blame."

Yakov's voice stalled as a tidal wave of love washed over his entire being. How he adored every man and woman before him. How fortunate he was to live by their side. "Don't fear Paulus," he said. "Don't let him stir up anger within you. Bless him, instead. He can't take anything from you. Remember that he acts from a place of suffering, of pain. Let's shower him with compassion, because kindness is the fruit that grows from the seeds that peacemakers plant."

In the coming weeks, Yakov and the other disciples resumed their daily journeys to the temple, nodding amiably at the Roman soldiers in an effort to build a reputation of placidity. Every new day, the wind blew fresher, letting them know the free days of spring had returned. By the time the almond trees sprang into bloom in the month of Adar, the disciples had overcome their anxieties. And the legionnaires who protected the walled city from rebel attacks now recognized Yakov and his band of peaceful Jews as part of what made the Holy City remarkable.

Although Yakov enjoyed the increasing sense of unity, of protection, he still missed Mariamne. Why hadn't she returned? He had expected she would soon realize her mistake and understand that her place was beside him. But when the years passed without a word from her, his hopes turned to dust. Surely, a beautiful woman like Mariamne must have remarried by now. And forgotten all about him. Oh, what a fool he had been. He should have let her speak more often before the Assembly, given her the platform she had always strived for. Why hadn't he? Had he feared she would outshine him? Had he allowed his ego to overshadow his faith? And if that was the case, did he have the right to ridicule Paulus for falling prey to his pride? Yakov's heart ached. He was just as guilty himself.

Still, whenever Yakov looked out across the hundreds of faces that viewed him with great anticipation, an immense wave of gratitude flushed over him. They had all come here because of him. Not anyone else. Not because of Yeshua, or Mariamne, or because they had to. They had come because his words gave them hope.

"You have united your perfect light with God," Yakov said. He allowed his heart chakra to open and shower the surrounding people with love. "God is our Father. Everything that belongs to God also belongs to us. You see, even if a pearl falls into mud, it will not lose its value. It will still be a pearl. Likewise, you will always be precious in the eyes of God, whatever life has thrown at you."

He closed his eyes and united with everyone in prayer:

"We thank you, dear Father;

Grant us your mind, word, and wisdom;

Mind, that we may know you;

Word, that we may understand you;

Wisdom, that we may be one with you."

When he fluttered his eyes open, the sun had already traveled behind the high walls of the temple, and the breeze carried the chill of dusk. It was time to return home before nightfall, have supper, tend to the animals, and rest before another day of serving God was upon them.

Yakov's heart felt lighter than it had in years. He had accomplished all he had ever aspired to. He could, with all the peace in his soul, finally claim he was the true leader of the disciples.

On their walk home, Yohannah took his hand, and this time he let her. The children behind them snickered. Youngsters always believed that love lived only in the hearts and loins of adolescents. Old people's love appeared absurd to them. But friends could also hold hands, couldn't they? What harm could it do?

He even found himself whistling, and Yohannah giggled. Spring was such a precious time. Every year, the season brought new life and fresh hope to the world, another chance to make things right. And this spring, Yakov promised himself, everything would change for the better.

It was time to call Mariamne back. She belonged here. He should never have let her go.

Yakov turned around to announce the good news to his dear brethren who shared his life, his vision, his dreams. Then he spied a familiar character trudging up the hill, only steps behind them.

Paulus.

CHAPTER 33

Surrounded by a crew of road-worn travelers and a donkey loaded with supplies, Paulus looked both well fed and annoyingly cavalier. When he offered his bearded cheek for a kiss, Yakov obliged. He focused on filling his heart with love and welcomed the man as an ally, not a foe.

Paulus's eyes went to Yohannah, who stood by Yakov's side.

Yakov blushed and let go of her hand.

"New wife?" Paulus smirked. "Second wife?"

Yakov opened his mouth to respond, then regretted it. He didn't owe Paulus an explanation. The man was neither his judge nor his superior.

"You've met our Yohannah before," he replied. "Phillipos's wife. His widow."

Yakov searched Paulus's face for any sign of guilt. Did he know how Phillipos had met his destiny? But Paulus showed no hint of recognition.

"If you wish, you may stay with us as long as you please," Yakov said. "We have plenty of space. Many of our apostles are out in the world, preaching the Good News. Their huts stand empty—for now."

A flash of annoyance shadowed Paulus's face before he adopted a mask of amiability. "We are much obliged."

Inside the compound, Paulus called his youngest servant closer: "Lucas, bring the sacks. Show our dear friends what fine produce we have brought them."

They unloaded bag after bag of wheat, barley, dried apples, and figs, and stacked them on top of each other at Yakov's side.

Paulus beamed. Then he reached a hand under his mantle and produced a heavy leather pouch, the size of a muskmelon, and handed it to Yakov.

Reluctantly, Yakov untied the string and peered inside. Hundreds of shekels and drachmas.

What was this? A bribe?

"Blessings, brothers in Christos," Paulus said. He called everyone closer to behold his gifts. "Most blessed are you who have accepted Yeshua Christos into your hearts, for he gave his life for our sins. May we glorify his name for all time to come."

"Sins?" Yakov asked, but Paulus ignored him.

"We heard you have come upon meager times again," Paulus's gaze traveled through the crowd, searching for something. Someone. "Your brethren across the empire have collected a substantial fortune to show their support, to help you."

Yakov shoved the purse back into Paulus's hands. "Thank you, but we don't need your help."

"Before you reject our gifts," Paulus said, with the purse resting in his lap, "let me explain what it represents. All around the coastal regions of the Great Sea, thousands of men and women have found mercy in their hearts for you. Some of them have made acquaintance with your apostles and heard about your unmovable faith, and your reluctance to abandon the law of Moses. But despite all that, they are driven by an astonishing faith in my gospel about Yeshua Christos. When I spoke of your needs, they offered me their last drachmas and begged me to help you."

"I'm pleased for you," Yakov said, "and grateful for your generosity. But honestly, this time we are not in need. God's grace is upon us."

Yakov sought the eyes of his brethren to garner their support before he changed the subject. "Tell me, though, what good tidings can you bring from our brother Kephas?"

Paulus chuckled. "My good man, there is no shame in accepting assistance. Remember what the scripture proclaims: 'Nations shall gather together and come to your light. The abundance of the sea and the wealth of all shall be brought to your feet.'"

Again, Paulus scanned the crowd, looking from one face to the next.

Yakov knew exactly whom he sought: the woman who had once rejected him. He bit the inside of his lip to keep his negativity at bay. *Love every man and woman as your brother,* he thought. Oh, how he missed Mariamne! She would have known how to handle Paulus. If she were here, Yakov could have focused on grace. On acceptance and forgiveness.

"Kephas," Yakov said again, more adamant this time. "What news can you share from him?"

"Last I heard, your friend went bearing the gospel of Yeshua Christos to Rome. But that was many years ago."

"Rome? You mean to tell me Kephas voluntarily walked straight into the jaws of the beast?"

Paulus chuckled. "That is the word that reached my ears." He grasped Yakov's shoulder affectionately. "The Romans are not the demons you imagine them to be." He signalled to Lucas to open a sack of figs, and at the sight of the luscious fruits, the children of the compound came running. They held their hands out for the treats.

"I know you have come in peace." Yakov squeezed Paulus's shoulder, returning the gesture of familiarity. "And you have traveled far to come see us. We will graciously accept your gift of food. May we leave the past behind and make this a new beginning?"

There, he had said it out loud. He had proved to the Assembly that one could respond respectfully, even to those you suspected of bearing an ulterior motive.

"The money, however," Yakov said with a genuine smile this time, "we may not accept for ourselves, but we'll gladly donate it to the temple."

Yakov searched Paulus's face for a reaction, but Paulus was as gifted as any actor at Herod's Theater.

"Welcome to Judea, my friends," Yakov said, instead, and spread his arms wide. "May your stay with us be long and restful."

In the days to come, Paulus, his five companions, and his servants joined the Assembly's morning baths and afternoon sermons at the temple. Yakov managed to keep his heart and mind open and to view Paulus as a reflection of himself. Clearly God had brought the Tarsian back to put Yakov to the ultimate test.

But despite his best effort to fit in, Paulus continued to argue with anyone who disagreed with him. One morning, after Yakov had come upon him squabbling with Yudah Tzaer over a sleeping mat, Yakov called Paulus aside for a chat.

The men sat on a fallen tree trunk by the brook, and Yakov handed Paulus a whetting stone and a sickle. He showed Paulus how to moisten the stone and hold the knife at the right angle and rub the blade against the coarse stone to sharpen the blade.

"I've been pondering something," Yakov said. "You claim you always act from a place of God. Then what makes you quarrel with everyone you meet? Not a day goes by without your anger waxing hot, without your seeing another man too close in the face. You claim to be a man of peace, and still they throw you out of every town you visit."

"I have never been banished…"

"You don't have to pretend with me." Yakov gently adjusted Paulus's hand to make sure the blade met the stone at the correct angle. "We're all perfect, and yet… Perfection is an illusion. If you must know, we've come upon some letters you sent to your churches in those places: Thessalonica, Corinth, Hierapolis. The words you use—it sounds as if you're begging them to allow you to return. And you denigrate other preachers, you defame our apostles, You even call *me* a sinner."

Paulus snorted, but Yakov could sense his words had taken root.

He sprinkled water on the whetting stone in Paulus's hand, then on his own. They sat in silence for a while, focusing on the steady rhythm of sharpening.

"You accuse us of preaching falsehoods," Yakov continued. "Yet you arrive at our compound and expect us to leap with joy when you share your wealth. I know you're not wicked, but I fear your hunger for fame has blinded you. You long to be admired."

Paulus stared at him. "Whatever makes you believe that?"

"And when you can't satisfy your needs," Yakov continued, "you spark arguments: you strive to prove others wrong. But let me ask you this: do you know why you have failed to achieve all you desire? It's because whenever you attack another, you are hurting yourself. Your anger toward others only reflects your displeasure with yourself. We are all one."

Paulus wiped the sickle clean, pressed the blade against his thumb, then slashed the sickle in the air a few times, as if testing its sharpness against the wind.

"Whom do you aspire to fool with this superior talk of equality?" Paulus said after a lengthy pause. "You portray yourself as an honorable man, yet you call yourself Yakov the Just." He chuckled. "Behold your own Assembly before you cast judgment upon me. They all left you, did they not? Your sons, your wife. Even that woman—what was her name? Magdalen? The one who disrobed in front of every man who cast their eyes upon her."

"I only want to help you," Yakov said, not taking the bait. "God resists the proud, but assists the humble. You can be better."

"She spread her legs for me, you know." Paulus grinned at the memory. Then he rose to stand, wide-legged, arms akimbo.

Yakov tried to push the image away, but his heart filled with jealousy.

"Did she tell you?" Paulus continued. "She opened her mouth and let me taste her, and then she let her tunic slip to the ground."

Paulus was lying. He had to be.

"In your fantasies, surely," Yakov shot back.

"I call God as my witness!" Paulus said jubilantly and raised his palms to the sky. "You may continue to believe what pleases you, but despite whatever you may have heard, I have Christos on my side. Yeshua might have been your brother while he walked this earth, but after his death, after his resurrection, he came to *me*. The sooner you accept this, the sooner you may be saved."

Yudah Tzaer and some of the other disciples had heard the fiery argument and had arrived at the brook with a basket of dishes: soiled ceramic platters and limestone mugs. They stepped into the water to wash them, close enough to listen. Close enough to provide protection.

"Nothing you say will change our minds," Yakov countered. "We were there, remember? We learned everything we know from Yeshua himself." He picked up the whetting stone Paulus had dropped on the ground and flung it to Yudah Tzaer, who caught it midair, rinsed it in the brook, and handed it back to Paulus.

Yakov motioned at the sickle. "Not sharp enough. Keep going."

Reluctantly, Paulus picked up the sickle and continued rubbing the stone against the blade.

"Your faithful servants in those churches," Yudah Tzaer said, "they've told us everything. How you say that all Yeshua's disciples— Uncle Yakov, Andreas, Bar-Tôlmay, Taddai, Levi, Shimon, Phillipos—they only thought they were the 'leaders' until we met you. What shadow lives in your heart and makes you spread lies about us?"

Paulus chuckled and shook off Yudah Tzaer's accusations like a dog shakes off water after a swim. "Easy now. You have all misunderstood: my aim is to work with you. I have spread the teachings of Christos like an aromatic fragrance all around the world. And yes, a few sinners may have been tempted by Satan and shunned me. But what I do not understand is why you keep sending your apostles to undo all my exemplary work. Our cause spreads like sweet incense to save those who are lost in the darkness."

"Lost?" Yakov almost spat out his words, laughing. "Those who haven't discovered oneness with God are not *lost*. You make it sound like they have done something wrong. They just haven't awakened yet."

Paulus squatted in the shallow brook to rinse the sickle and stone: "I am different from you, Yakov. And unlike Moses, I never covered my brightness with a veil. I feel no shame about my power, my connection with Christos. Moses's followers were simple men, with closed minds. And to this day, their minds are covered by that same embarrassing veil."

"Moses's followers?" Yakov said. "You mean to say Jews? But haven't you always claimed you're Jewish?"

"This veil of sin can be removed by joining Christos," Paulus continued. "Besides, who are you to accuse me of lying, of creating wild tales about your lot? Your own apostles approach my churches and claim *my* gospel is untrue."

Paulus shook his head, frustrated. "How many times must I explain that my gospel is not of human origin? I did not receive it from a friend or a brother or some simple pilgrim I met while I traveled through the wilderness. No one taught me a false gospel. God's own son, Yeshua Christos himself, revealed it to me. God selected *me* among hundreds of thousands of Jews and called me to serve him. I did not approach anyone for advice, not even you. Because I knew what I had seen, what I had heard, was the truth."

Paulus didn't even wait for a response. He marched up the path back to the compound, slashing the air with his sharpened sickle.

Everyone laughed at his outburst.

Yakov laughed, too, but a stone had formed in his gut. He tried to focus on forgiveness, envelop Paulus in a sphere of compassion, and connect with the wounded child within, the one crying for love. But nothing seemed to help remove the shadow of doom that had darkened his mind.

The next morning, Yakov woke with a splitting headache. He asked Yohannah to heal his pain with her hands. But even after the pain subsided, he couldn't bear to trek all the way to the temple. He needed time to focus, decide what to do about that headstrong, stiff-necked man. Perhaps they should bid Paulus goodbye and let him return to Antioch and then forget he even existed. But blinding their eyes to their problems would only bring them back to the same conundrum they had faced the last few years, where Paulus was preaching a message opposite to their own, and everyone they taught became increasingly confused. They had to come to an agreement sooner or later. They had to bring Paulus over to their side.

Instead of visiting the temple, the disciples hiked up the nearest hill to the peak where the sky seemed to go on forever. Yakov smoothed out his robe, placed it on the ground, and invited Paulus to share it.

"Let's ponder this…" Yakov looked out across a dozen of his closest followers and Paulus's kinsmen and servants. "What good is having faith without good deeds? Suppose you know of brothers or sisters who don't have enough to eat. You may bless them, and tell them, 'May you keep warm and eat well,' but if you don't offer them help, how will they survive? Let's all give thanks to Paulus, who traveled hundreds of miles to aid us."

Yakov sensed how Paulus relaxed beside him. They had to lead with graciousness and shower him with love. "Will you share a few words?"

"Allow me to tell you a story about a simple man," Paulus said, "one who was raised up to the highest of heaven, where he heard things that cannot be put into words, that human lips may not speak."

"He experienced a moment of enlightenment," Yakov said.

"That man was me," Paulus continued. "Yeshua Christos, your teacher, encountered me lifeless on a deserted road. He lifted me up and blessed me. But Satan was jealous of my relationship with God. He assaulted me with a painful ailment to thwart my salvation. But

Christos said, 'My grace is all you need, for my power is greatest when you are weak.' Those are the exact words your teacher Yeshua Christos told me."

"We have all experienced moments of enlightenment," Yakov said. "What you saw and heard was God, not Yeshua."

"Oh, no!" Paulus objected. "You must remember I am the only one who has met Yeshua Christos after his resurrection. I saw him!"

"And you never considered that you might have been hallucinating?" Yudah Tzaer asked.

Everyone snickered and Paulus's face turned red.

"Not at all," he said, but his voice held a shiver of doubt. "The day our earthly bodies pass away, God will invite us to his house in heaven, into the home he made for us all, for all time."

"According to Yeshua," Yakov said with as much love as he could muster, "you must find the Kingdom of Heaven *before* the flame in your body extinguishes. Heaven already exists inside of us, around us. It's not a place where our souls will go."

Paulus shrugged, unperturbed, while watching his kinsmen. "One day, we will stand before Christos and he will judge us all."

"That's where you're mistaken," Yudah Tzaer interrupted. "One of the remarkable things about my father was that he judged no one."

"And I remained under the impression you had never met your father," Paulus said with a snigger. "Perhaps your father did not judge as a man while he was alive. But in his spirit of the Messiah or Yeshua Christos, he does judge. And we should all aspire to please him, lest we go to hell."

"My brother was nothing like the divisive being you speak of," Yakov said, "but then, we all know you never met him."

"I did meet him. And I know him considerably better than any of you ever did. Christos was without sin, but God made him share our sin for our sake. And the day we unite with Christos, we will share in the righteousness of God."

Yakov saw the doubt that flashed across the faces around him and hoped they would all remember to react with compassion and protect with love.

Paulus closed his eyes and stretched his arms out, as if to embrace the clouds that lingered above. Then he returned his gaze to Yakov and the disciples. "Does God grant you the power to work miracles because you follow the law? Or because you believe in the Good News?"

"One doesn't have to be separate from the other," Yakov said.

"Perhaps." Paulus looked across the men and women around him, chin up, confident his words would tear down any walls of confusion. "Four hundred and thirty years before God gave Moses the law, he made a covenant with Abraham."

They all nodded in careful agreement.

"God gave his word to Abraham and his descendant," Paulus continued. "Not *all* descendants, mind you—*one* descendant!"

Paulus paused for effect. "The scripture says, 'Whoever does not obey the law is cursed by God' and that 'anyone hanged on a tree is cursed by God.'" He lifted his chin and combed his fingers through his beard. "Christos redeemed us from that curse. He died on a cross to help share God's blessing with Jews and gentiles alike. Through faith in Yeshua Christos, we may all receive the spirit promised by God."

"That's one way of seeing it," Yakov answered. He tried to make sense of what he had just heard. "Or perhaps you're only drawing conclusions that support your beliefs."

"I know your scheme." Paulus tapped Yakov's knee with his walking stick, just a touch too hard. "I have dwelled among you from new moon to full, and I have watched you. You pretend to be righteous, yet none of you follow the law to the letter. And you force others to be circumcised so you can brag about how many followers you have gained compared with me." Paulus chuckled. "Oh, do not dare deny this; it's utterly useless."

He studied his fingernails and cleaned them with a thin stick before he continued. "The law has become obsolete. Yeshua's death annulled it. Why do you find that so hard to accept? We only need to learn the truth about Lord Christos and how he died on the cross for us."

Yakov drew a cross in the mud with his finger, then scratched it out. "Everyone's truth is different. And I've come to understand that the more facts I present, the less you believe me. I clearly can't change your mind, and I must accept that. But don't go around telling people that if they're circumcised, Yeshua's message won't be any use to them at all." He sought strength from the faces of Yudah Tzaer and Yohannah, who urged him on. "That's not only misguided… it's insulting. And don't spread lies about those of us who obey the law, that God will never grace us."

"But you won't be," Paulus said. He cleaned a tuft of lint from his mantle and flicked it into the air.

"*We* aren't graced by God?" Yakov wanted to shake the man until he came to his senses. Instead, he filled his heart with love and added, in the sweetest voice possible, "We live in God's grace. We *are* God's grace."

"A circumcised man must obey the whole law. But the law is dead and cannot save anyone. What matters is faith in Christos."

"Neither following the law nor ignoring it can secure salvation." Yakov countered. He tried to view Paulus as a stubborn child who yearned to be heard. If only he would listen.

"See, we are not that different." Paulus patted Yakov's shoulder. "We can reach salvation only through belief in Christos the Messiah and his resurrection."

"As long as your heart is closed, I cannot persuade you to see the truth." Yakov felt dizzy all of a sudden. "But Yeshua's own disciples, and the temple priests, and any other Jewish leaders will never agree with you."

Paulus smiled. "How can Christos and Satan agree?" He stood and smoothed out his robe. "My men and I, we don't need temple priests. We don't even need the temple. We are the temple of the living God, of Christos. We can never work together with unbelievers—it cannot be done. Light and darkness can never exist together."

"They can! Once you stop seeing the world in polarities of good and evil," Yakov responded, having regained the power in his core. He connected with God and filled himself with abundant love and infinite light. "Once we realize we are all one, we can all live side by side in peace. That's what Yeshua taught. And that's what our apostles teach all over the world. Even some of your own disciples understand this. That's why you're sometimes not welcomed back in places where you have taught before, even in churches you have founded."

Paulus laughed, shaking his head. "Even Satan can disguise himself in the robe of an angel. My service to God far outshines yours. I have worked harder. I have been cast in prison and have been whipped many times. I was even stoned once! I have often gone without sleep, without food and water."

Yakov sensed the pain in Paulus's voice. "I'm sorry you have endured such hardship." He patted the spot next to him to get Paulus to sit down, to relax, to feel he was among friends. But Paulus just looked out across the peaks, his gaze following the wispy clouds that sailed lazily across the sky.

"No man may consider me a fool," Paulus said as if to himself.

"You're not a fool." Yakov searched his mind for a quote from the scriptures that would appease the man beside him. But no words could be found.

Scarlet anemones and golden daisies fought for attention with pink rock roses in the fields of wildflowers that carpeted the hills. The spring rains and heavy winds had finally abated and moved on to other continents. Yakov had awakened past midnight, and however he tossed and turned, had not fallen back to sleep. Instead, he had followed the moonlit path down to the brook and bathed in the fresh stream under a canopy of twinkling stars.

Today was the big day. After weeks of arguments, Paulus had finally succumbed and consented to follow the Assembly's rules. He had agreed to go through the purification ritual at the temple as a token of dedication and would even pay the temple fees of four new Assembly members. It was a massive victory.

Then why did Yakov feel so disillusioned?

The sun stood high in the sky by the time Yakov guided Paulus and the others to the recently renovated immersion pools at the temple. Living water whirled from large pipes into the square basin and kept the water fresh at all times.

Paulus looked uncomfortable in his near nakedness, wearing only a loincloth, as he descended the slippery stairs into the mikvah. He cupped his hands over his genitals, as if afraid someone would take a measure of his manhood. His muscular body, which normally held so much strength, was hunched over in bashfulness and seemed to shiver as he lowered his head under the water.

For the first time in his life, Yakov knew that he was the right man in the right place. He had earned this triumph, and Yeshua would have been proud. Even his father would have been proud. Yakov glowed as he accompanied Paulus and his men through the Court of the Gentiles to Solomon's Portico.

"There's never a need to fear," he said once all the Assembly members had gathered around him. "As long as we move forth in love and kindness, we cannot fail."

Paulus sat with his eyes closed, his back straight, seemingly in bliss.

"Then why do some people act with hatred and violence?" a young boy asked.

"Because they have no faith. They are blind."

The boy frowned.

"To perceive their blindness," Yakov said, "cover your eyes with your hands, press gently, and tell me what you see."

The boy closed his eyes and knitted his brow.

"Uncle, no one sees this way," Yudah Tzaer interrupted.

"Do it again!" Yakov commanded. All around him, everyone but Paulus placed their hands over their eyes. "Now, what do you see?"

The little boy let out a shrill laugh. "Light! Teacher, I see light!"

Yakov's heart filled with gratitude. "Go on," he prompted. "What more can you tell me?"

"It's a light brighter than the light of day. The light of God."

"Now," Yakov continued, "cover your ears with your hands, and tell me what you hear."

Yakov placed his hands over his own ears and listened, to demonstrate that he, too, needed to listen inside.

At first, all he heard were the voices of the surrounding crowd, of merchants shouting. And then, he heard the voices of angels. The voice of God.

"They're praising you," the boy said, eyes wide in awe at his newfound wisdom.

"They praise me, yes," Yakov answered. "And they also praise *you*, because you have seen and heard God, and they are thankful. But those who live and act in fear remain blind and deaf. They cannot perceive the light inside until they awaken."

Yudah Tzaer raised his hand and waved. "May I?"

"Of course."

Yudah Tzaer cleared his throat and said, "When you go out into the world to teach, many will accept our message of love and oneness. But when they realize how much effort it involves, some become discouraged. They'll look for an immediate solution, something simple. And if they're told of an effortless way, where they will not need to change their ways to reap the rewards, they may become confused. They'll wonder who's telling the truth."

Yakov opened his eyes slightly to glance at Paulus, but the man seemed absorbed in Yudah Tzaer's words and thankfully did not seem to take offense.

"What Yudah Tzaer here is trying to say," Yakov said, "is that if you listen within, God will guide you. Because what is real cannot be threatened, it will always remain. Nothing unreal exists. The deaf and blind will associate with like-minded people, because they don't know better. As long as you are one with God, no one can taint your mind."

During the thirty days of purification, Paulus shadowed Yakov's every step. At dawn, when Yakov woke up, Paulus was already waiting by the entrance of his courtyard to accompany Yakov to the brook. They ate together, meditated together, prayed together, walked to the temple together. The more Yakov tried to keep a distance, the more Paulus pegged himself to his side. But Paulus worked hard, as he had promised to do. He milked the cows, plowed the fields, and mended the roofs of any huts that were falling apart. He even brought firewood from the forests. Fortunately for Yakov, Yohannah's amorous attention had also shifted over to Paulus, and she no longer tried to take Yakov's hand or snuggle up to him by the fire. For the first time in years, Yakov felt at peace.

"Today's the last day of your purification," Yakov told Paulus one morning as they herded a half-dozen sheep into a shearing pen. "And as a reward I would like you to deliver the sermon at the temple."

Paulus chewed his lip to conceal his eagerness. Together, they grabbed one of the sheep and tipped it gently onto its back. Paulus propped the body against his to make sure the animal was comfortable and would not struggle during the shearing. With the ewe's shoulders between his knees and her four legs in the air, he held on to the front legs and signalled to Yakov to start shearing.

"Are you willing?" Yakov asked again. He put the sharp shearing knife to the sheep's fleece and used long, confident strokes to shear the wool from the top of the breastbone to the flanks.

Paulus remained silent.

"You're a gifted speaker." Yakov placed a hand over the animal's teats, careful not to nick them. "This would not differ from when you speak in your churches."

"And you don't consider it a test?" Paulus moved the sheep to its side, giving Yakov access to the wool on its back.

So combative! Yakov chuckled to himself. But in truth, wasn't it really a test? "Tradition," he responded instead, and dug his hand into the thick wool on the ewe's back, keeping the blade as close to the skin as possible. "A sermon at the temple will show God that you are willing to do his work. But if you'd rather not—"

"I will," Paulus said as if it were the most natural thing in the world. He raised the animal onto its feet to allow Yakov reach of the last section of its back. "If it would please you."

Yakov kissed the sheep's head and sent a word of gratitude to God for the gift of the wool that they would sell in the market.

"Indeed, it would." Yakov released the ewe to join the others and watched her bounce around the meadow, delirious in her newfound lightness and freedom. "That's exactly what I like to hear."

The shearing of the sheep took much longer than planned, and by the time they reached the temple, the day had already cooled off.

"Come forth, Paulus and Timotheos, Mattai and Symeon," Yakov called out once everyone had taken their seat. "You have completed your thirty days of purification and become genuine servants of God. It pleases me more than words can say. But before you leave us, let me offer a few words of advice. If you go forth and put God's word into practice, God will bless you for all the unselfish deeds you do for others."

A light descended upon the four recently purified men, and Yakov's heart brimmed with gratitude. He bowed his head and thanked God for allowing him to lead others into the light. "Timotheos, Mattai, would you like to say a few words?"

The new disciples looked uneasy.

"Have courage, my men." Yakov stretched out his hands to help them up from their seats. "A few words of gratitude, that's all."

"We offer thanks," Timotheos said as his face turned scarlet, "to every soul among us, and to our honored God. We're so grateful for your wisdom. And I—we—ask for your protection that we may not stumble in this life."

Yakov patted Timotheos's shoulder and showed the blushing youngster to his seat. "Well done."

He turned to the young Mattai, a Samarian shepherd whom his men had rescued from the hands of Judean bandits. "Would you like to offer a sentiment?"

Mattai scratched the thick blond hair under his headscarf, cleared his throat, and looked out across the Assembly. "Praise be to God, for your fatherly mercy and love. And to Yakov, for the sweet and simple instructions that we may hear God's words."

Yakov patted Mattai's shoulder with satisfaction. A wise and honorable youngster, he would go far. "And Symeon?"

"I would like to speak." Paulus made his way to the front. "If I may."

"Of course," Yakov said, surprised at the interruption.

"First, I would like to offer my sincere gratitude to all of you for welcoming us into your midst. We will be forever in your debt. As

God is my witness, I will serve God with all my heart and soul by preaching the Good News. Wherever I am in the world, I will always include you in my prayers. I have complete faith in the gospel your brother Yeshua taught, and have an obligation to all people, the civilized and the savage, the educated and the ignorant, both Jews and gentiles."

Yakov drew a breath of relief. "And you will follow the law from now on?" he asked.

"I will." Paulus rubbed his chin pensively. "I will, and I always have. As God is my witness, I have always been a good and faithful Jew."

As Paulus sat down, an elderly Pisidian pilgrim burst forward. "This man is a fraud," he yelled, and wagged his finger at Paulus.

"Now, now," Yakov said, and he grabbed the man by the shoulders to hold him back. If the guardsmen noticed any trouble, they might arrest them all.

The Pisidian shook himself loose. "This man's an impostor!" he yelled.

The surrounding crowd drew closer, grew denser, as everyone within earshot of the ruckus leaned in to catch a glimpse of the accused impostor.

Paulus just laughed. "You're confused."

Yakov moved in between them and faced the Pisidian. "My good man, this is my guest, my friend. Whatever he may have done, or you think he may have done, the law asks us to forgive our trespassers. Will you please find it in your heart to forgive him?"

"Forgive?" Paulus scoffed. He pushed Yakov aside. "For what?"

"He's not a Jew!" the Pisidian scowled, his face red with anger. "And now he's brought other gentiles here, too. He's defiled God's holy abode."

A couple of temple priests infiltrated the crowd and called on the soldiers for help.

"I *am* a Jew!" Paulus insisted, softening his voice. "I was born from the tribe of Benjamin. And how dare you approach me in this sacred space and cast out my name as evil?"

"How dare you pretend you're a Jew?" the Pisidian screamed. "And how dare you speak here, in our Holy Temple, pretending to be a man of faith? I've heard you speak words against this holy place; you call it superfluous."

He turned to the temple priests and the soldiers who had surrounded them. "I've seen this man preach against our people in Sardis, in Hierapolis, in Perga. He ridicules the law of Moses and urges all Jews to abandon their faith. He claims our law has been annulled because some half man, half god called Christos was nailed to a cross. And then he says God raised him from death like a common Apollo."

"He's changed," Yakov tried. He grabbed the old man's arms, looked deep into his eyes, and connected with him through his heart. "He's been purified. He obeys the law now."

The Pisidian laughed and shoved Yakov away. "This man, Paulus, says the Jews murdered the Christos-god who died because of *our* sins. Then he rose to life as some Orpheus to make us right with God. In this crazy man's head, we should believe his fantastical god was the Messiah, although he didn't save any of us. And no one else has seen him. Because of this figment of his imagination, we must now abandon the law that has guided us through centuries, because our law cuts us off from God?" The man wiped some spit from the corners of his mouth before he continued. "You say he's changed? You've been fooled. He's nothing but a lying hypocrite. He has no right to speak here."

Paulus's servants and companions closed up around him.

"I have only sought to help carry your burden," Paulus said to the Assembly members, ignoring the Pisidian. "Because in the goodness of my heart, it was the only manner by which you would open your eyes and see the truth. Once you understand, you will no longer care for the law of Moses. You will yearn to obey the law of Christos, our Messiah."

Yakov stood frozen as an angry mob closed in around them. Had everything Paulus said in the last few weeks been a lie?

The guardsmen pushed through the crowd toward Paulus, swords raised. Yakov's entire body trembled with fear when he saw them raise their swords. He had to protect his guest, his disciple. His friend. But he didn't want to die.

"They warned me not to come." Paulus raised his voice to overpower the screams. "A seer told me you and your kind would tie me up and cast me to the soldiers like meat to a lion. My disciples in Caesarea asked me not to travel here. But I had to. I had promised to help you."

An icy shiver snaked up Yakov's spine. Had Paulus deceived him again?

"They cried, they begged me on their bare knees not to come," Paulus shouted as the soldiers pushed forward. "But I told them I am ready, if it would come to it. I am prepared to be tortured and spat on, even die in the name of Lord Yeshua."

"Oh, Paulus." Yakov said in disbelief. "How many times do I have to tell you that Yeshua was just a man, a humble preacher?"

"No," Paulus said, smiling now, eyes ablaze. "He was Christos, the Messiah. And you will see. The end of the world is upon us. When our savior, the Lord Yeshua Christos, descends from heaven and unites with us, he will change the mortal bodies of all believers into glorious beings. And the rest, I am afraid, will burn in the fires of Gehinnom for all time. Save yourself, Yakov."

As the guards closed in, Yakov stepped in front of Paulus and crossed his arms like a shield. He hadn't protected Yeshua. He had been a coward then. But not this time. Come what may, he would protect Paulus.

"Uncle," Yudah Tzaer called. "We must leave, get out of here!"

Yakov was scarcely aware that the crowd had dispersed. Everyone but Paulus's men had fled for safety. But his feet were nailed to the ground. He couldn't move.

"It was all part of your scheme, was it not?" Paulus said, his face contorted in fury as he faced Yakov. "You called for them, the Pisidians. You made me stand up and preach here. You caught me in your fraudulent scheme."

"Paulus," Yakov tried, "you're my guest. It's my obligation to protect you, to care for you. I would never—"

"Uncle! It's not worth it. We need to get out of here." Yudah Tzaer grabbed Yakov's arm just as the guards barged through the circle of Paulus's protectors and yanked Paulus away.

Yakov rushed after the guardsmen. "No. Stop!"

A guardsman pointed his sword at Yakov. "You'd better leave. Go home."

"That man is my friend," Yakov said. "My guest."

The guard raised his sword higher. "You didn't hear me? Leave, or we will arrest you, too. And stay away from the temple. You're not welcome here anymore."

As if in a nightmare, Yakov watched the Roman soldiers drag Paulus, Timotheos, and his other men away, like they had once dragged Yeshua, all those years ago.

Paulus was right: it was his fault. He had made Paulus speak. He had put him to a test to see if Paulus had truly changed.

What had the world come to, when they could no longer preach in their own temple?

Bile rose up Yakov's throat, and he doubled over and vomited on the ground.

Magdala Nunayya, Galilee, AD 60

Mariamne tended to the fragrant roses in her garden, snipping the yellowed deadheads with sharp shears and collecting petals she would use for scented oils in a basket. She knelt down to pull out the weeds that had sprouted between rows of the healing herbs, determined to put to use everything Yeshua had prescribed.

Inside the house, her father was lying on his deathbed. Although he was too old for a cure, Mariamne vowed to make his last days more comfortable. She brewed him earthy chamomile and spicy cinnamon potions for his fever and added ground cloves to ease the pain.

What would she do once he was gone? She rubbed her forehead to ease the tension, the worry. Her mother had passed long ago. And her son, Yudah Tzaer? God only knew where he roamed these days.

Mariamne entered the darkened room at the back of the house to tend to her father. He lay in the same bed where she had once suffered, moments away from death, when Yeshua had arrived to heal her all those years ago. He had brought her back to life. And what a life! Those two short years with Yeshua had been her best. And since then, only sorrow. Her thoughts wandered to Yakov. Had he married Talitha? Reared children with her? A tear escaped her eye. But she had no right to feel sorry for herself. She should have been bolder, more courageous. If only she had dared to confess her love for him, her life could have taken a different path. Mariamne jerked her head to rid her mind of the pointless contemplations. It was too late now. No use to dream of what could have been.

She soaked a towel in a bowl of steaming water and placed it on her father's forehead. Once he had passed, there would be no one to care for. No one to love.

Mother.

She thought she heard a soft voice, a whisper.

Mother, it called again.

The auditory hallucinations, those voices, occurred more often now that she had no one to talk to.

Mother.

She could have sworn that this time the voice was real.

Mariamne turned to re-moisten the towel and almost jumped with shock. Someone was standing in the shadows by the door.

Yeshua?

She rubbed her eyes and opened them again. Still there. Slowly, the apparition morphed into a solid figure of flesh and blood.

It wasn't a ghost.

"Yudah Tzaer!" Mariamne struggled to her feet and fell into her son's embrace. She melted into his arms: the warmth of his skin, the softness of his beard. He was really here! Mariamne pressed her lips to his cheeks, and her eyes overflowed. He had come back for her! She clung to him, as if he were the last person alive. Her son, her love, her treasure.

"And Grandfather?" Yudah Tzaer gestured to the bed where her father lay under layers of coarse blankets. "He's gone?"

"No, not yet."

Yudah Tzaer knelt by his grandfather's bed. He placed one palm on the old man's forehead and the other on his chest to send him divine healing. In a low voice, a murmur, he prayed over the old man's soul.

Mariamne's entire being filled with love and pride. Soft rays of light strained through covered windows and illuminated Yudah Tzaer's face, and for a moment she believed she saw God.

Her father's chest heaved and almost rose from the bed under the pressure of Yudah Tzaer's hands, and then his torso sank back into the mattress.

A bird tweeted outside the window, releasing the stillness from the room.

Her father's spirit had finally passed.

A few days later, when they had properly buried her father's remains and purified the house, Mariamne lit a fire in the garden and burned the clothes she had been wearing during her father's last days. The time had come for a new beginning.

Yudah Tzaer watched her as he gathered grapes into a basket. "I'll take these fruits to the market." He picked up a grape, looked at it, and put it in his mouth.

"That's women's work," Mariamne said, but Yudah Tzaer laughed.

"These fine fruits will fill my purse with copper coins. And we'll need money for our travels."

"*Your* travels," Mariamne corrected him.

Yudah Tzaer placed the basket on the ground and enveloped his mother in his arms, lifting her off the ground. He had grown so strong since she'd last seen him. If he squeezed any harder, her ribs would break.

"You think I'll leave you here all alone to rot in this village, doused in the stench of dried fish?" He laughed.

"It's not a stench. Besides, where would I go? My place is here." But a faint stream of hope, of release, emerged within her. She pushed it away. "I'm not going anywhere."

"What do you mean, where would you go? You have a home, remember? A son. Grandchildren. We all miss you."

"Grandchildren?"

"Didn't I tell you? Miriam and I have two young ones, Elazar and Maryam Salome."

A flood of love swept through her. *Imagine that: grandchildren!*

"Do they look like me? Like Yeshua?" A sharp pain clutched her heart, and she heaved, at once overwhelmed by sorrow. "I can't go back," she said and poked the fire. The ashes from her old clothes rose to the skies and soared away in the wind.

"You haven't heard, then, have you? About our old friend Paulus? He was arrested in Jerusalem for stirring up trouble in the temple. They sent him to Caesarea. I think they want to ship him to Rome."

"My dear boy, I have other worries besides him. And I forgave him long ago." *What about Yakov?* she wanted to ask. Did he miss her? But their chance at love had come and gone. It was foolish to expect anything else.

"Uncle Yakov sent me," Yudah Tzaer said and winked.

Mariamne turned so fast, her neck almost snapped. She stared at her son. "Yakov sent you? Why?"

Yudah Tzaer laughed.

She blushed. Her son was mocking her.

"He wants you to come back."

Mariamne's knees buckled beneath her, and she had to grab on to a rosebush for balance. The thorns cut into her skin, and she winced.

Yudah Tzaer rushed to her aid. "Do you think I'm blind?" He caressed a strand of gray hair from her face. "You're his best friend, his confidante."

Friend. What an awful word. Still, a ray of hope flourished inside her. Maybe having a wonderful friend could be enough. Besides, what else would she do here in Magdala, except rot to death, as her son was suggesting?

"He never married Talitha, then?"

"Who's Talitha?" Yudah Tzaer looked at her, confused. Then a distant memory lit his eyes. "Oh, the maid? She's long gone. Yohannah sent her away when she moved into Uncle Yakov's house."

Of course she did. Mariamne inhaled deeply through her nose to chase the fog of jealousy away. They were both widowed, and no law spoke against it. Quite a logical development. "He married Yohannah, then." She tried not to let her disappointment color her voice.

"Married her? No, she just takes care of his household."

Mariamne wanted to cry with relief. He hadn't remarried! Even if he would never love her, she could return to Jerusalem and be his closest friend again.

"When are we leaving?" she asked, grinning like a simpleton.

Three days later, Mariamne and Yudah Tzaer arrived at the compound long before dawn. They had traveled through the night despite the risk of falling prey to bandits or zealots. She couldn't wait another moment to see Yakov again.

The compound hadn't changed much since she left five years ago. They hadn't raised the height of the stone wall surrounding the compound, and the gate still hung loose on its hinges, a poor protection against intruders. And Yakov's mud-brick house stood as powerful as ever, a stronghold encircled by everyone else's single-room huts, and the fields brimmed with healthy grains and vegetables.

Yudah Tzaer unfastened the bundles of clothing tied to the back of their mule.

"Go," he said to his mother. "He's been waiting."

Mariamne's legs trembled as she made her way through the familiar courtyard, past the fire pit where she and Michal had spent years cooking and quarreling. Through the door that led to her old room, where Yohannah was curled up in deep sleep, and to his room. She pushed the curtain door aside, and sniffed the unique scent of parsley, sweat, and animals: Yakov.

Moonlight sifted through the narrow window, and there he was, fast asleep on a simple mattress of stuffed hay. In the same bed where Talitha had spent all those nights when Yakov should have been with her, with Mariamne. But now the young servant was gone. No sense in dwelling on the past.

Mariamne knelt on the floor next to Yakov and watched him sleep. Oh, how she loved this kind and gentle man. When she rested her cheek on his chest. He stirred. But she didn't look up, didn't move. For now, she just wanted to lie there with him, without words, without explanations. Just be together.

Yakov jerked awake from his deep sleep. Something heavy was pressing down on his chest. He wriggled in the dark to free himself from the burden that cramped his lungs.

He gasped for air, then startled when the pressure shifted its location. What on earth could it be? Had a puppy sought refuge on his chest? A baby goat?

When he stretched his hand down to push the animal away, his hand did not grasp fur. Instead, his fingers ran through long curls of human hair. A woman? He flickered his eyes open and rubbed them awake while adjusting to the dim light. And then he caught sight of the face of the most beautiful woman in the world, resting peacefully on his chest.

Mariamne.

This time, it wasn't a dream. His head sank back onto the pillow, and he let his heart fill with infinite love. With happiness.

He didn't want to move.

He wanted to stay like this forever.

Jerusalem, Judea, AD 60

While summer sailed by in its perfect glory, Mariamne and Yakov rekindled their friendship. Inseparable friends again, as if no time had passed. They walked to the temple together, meditated together, and worked together to resolve any issues raised in the compound. The moon had traveled three full cycles since Mariamne's return, illuminating endless nights of desperate longing. Like two innocent bees, Yakov and Mariamne buzzed around the honeypot, in fear of making the wrong move, of committing an error that could not be reversed.

Mariamne blushed every time she remembered how surprised Yakov had been to find her sleeping on his chest the morning of her return. She had pretended to be asleep, heart throbbing and delirious with the joy of finally lying in the arms of the man she had loved for so long. He, too, had pretended to slumber, although the smile on his lips had betrayed him. Oh, how she had longed to kiss him, to dive into his arms and abandon all the rules of courtship, of decency. In the end, however, the fatigue from the arduous journey had overwhelmed her, and she had succumbed to deep sleep. And when she had finally awakened, he had already risen and left.

Without a word of complaint, Yohannah had moved back into her own house, and by new moon, she had married Zacchaeus.

To Mariamne's dismay, she and Yakov had quickly slipped into their old habits. Once again, Mariamne was sleeping alone in her old bed, listening to Yakov's soft snores in the next room. Although some things had changed since her return. These days they flirted with each other. They laughed and joked and danced, oblivious of anyone watching. She could have sworn he loved her, too. Then why did he keep his distance? Not once had he brought his lips to hers or left his curtain door open with a hint of an invitation. Even so, she was happier than she had been in a long time. Ever since Yeshua passed away.

In the days leading up to Sukkot, the harvest celebration that commemorated the forty years Moses and his people wandered lost in the wilderness, the compound changed into a village. Yakov invited any passing strangers on their pilgrimage to the temple to stay. Hundreds of makeshift huts and tents covered the hillside, and the air filled with song.

The adolescent boys climbed high in nearby palm trees and slashed the fronds that would make the roofs of the temporary huts, while the younger ones beat the fig trees with sticks and collected the ripe fruits that fell to the ground.

Like all other women and young children, Mariamne and her grandchildren, Elazar and Maryam Salome, kept busy building a temporary hut where Yakov would sleep during the holy days. They wove boughs of willow and leafy myrtle into walls, tied them together, and pressed fistfuls of mud and straw between the boughs to fill the gaps in the foliage.

Mariamne hummed to herself in an attempt to enjoy the moment and to pacify her impatient, pounding heart. Tomorrow night, the first eve of the holiday, she and Yakov would dine in the provisional hut, and if she were lucky, he would invite her to spend the night there with him. For the first time ever, they would sleep in the same space, mere inches apart, breathing the same air. And their limbs would touch. Mariamne's cheeks blossomed at the thought. At last, the light of their love would conquer any fears.

It had to.

"Sour fruits for the sweet ladies," Yakov called from a distance.

Mariamne stepped outside the hut and saw that Yakov and the other men had returned from picking wild citrons in the woods.

"Anyone need citron fruits for their arba'ah minim? Anyone?" Yakov laughed and swooshed the basket of green lemonlike fruits around and around, as if ready to discard them to the ground.

All the women came out of their huts and surged forward to collect one citron each. The rare fruit was one of four plants needed for the arba'ah minim bundle of plants, which the men would use during prayer on the first morning of Sukkot. Mariamne's heart ached when she watched Yohannah elbow through the crowd to collect her citron. Right after Mariamne's return, Yohannah had married the short-tempered Zacchaeus to save face. And now she suffered from the bruises and black eyes that only a distrustful man would dispose upon his wife. Still, Yohannah never stopped smiling. She never lost faith.

Mariamne waited patiently for her turn, content to be the last in line behind the other women. She tilted her head and pouted coyly as Yakov handed her the last citron. *Oh, those eyes!* She wanted to drown in their soulful depth. When their hands touched, the warmth of his rough skin radiated through her, and she closed her eyes as she brought the citron to her nose to enjoy its fresh scent.

Yakov slapped her hand, causing the fruit to drop back into the basket. "It's not perfume, young lady, it's a holy fruit."

She giggled and picked it up again, but this time she scooted away before he could slap her again. Behind her, she heard him chuckle, and she flirtatiously swayed her hips to tempt him.

Inside the still-roofless hut, Mariamne bound her arba'ah minim bundle together: a date palm frond, two boughs of willow, and three boughs of myrtle. *Perfect.* It would serve Yakov well when he blessed the Assembly in the morning.

Yudah Tzaer peeked into the hut, his arms full of palm fronds.

"Ready to cover up the roof, Mother?"

"Ready," she answered.

She was as ready as she would ever be.

*

On the first morning of Sukkot, Mariamne woke to the sound of singing from the adjacent room, and she pressed her ear to the wall.

"Ba-a-ruch ado-o-oneinu," Yakov's voice rose in singsong, smooth as frothy cream on fresh milk.

Mariamne drank in the beauty of the melody and relished the sense of peace that permeated her core.

Then again, "Blessed is the Lord," he sang.

Mariamne propped herself up on her elbow.

"Blessed are you, my Lord," he sang as he stepped through the curtained doorway and smiled at Mariamne. "Can't sleep? Was I singing too loud?"

She fluffed her hair and glanced at him seductively over her shoulder like an adolescent girl, but then she caught herself. She shouldn't tempt him on this holy day. Instead, she rose from her bed and looked out the window.

"It's windy," she said. "Do you think the huts will stand?"

"They always do," he said behind her.

She hoped he would come closer, put his arms around her, hold her. Instead, he passed her by and stepped out into the courtyard.

Mariamne grabbed the arba'ah minim bundle and hurried after him. Outside, the clear blue skies promised a beautiful day. The wind had quieted to a faint rustle. She felt like a fool.

Yakov graciously took the arba'ah minim from her hands. He held the citron fruit in his left hand and the leafy bundle in his right and stretched his arms out toward the rising sun.

"Ba-a-ruch ado-o-oneinu!" He gestured for Mariamne to come closer, to stand by his side. "Together?"

"Blessed are you, Lord our God," she said as she snuggled closer. "Are we singing?"

Yakov's chin dropped in a slight nod, and he closed his eyes. With the voice of an angel—a booming angel—he let the blessing ring out over the compound, its inhabitants and guests. "Blessed are you, Lord

of the Universe, who has sanctioned us with your commandments."
He brought his hands together, allowing the fruit and leafy bundle to
touch in a gentle kiss.

The village stirred. One by one, their companions joined them in
a circle, holding their arba'ah minim up to the invisible God above.

Yakov raised the citron fruit and leafy bundle toward the sun
again and shook them gently three times to the east. All the men
followed suit. Then he turned to the south, shook them three times
again, waited for the men to shake their bundles, then shook them
three times to the west. At last to the north.

A sacred stillness spread among them as the women pressed their
palms together in gratitude to God and his mastery over all creation.

Mariamne's fingers slid up the small of Yakov's back, along his
spine. She rubbed his broad shoulders, then the nape of his neck. His
skin prickled beneath her touch. When she peeked at him from under
half-closed lids, she caught him smiling.

Once again, his smooth voice echoed into the valley.

"Blessed are you, my Lord," they all sang.

Overcome with joy, Mariamne silently added, "who has brought
this wonderful man into my life."

The temple vibrated with the ethereal energy that always filled the
courtyards during major holidays, despite the hundreds of Roman
legionnaires keeping guard. Yakov and his companions merged with
the masses and became indistinguishable among the throngs of people
who carried vats of water to the temple for the libation ceremony.
They held their heads down as they passed the temple guards and the
foot soldiers who stood ready to enforce the rules of the new
procurator, Porcius Festus. Although petty crime was down since
Festus had replaced the ruthless Antonius Felix, the number of armed
Roman soldiers on the streets had quadrupled. Festus had also
continued his predecessor's reign of fear, taking advantage of the
discord between Jews and Syrians, and did not hesitate to arrest,
torture, and even crucify any suspected rebels. This very morning,

Yakov had told the Assembly members they must stay quiet and out of sight, and blend in.

In silent reverence, they listened as King Agrippa II and his handsome friend, the high priest Ishmael ben Fabus, took turns reading sections from the Torah. And on their walk back to the compound, they joined thousands of other faithful Jews in dancing and singing praises to God by the Pool of Siloam.

When at last they returned home, everyone was exhausted after an interminable day of prayers parading around the altar where thousands of worshippers had left boughs of willow had in an ever increasing pile. Hunger was the least of Mariamne's concerns when she took a seat beside Yakov in their temporary hut for their evening meal.

As always, the conversation between them flowed freely as they enjoyed the lentil stew, grilled leeks, and flatbreads drizzled with honey. Every time Yakov paused, Marianne waited eagerly for his invitation to spend the night. Each time he stretched his hand out to scoop up another mouthful of lentils, she wished he would reach out and touch her, caress her. Instead, Yakov finished his meal, lounged back on his sleeping mat, and closed his eyes. With a flick of his wrist, he indicated for her to leave.

"Good night, then," she whispered, her heart caught in her throat. "May your night be blessed. I will see you in the morning."

Yakov didn't respond. Instead, he yawned and turned his back.

She was not welcomed to stay.

That night, Mariamne tossed and turned on her knotty mattress inside the house. The thin linen sheet caught in her limbs, and she had to pull it free again and again. At last she gave up trying. She couldn't sleep. She had waited all day for Yakov to invite her to spend the night, but to no avail. Of course it wasn't customary for an unmarried man to bring a woman into the provisional hut, but they *did* live together. Surely everyone thought of them as a couple. He could have at least given her an encouraging hint. Instead, the day had passed like any typical first day of Sukkot.

And now, in the middle of the night, she couldn't help but wonder. What if Yakov had expected her to stay? Had he not left ample space for her? No, that didn't make any sense. Before turning in, she'd had to wash the platters, put the food away, and extinguish the fire. But had he expected her to return once the others were asleep?

There was only one way to find out. If he rejected her, no one would ever know, and tomorrow she could pretend nothing had changed. But she had to find out. She combed her fingers through her long, curly hair, pinched her cheeks for color, and rubbed rose petals against her neck for a sweet scent.

The moon stood high in the sky, illuminating the sleeping landscape of hundreds of Sukkot huts that stood protected in the cradle of the high hills. A sheep bleated, unhappy to be confined inside the stable, away from the tasty fresh leaves adorning the huts.

Mariamne lifted her tunic and walked barefoot through the dewy grass to Yakov's hut. She squatted outside the doorway and pushed aside the sheet that covered the opening.

Yakov was sleeping on his back, shoved against the back wall. As if to leave space for her? She hesitated. What if he rejected her? What if he didn't want her at all?

But Yakov had barely slept a wink. He had awakened a thousand times to see if she had finally come back. How had she misunderstood him? He had meant for her to return after her chores. He had even made room for her. But now she was finally here. And she wouldn't have come here for nothing, only to look at him. Would she?

He patted the space beside him on his sleeping mat, and hoped she would at least enter, lie beside him, keep him warm.

But she hesitated.

Yakov's cheeks burned with humiliation. Had he read her wrong? Did she regret coming here? But just as he was about to say something, she crawled in and closed the curtain behind her.

He pulled her into his arms, and before he could stop himself, his mouth covered hers. His tongue pressed into her mouth. His hands traced her body from her hair to her breasts, across her stomach and thighs, and then he lifted her tunic over her head. Without knowing how to stop himself, his face dove into the space between her breasts, and his tongue tasted the heavenly nectar that covered her skin, from her nipples down the roundness of her belly to the wetness between her legs that proved she was willing. His tunic fell to the side, and he raised his pelvis. Without hesitation, he thrust himself into her. With his eyes closed, he moved faster and faster, as if afraid to pause and find her eyes filled with horror. He wanted to apologize, tell her he was sorry, but he wasn't sorry. She had to be his, if only in this moment, if only for tonight. When she lifted her body to meet him, he pushed deeper, deeper, losing himself in the rhythm, until he finally exploded with ecstasy.

Bashfully, and soaked with sweat, he swept her hair back from her face to look at her. The happiness, the love, that radiated from her eyes washed away any remaining doubts, any feeling of guilt.

She wanted him as much as he wanted her.

His entire body trembled with satisfaction as he stared at the stars through the palm fronds that covered the hut, and he wanted to weep with gratitude.

"I love you," she said softly as she rested her head on his shoulder.

You're mine now, he thought.

And suddenly everything in the world made much more sense.

CHAPTER 37

Jerusalem, Judea, AD 62

At last, love had blossomed. Mariamne and Yakov spent the next two years relishing life, safely protected by the cocoon of the compound, while the Romans ran riot outside its walls. Ever since Festus had raised the taxes to finance his extravagances, the people of Judea had suffered, and the rebellion against the Romans had spiraled out of control. In the past few years, the Sicarii had carried out several attacks at public gatherings, where they had stabbed Jews and gentiles alike with daggers they kept concealed in their cloaks. As a result, Festus had granted the legionnaires free rein, and killings of unarmed civilians had increased rampantly.

The Assembly members rarely ventured outside the compound these days and had not worshipped at the temple in over a year. They rarely visited the market, and then only to sell their wool, clothing, and animals, if absolutely necessary.

Inside the stable, Yakov brushed the mule with short, straight, flicking motions, as he rubbed its coat clean and shiny. He glanced at his beloved wife, Mariamne, who squatted at the teats of a doe, draining its udder of milk. He couldn't stop adoring her. Yeshua's wife was now his own. Everything that had once belonged to his older brother was his: recognition, disciples, wife—as if he had stepped into Yeshua's sandals and taken over his life. But it hadn't been easy.

"Merely a pint." Mariamne held up the jar of milk. "Two copper coins, maybe three, that's all."

"If that's the case, we must keep it for ourselves," Yakov said. The end of winter always brought a certain threat of famine. The stocks of fruits and legumes from the fall harvest were withering, and the springtime yield of barley and wheat still loomed like unfulfilled promises. No one knew what the weather would bring: sunny days and plentiful rains, or only one or the other.

Mariamne watched as Yakov gulped down the frothy liquid. The fresh milk warmed his throat, his stomach.

"Patience, my dear." Her hands sought their way around his waist.

"Not here," he said, his voice already hoarse with desire.

But she never obeyed him. She lifted his cloak and undid his loincloth. Yakov leaned against the wall and watched her. At times, her playfulness embarrassed him, but his body couldn't deny her. He let her have her way with him. Like he always did. He moaned louder and louder until she came with a muffled scream and he climaxed into her.

With a wink, she released him, pulled down her tunic, and grabbed the jar of milk. Then she left the stable, whistling.

Yakov chuckled to himself. He must be the luckiest man in the entire world. But also the most foolish. He could have married her right after Michal passed away. Like a dunce, he had yearned to do the right thing, to live up to his moniker of Yakov the Just, behave like the decent man they all expected him to be. As a result, he had denied himself—and her—the happiness God had offered them.

But at last everything had finally fallen into place. Paulus was gone, imprisoned, shipped away to Rome and, from what they had heard, under house arrest. Now, if only the Romans would leave Judea and render the country back to the Jews, Mariamne and Yakov could pass their last days in complete and utter bliss.

*

"Do this for them. Not you," Mariamne said to Yakov a few days later as she stood knee-high in the frigid brook. She bent over and scrubbed a clay platter with a bundle of wool, forever concerned with cleanliness. Whenever Yakov offered to have the young men bring up vats of water to heat over the fire, she frowned at the idea. There was nothing cleaner than flowing water.

"Did you hear me?" She flung a platter at him. He caught it before it crashed on the rocks.

"Like Yeshua, you mean?" Yakov asked, surprised at the absence of jealousy in his heart. He stacked the clean platter on top of a pile of dishes on a sheet. "Do everything for others?"

Mariamne stepped out of the water, wiped her feet on a towel, and snuggled up to him. "Like *you* do." She stroked a wisp of white hair from his eyes and pinched his chin through the gray beard. "You're the one who shouldered your brother's yoke."

"Reluctantly. Don't you remember?" He smiled.

"But you did. You brought us here to safety. You've kept us all alive. Fed. Clothed."

"We did that together. All of us."

"You remembered all of Yeshua's lessons. You've taught us what you know. You've kept us alive in spirit. In God."

"*You* wanted to be our leader." Yakov picked up a flat stone and flipped it into the brook, making it skip once, twice, three times before it sank into the water. "Without you I would have been no one."

Mariamne took his hands between hers and turned him toward her. Her eyes were still as bright as Lake Kinneret on a sunny day, although she had aged. They both had.

"You've been a remarkable leader," she said.

"I was guessing."

Mariamne laughed. "Guessing? You should be a fortune-teller, then, who can guess everything correctly."

He kissed her wrinkled forehead.

"Let's return to the temple, my love," she said.

"I don't know." He gazed up the path that led to Jerusalem. "It's too dangerous. We can't risk our lives. Not now. There are too few of us still here. We don't even know where the others have gone. If they're still alive—"

"Yakov." Mariamne turned his face toward her and looked deep into his eyes. "How can you tell others there is no death and still be afraid of dying? Where is your faith?"

"I'm not afraid. It's just that…"

"Yes, you are. Although you know perfectly well that nothing real can be threatened, and nothing unreal exists."

Yakov rubbed his bald head. Was there any truth in her words? Was he afraid? When they had stopped visiting the temple months ago, he had always blamed it on being too tired, too weary to make the long trek there and back. But the truth was he had a bad feeling. Too many of their friends had been arrested and killed without cause. The world outside had become a death trap.

"A shekel for your thoughts." Mariamne's gaze bore into his eyes. She lifted his chin with her finger and brought his lips to hers. "Yeshua will protect us."

How can she stay so calm?

"What are you thinking, my love? What worries you?"

Yakov ignored her. He gathered the corners of the linen sheet and tied them together to form a sack around the clean dishes. But Mariamne pulled him down to sit beside her. She drew him close.

"Don't hide your face from me," she said.

Yakov rested his cheek on her shoulder and sighed. How could he tell her about his dreams? The nightmares where he morphed into Yeshua and was nailed to a cross. About the vultures that circled around him, day and night, as if he gave off a scent of death. And the black ravens who called to him from the other side.

"Yeshua will protect us," Mariamne said again that night as they lay down to sleep. She drew a line with her finger across her husband's furrowed forehead to his lips. He always worried too much.

Yakov pulled the sheet around him and scrambled up to the window. "I don't want to die like him. Like Yeshua."

Mariamne followed him, pressed her body against his back, and embraced him. "You're not going to die. You're wiser than he was."

Yakov chortled. "Wiser? How can you say that?"

"Yeshua was a wonderful man. Kind and compassionate. He meant well. But he was impatient and rash. He couldn't understand when someone didn't agree with him. He was convinced that everything he believed was the absolute truth. He would never listen to anyone else."

"Everything he believed *was* the absolute truth."

"Yes, but he wouldn't listen to anyone else. He could never have dealt with Paulus like you have."

"I had you. Without you I would have been lost."

"He also had me, Yakov. And I let him down. When he wanted to leave and begged me to run away with him, I refused."

"You were so young."

Mariamne nodded. "I was young and foolish." She covered his back with kisses. "Remember, God favors the humble. And I meant what I said earlier: you *have* to return to the temple to preach. Do it for the Assembly, and for all the others who have yet to learn they are one with God. For those who need hope, who need to be rescued from error and won back for truth. And for those who need to believe in a better future, one where Judea and Samaria and Galilee are free from foreign rule."

Yakov took her into his arms. He lifted her up as if she weighed nothing, carried her to their bed, and placed her on the mattress.

"You don't have to try to become perfect," she said. "God already made you perfect. Your only task is to allow God to remove all the fears from your mind, like the shavings of wood when you carve a chair. You are loved by all. By me. What else do you need?"

He pulled the sheet up to her chin and kissed her lips. "Sleep now."

"Where are you going?"

"I have to prepare my sermon. We'll return to the temple tomorrow."

Ominous clouds covered the sky the following afternoon when Yakov, Mariamne, and the other disciples made their way through dozens of checkpoints on their way to the temple. The wind wailed through the stalls at the market, and an unseasonal chill in the air crept under their skin. When they reached the temple gates and heard the tax had increased to four drachmas, Yakov was ready to give up and go home. But fortunately, Mariamne egged him on.

As soon as they entered the Court of the Gentiles, an awestruck murmur went through the crowd.

"Look, there he is! Yakov the Just!"

Everyone turned to stare at them.

A warm glow spread across Yakov's face. Mariamne was right. He belonged here, in the temple. These outstanding men and women needed him. A swarm of people escorted him to Solomon's Portico, and when he stepped onto a raised platform, they settled down to hear what the famous wise man had to share. A couple of Roman soldiers in iron helmets and full armor trailed the crowd, but they stopped at an appropriate distance, ready to act only if the commotion turned unruly.

Yakov closed his eyes and focused on the light of God. In his mind's eye, he imagined how this divine glow spread out from his heart and enveloped every person around him. He opened his eyes and gazed out across the hundreds of listeners who had gathered to hear him speak. When he saw the adoring faces of Mariamne, Iosa, Abram, Yohannah, and all the other disciples who had loyally remained by his side through years of hardship, his heart filled with gratitude.

"Blessed are those who will listen without prejudice," he called out, with a tremble of excitement. "Some of you know me as Yakov the Just, the teacher who obeys the rules established by my brother Yeshua the Nazarene." Yakov swallowed. He had never mentioned Yeshua's name in the temple before. Nerves tingled his spine, and for a moment no air entered his lungs. He scanned the courtyard to see if any soldiers were approaching, but apart from the devotees before him, no one paid him any attention. Thirty years had passed since Yeshua's arrest. How foolish of him to fear that the new high priest could have heard about his brother. Hundreds of rebels, field preachers, and innocents had been executed, and even crucified, since that day. Why would anyone remember Yeshua?

Mariamne urged him to continue.

"Our teacher, Yeshua, taught us to connect with God. To be one with the Father. He revealed to us all that's been hidden—we all saw it revealed through him, and then we all learned to see."

At the back of the court, a handful of temple priests had gathered. They held a small group of believers at bay while they waited to hear the high priest speak. One priest turned and pointed at Yakov and the much larger crowd that surrounded him.

Yakov gulped. Why were they watching him? Did they suspect he was planning an uprising? He pushed the thought away. Surely, he was overreacting.

He turned his attention back to the people before him.

"Yeshua believed all men and women are worthy of God's love," he continued. "He showed us why it's wrong to judge others, to condemn those who differ from us, because we are all one. Only those who never judge others can ever find peace."

The soldiers stood at guard, their hands clutching the handles of their swords, prepared to attack. But Yakov wasn't afraid. Mariamne had been right: the time had come to reveal the truth to one and all.

"A few years ago, a man called Paulus of Tarsus approached me here in Solomon's Portico," Yakov said. "He spoke of my brother Yeshua and how he had met him in a state of delirium."

The growing crowd around him stirred. Some of them knew of Paulus. A few had even heard him speak.

Yakov closed his eyes and focused. He had to communicate from a place of love. The truth would set them all free. He didn't want to lie any longer or hide his true identity. "But the Yeshua Christos that Paulus spoke of had nothing in common with my brother. His 'Lord Christos' is a figment of Paulus's imagination, a deity that sprang from Paulus's desire to be heard and admired. We all know that only *God* can be our Lord. No one else."

Yakov stopped to wipe his nose, which was dripping from the cold. "Paulus arrived in Jerusalem with one sole intent: to cause confusion. He was arrested, right here in this very temple, when his lies were finally exposed. But let's not judge him. Paulus acted from a place of fear, of separation from the love that is God."

The cluster of temple priests and soldiers seemed to expand and move closer.

Yakov tried to calm his tumultuous heart. He focused again on the sphere of divine light and love, this time expanding it even further to envelop the soldiers, temple priests, and every other person in the temple. Peace must be possible if the world before them was a mass illusion. If only he could help them see.

He cleared his throat. This was his chance to show the world that what he preached was the true word of God. "The Yeshua of whom I speak—my dear achui, my brother—had nothing in common with this Christos. My brother never claimed to be the savior. He was not the Messiah you are all waiting for. Yeshua was a simple man of peace, of humility. He taught us that God is love, and that we are all sons of God."

"Have you finished speaking?" A soldier stood below the raised platform. "Your sermon... Make it end."

The soldier turned to address the crowd. "Scram! No large groups allowed here today."

Yakov gave a quick nod and stepped off the platform, his cheeks flushed. He tried to read the expressions on the faces that watched him. Did they understand now that, unlike Paulus, his Assembly had no wish to conquer the world? All they wanted was to spread a message of peace. Of oneness and love. Of enlightenment.

Mariamne gave his hand a quick squeeze before she let go, lest anyone notice their inappropriate display of affection in the sacred temple.

"Look!" Yudah Tzaer pointed at the entrance to the Holy Place, the most sacred construct of the temple, where the high priest ben Fabus had appeared in all his glory to address the small congregation waiting for him. The gemstones in ben Fabus's breastplate dazzled in the high midday sun, and his white tunic shimmered like marble under his heavy blue coat.

In no time, all the temple priests had gathered around ben Fabus to pay their respects. And with their heads leaning in, they seemed to deliberate something. Ben Fabus looked up, as if scanning the courtyard. Then, one by one, each of the priests pointed in Yakov's direction.

A shiver ran up Yakov's spine. He looked up and saw that hundreds of soldiers had gathered around him, positioned in every corner, in front of every exit. Where had they all come from? And where had all the other worshippers gone?

"We should never have returned to the temple," he said quietly.

Beside him, Mariamne's face had stiffened.

"Mari." Yakov grabbed Mariamne's hand. His heart beat wildly. "Listen to me: you must leave. And if I fall behind, keep walking."

"Don't be foolish," she said, but her desperate grasp confirmed her fear.

Instinctively, the disciples formed a protective ring around Yakov. As one, they moved as fast as they could toward the closest gate.

From the corner of his eye, Yakov observed dozens of legionnaires moving in their direction, like lions on a hunt.

"Run!" Yakov yelled.

And he ran, as fast as his legs would bear him. His sandals caught on the skirt of his tunic, and he stumbled. Regaining his balance, he sped toward the nearest entrance. Every time he fell to his knees, his fellow disciples magically appeared and pulled him to his feet.

Time and time again.

Until he stumbled over someone's leg and crashed headfirst to the ground. When he tried to scramble to his feet, his legs wouldn't move. He reached up for help, but his hands grasped empty air.

He was alone. The others had fled.

A legionnaire positioned himself, wide-legged, with one foot on either side of Yakov's torso. He pointed the tip of his sword against Yakov's throat.

"You speak of Paulus of Tarsus," he said with a vicious sneer. "Someone of such low stature as yours should not speak ill of King Agrippa's friend."

"Friend?" Yakov wiped gravel from his bleeding lip. "No, Paulus isn't a friend of… Agrippa arrested him."

The soldier laughed. "The king protects his own. And some of us,"—he pointed at one of the priests who stood on the sideline watching them—"remember you well from the day Paulus was arrested. You were there."

"Yes, but I tried to protect him. He was my guest."

"Protect? The poor man cursed and yelled at you as he was dragged away."

Yakov clambered to his feet and brushed the dirt from his tunic. "Paulus was confused, sometimes delirious, but that doesn't mean he wasn't a son of God."

The soldier snickered. By now, the other legionnaires had joined him. They formed a circle around Yakov.

"Yakov the Just, am I correct?" the high priest ben Fabus asked. He had pushed his way through the crowd, striking anyone who stood in his way with his bejeweled staff.

Yakov nodded. "Y-you are. I mean, I am he."

"Much time has passed since you last visited me. I was under the impression that you had long since escaped Judea. Left, I mean. For the good of one and all."

"For the *good*?" Yakov said, not sure what ben Fabus was insinuating.

"May I have a word?" The high priest scrutinized Yakov from beneath his gold-rimmed turban. "Away from the crowds."

The question had only one answer.

Inside the Chamber of Hewn Stones, at the north side of the temple, Ben Fabus guided Yakov onto a Roman chair in the middle of a bright hall. Torches lit up the high ceilings and cast shadows on the lush scarlet carpet below. All around him, dozens of aristocratic-looking men sat upon their chairs, chatting away, watching him. They were all clad in similar cream-colored tunics and tasseled headscarves, like priests, but without their priestly turbans. Yakov looked from one face to another, but he didn't recognize anyone. What was this? A council of judges?

"Harrumph," one of the men cleared his throat. "What have we here?"

Is this what Yeshua went through?

"A-am I under arrest?" Yakov turned around to ask ben Fabus.

But the high priest was nowhere to be seen.

Four armed soldiers blocked the exit.

Surely this could not be the Great Sanhedrin, the Supreme Court of the Jews. They would never allow Roman soldiers entry. Could it be one of King Agrippa's modern ideas?

"W-what am I doing here?" Yakov asked.

"You have blasphemed against God," one of the seated men said politely. "You have broken the law. You will confess?"

"N-no," Yakov said. He looked around the room in confusion. His head throbbed. Why was he here? Could Paulus have anything to do with this?

"You claimed you are God."

Yakov sighed. They had taken the statement out of context and offered it as bait. But he couldn't deny he had uttered those exact words only moments earlier. "Yes, but we are all sons of God," he said at last. "I am. You are. Paulus, bless his soul, is too."

Yakov racked his brain for something clever to say. He inhaled deeply to steady his voice. "As God is my witness, I have not blasphemed against God."

The men chuckled. But it wasn't amusing. At all.

Yakov turned slowly. All those eyes staring at him, judging him. His head spun with fear.

"Are you not the man they call Yakov the Just? Who lures people into his compound and convinces them they are equal to God?"

The blood drained from Yakov's face. He struggled to find the right words. Deny their accusations. Beg them to spare his life. But his tongue had swollen. His lips were numb. He closed his eyes and focused on his heart chakra. *God, please save me.*

He filled himself with love until his heartbeat stilled to a hum.

Without a tremor, he opened his eyes and said, "I am Yakov bar Yosef, brother of Yeshua the Nazarene. I am who they call Yakov the Just."

"Thus, you confess you refer to your own self as God."

Yakov had to laugh. They were using his own words against him.

"I've already told you. I'm not a god, or any kind of messiah, if that's what you infer. But what I know for sure is that I'm *one* with God. As are you. And you. And you." He pointed from one man to another, turning around the room until his head swirled.

Laughter. Snickers.

No one took him seriously.

"Hence, you have confessed to blasphemy," said a tall man in a stitched golden robe. He appeared to be their leader. "Accordingly, we had resolved not to stone you for your crimes, but…"

The man paused and scratched his beard. He looked around the room, bobbing his head toward each one of the judges, as if to garner support from his colleagues.

"G-good men…" Yakov's voice caught, and he pressed his hands to his chest in an effort to look humble. "I'm not trying to fool you. I only wish to help you understand that all you see around you is an illusion, created by your own minds. Once you understand this, you'll have eternal life."

A warm wave of divine love swept through him, and he mumbled to himself, "There is no death." Then louder, for everyone to hear, "You can kill my body, the man you see before you. But *I* will never die."

He ran out of breath. His lungs seemed to shrivel. He heard himself pant, gasp for air.

At the other end of the room, the guarded door shone like a bright passage.

The judges stared at him, at one another, confused.

Yakov rose from his seat and took one step, then another, toward the door.

He had to get out of here.

The soldiers who guarded the door raised their swords, ready to bring them down in attack, but Yakov moved as if in a dream. His heart throbbed in his throat as he pushed the surprised soldiers aside and stumbled into the temple courtyard.

The stark blue sky opened up before him. Snowflakes glistened in the air like angelic feathers, casting a blanket of silence over the world.

He ran toward the nearest gate, but then he stopped short. Amazed. Something magical had happened. His head was clear. His heart was light.

All his fears had evaporated.

The daylight shifted into a higher vibration, and the air sparkled like a thousand stars. Completely stunned, he realized he could see farther, and more clearly than ever before. The sky had magnified into an eternity, and he watched the snowflakes fly up and away. He rose up with them, swirled through the air, and from their perspective he could see beyond the temple walls and view lands and seas and people in every corner of the world. He could hear the flutter of butterfly wings and of flower petals opening up before the sun. He heard the soft voices of people in Rome, Mesopotamia, and Gallia. The blood in his body pulsed at striking speed and brought life to every particle of his body. A sheer violet light surrounded him, and he expanded his consciousness far beyond his body, erasing the borders between himself and all others. Everything in the entire world had melted into one and shimmered in the vibrant light. He had never felt so alive.

When he turned to look upon the surprised faces of the judges who watched him from the doorway of the Hall of Hewn Stones, his heart filled with unconditional love. All distinction between himself as a perceiver and himself as the perceived, as an external being, disappeared. A godlike light shone from each and every one of the judges. They were one with him. With God. With all.

A smile spread across Yakov's lips. He filled with euphoria.

Someone yanked his shoulder.

"Where do you think you're going?"

When Yakov turned around, he saw that a beautiful spirit dressed in the body of a legionnaire was holding his arm. The soldier pushed the tip of his dagger against Yakov's throat. "If you're looking for the exit, it's right there."

The soldier pointed to a cornerstone at the pinnacle of the high temple wall. With the dagger still pushing into Yakov's skin, the soldier pushed him up onto the stone and forced him to look down into the gaping valley far below.

Yakov laughed. The stones of the wall glimmered in the divine light. The grass and the bushes in the valley below danced in colors that morphed from deep green to light blue and pink, to olive, to violet. The eyes of the people who had gathered below to watch his fall sparkled like the brightest stars. The entire world blazed in a magnificent glimmer.

Then, as if someone had whacked his head, Yakov crashed back into reality and into his body. He looked down into the valley again, but this time he noticed the towering height of the pinnacle where he stood and the depth of the abyss below. A wave of nausea swept over him as his head spun. His body swayed, delirious from the altitude. If he fell, he would most definitely die. He tried to back up, push the soldier away. But the soldier held him in a firm grip and did not budge.

Yakov's mouth filled with the taste of metal. He didn't want to die.

Mariamne. Where was she?

Everything you see is an illusion.

The words seemed to appear from nowhere. A sense of peace enveloped him. His heartbeat calmed to a gentle hum. He relaxed.

There is no death.

His eyes seemed to open wider. The world shimmered around him. Light sprang from every being, every plant, and every stone around him. His soul filled with euphoria. Death no longer frightened him.

Only love is real.

A stone hit the back of his head, and he looked back at the judges of the Great Sanhedrin. They stared at him, stones in their hands, ready to kill. To wipe Yakov off the face of the earth.

Yakov viewed them through a mist of limitless love, and he forgave them.

He thought of Paulus. Had he egged the temple priests into action? But why?

Then he closed his eyes and sent his enemy, his friend, pure love from his heart. He now saw Paulus only as a reflection of the divine and the wicked within himself. He connected with him, became one with him. Loved him with all his heart. Paulus had been his best teacher.

It's not about me.

He laughed. Of course not.

"My God and Father…" Yakov's heart filled with love for all the judges, the legionnaires, the priests, and every person staring at him, "let your light shine upon me and bring me salvation. Save me from death, for your grace is alive in me—"

Yeshua appeared in a tunnel of bright light before him and beckoned him closer.

With a jolt, Yakov ejected from his body and floated into the light.

Someone struck the back of his head with a club.

And then his body fell.

Off the Coast of Alexandria, Aegyptos, AD 62

Mariamne's fingers swept the waves while her arm rested over the rim of the boat. She looked back toward the disappearing skyline of Alexandria. With her other hand, she clasped Yudah Tzaer's hand. Tears streamed down her face.

Yakov watched her from above. He wanted to lift her up in his arms and tell her she was safe.

I'm right here, he said, but Mariamne couldn't hear him. He kissed her cheek, and for a moment she looked up, as if she had felt his lips on her skin. But then she shook her head.

You're not hallucinating, my love.

In the back of the boat, Yudah Tzaer's wife rested under a blanket with their children, Elazar and Maryam Salome, and the childlike servant girl they had met in Alexandria, Sara-la-Kali.

Yakov calmed the waves and directed the boat safely toward their new life in Gallia. There, in the town of Provincia, Mariamne would seek out Shemuel bar Azai, the carpet weaver to whom they had given refuge after the uprising in the temple many years ago. And Yakov would do all he could to pave her way and shelter her from any dangers.

Gallia Narbonensis, he had whispered to her, night after night. *Go to Gallia.* A place where she could start anew, among people who had never heard of her, or Yeshua, or Yakov. A part of the Roman

Empire where no one would bother her. Where Paulus could never find her.

Yakov had guided her to a fisherman's port in Aegyptos and showed her to the only boat they could afford: one with no sails and no oars. But Yakov, together with Yeshua, would bring her safely across the Great Sea. The men she had loved, the two brothers whose deaths would always haunt her.

You're not to blame, he whispered. *Everything happens exactly as it should.*

Mariamne clutched a stone to her chest. Engraved with the letter Yudh, the stone had once been used to cast lots. She kissed the stone, dropped it into the sea, and watched it sink slowly into the abyss. Then she closed her eyes and united with God.

Yakov enveloped her with light.

At last she was safe.

Author's Note

The seed of this story sprouted when I read the New Testament for the first time while doing research for *The Transmigrant*, a novel about the "lost years" of Jesus. I was not raised in a religious home and therefore could read the Bible without a preconceived understanding of its content. It quickly became evident that James, the brother of Jesus, had once been the chosen successor of Jesus who led the first community of disciples, and that Paul was an intruder and troublemaker. Despite the bitter battles between James and Paul for leadership of the "church," Paul's beliefs ultimately prevailed and formed the fundamental doctrinal tenets of Christianity. They include the beliefs that Christ is God in the form of man, that his death atones for the sins of humankind, and that belief in his resurrection guarantees eternal life. These tenets are in many ways a betrayal of Jesus's teachings.

Why do we never hear about James?
And why was his legacy erased from history?

Five years of research into sources that speak of James and the Jerusalem Assembly (the commune of Jesus's disciples) has proved that I'm not alone in wanting to vindicate James and bring forth the original message of Jesus. Several eminent historians, Bible scholars, and professors of religion, such as Robert Eisenman, Barrie Wilson, Bruce Chilton, James D. Tabor, and Jeffrey J. Bütz, have written books about James.

The time has finally come to celebrate James
and bring his story to life.

Who's Who in *The Holy Conspiracy*

Many of the people mentioned in the New Testament share names that were popular in the first century, names such as James (Yakov), John (Yochanan), Judas/Jude (Yudah), Mary (Mariamne), and Simon (Shimon). For clarity's sake, I have changed some of the names in the novel and have disregarded a few characters. I've used the Aramaic versions of the names where possible.

Yakov (James the Just, Brother of Jesus)

James the Just, or "brother of the Lord," was Jesus's younger brother and chosen successor, and leader of the first "church," the Jerusalem Assembly. He is one of the few characters in the New Testament whom we can prove actually existed. Besides the New Testament, James is mentioned by more than thirteen extra-biblical sources, including first-century Roman-Jewish historian Josephus Flavius (AD 37–100), Papias of Hierapolis (AD 60–163), Titus Flavius Clemens of Alexandria (AD 150–c. 215), the early church historian Eusebius, Origen of Alexandria (AD 184–c. 253), and the Gospel of Thomas (first or second century at the latest). Even in the book of Acts, written between AD 80 and 90, James suddenly appears in Acts 15, and even though he was never mentioned by name before, now he's in charge of the entire Jerusalem movement.

James was clearly a well-known figure in the first century, since the contemporary historian Josephus and many others regarded the Roman destruction of Jerusalem in AD 70 as divine revenge for the death of James in AD 62.

The New Testament mentions James as: James the brother of Jesus, James whose mother is Mary, James the bishop of Jerusalem, and James the father of the apostle Judas Thaddeus. Other (different) Jameses in the New Testament include James Zebedee and James, son of Alpheus.

Saul of Tarsus/Paulus (Paul)

Paul was a tentmaker from Tarsus in today's Turkey, who claimed he was Jewish while also a Roman citizen. Paul and Jesus never met in the course of Jesus's lifetime. Instead, Paul had a vision of Christ during a possible fit of epilepsy, which could explain the blinding white light he experienced. Although Paul is often viewed as one of the most important figures of Christianity, it's important to note that his faith did not stem from the historical Jesus. But why did Paul feel the need to create his Christ from Jesus the Nazarene, instead of creating a completely separate figure that no one could question? His (seven authentic) letters reveal the bitter battles between him and Jesus's disciples, the so-called "pillars of the Jerusalem church." He speaks condescendingly about James and Peter and the rest of the Jerusalem Assembly as "those who were supposed to be the acknowledged leaders," although he also claims that "what they are means nothing to me." In his letters, he calls them "false apostles, deceitful workmen, disguising themselves as apostles of Christ."

Paul created today's Christianity, including the Christ character who was born in the flesh, sacrificed to atone for our sins, and resurrected after three days. Paul also laid the groundwork for the story of Jesus's mother, Mary, as the immaculate Virgin, and invented the Last Supper and Communion, where the faithful can become one with Jesus by symbolically ingesting his body and drinking his blood. Paul died in Rome around the same time as James, in AD 62–64.

Mariamne (Mary Magdalen)

Mary Magdalen was one of Jesus's most loyal followers, and most likely his wife. She is mentioned more times in the New Testament than most of the other apostles. The Gospel of Mary, believed to have been written in the third century, reveals a Mary Magdalen who had a special relationship with Jesus and possessed a deeper understanding of his teachings. In the Gnostic Gospel of Philip, Mary Magdalen is described as Jesus's intimate partner and companion. The image of

Mary Magdalen was transformed into that of a harlot by Pope Gregory I in AD 591, when he associated Mary Magdalen with the sinful woman who anoints Jesus's feet in Luke (7:36–50).

Mother Maryam (Mary, Mother of Jesus)

The myth of Jesus's mother as the perpetual virgin originated in the Gospels of Matthew and Luke, which were written sixty to eighty years after Jesus's death by people who had never met him (or her). In the most contemporaneous authentic sources, Mary is described as a common Jewish woman with five sons and several daughters. We don't know much about Mary's death. Some Catholics believe that she, like Jesus, rose to heaven in her full body. Others believe she died near Ephesus in Turkey. I have assumed the more logical theory that she went to live with her oldest living son and "the beloved disciple," aka Mary Magdalen, her daughter-in-law.

Kephas (Simon Peter)

According to Christian tradition, Peter was a fisherman and among the first of the disciples called during Jesus's ministry. His nickname Peter (Kephas in Aramaic) means "Rock." His stature as the first leader of the disciples originates in Matthew 16:18, which says, "You are Peter, and on this rock I will build my Church, and the gates of hell will not prevail against it." However, the earliest authenticated sources, the seven letters written by Paul, contradict the claim that Peter was the leader of Jesus's disciples. Peter is believed to have been crucified in Rome under Emperor Nero between AD 64 and 68.

Yudah Tzaer

Based on inscriptions found on ossuaries discovered in Jerusalem in 1980, it is possible that Jesus was married to Mary Magdalen and that they had a son named Judah. The 2007 documentary *The Lost Tomb of Jesus* supports this theory, and many theologians, including Bible scholar and author James Tabor, have affirmed their belief in a married Jesus.

Taddai (Jude Thaddeus)

One of the lesser-known disciples, Jude Thaddeus, is commonly identified as the son of James. After the crucifixion of Jesus, he is believed to have traveled throughout Mesopotamia, Libya, and Persia with Simon the Zealot.

Andreas (Andrew)

The brother of Kephas (Peter) and also a fisherman, Andrew is believed to have preached in Asia Minor (Turkey) and Greece together with another disciple called Levi. According to tradition, he was crucified on an X-shaped cross around AD 70 in Achaia (Greece).

Phillipos (Philip)

As one of the "traditional" disciples of Jesus from the town of Bethsaida in Galilee, Philip is believed to have preached in Greece, Phrygia, Syria, and Turkey. In Hierapolis, he is said to have converted the proconsul's wife, which eventually led to his crucifixion. In 2011, archeologists unearthed a tomb in Hierapolis that may have belonged to Philip. The marriage to Yohannah in this novel is purely fictional.

Yohannah (Joanna, wife of Chuza)

Joanna is one of three women mentioned in the New Testament as part of the group of disciples that followed Jesus from town to town. As stated by the Gospel of Luke, she was the wife of Chuza, Herod's steward. As the wife of an important court official, she would have had sufficient means to travel and contribute to the support of Jesus and the disciples. The marriage to Phillipos in this novel is purely fictional.

Bar-Tôlmay (Simon Bartholomew)

We know little about the apostle Bartholomew. Some claim he was the same person as Nathanael, but it's presumably just an effort to combine the many disciples into a firm number of twelve. Logic contradicts there were only twelve disciples. Bartholomew may have died in Armenia, although a second-century teacher, Pantaenus of Alexandria, said he found a Hebrew copy of the Gospel of Matthew in India that Bartholomew had left behind.

Barzebedee (James, son of Zebedee)

One of Jesus's first disciples. James, like his brother John, was a fisherman. According to (the anecdotal) Acts, Herod Agrippa beheaded him in AD 44. To avoid confusion with other characters named Yakov, I have called him Barzebedee in this novel.

Levi (Levi/Matthew)

Levi is the Hebrew name, and Matthew is the Greek name. As a tax collector, Levi worked for Greek-speaking Romans and gathered taxes from Hebrew-speaking Jews. He might have been the only disciple who was educated and knew how to read. Believed to have preached in Judea, Syria, Persia, and the Parthian Empire, he died between AD 60 and 70, not martyred.

Barnabas

Barnabas was Paul's right-hand man and travel companion. He is mentioned in Paul's letters to the Galatians and Corinthians.

Shimon (Simon the Zealot)

Simon supposedly preached in Egypt and later joined the apostle Taddai (Jude Thaddeus) in Persia, where, as attested by the apocryphal Acts of Simon and Judas, he was martyred by being cut in half with a saw.

Iosa (Joses)

Joses was one of the younger brothers of Jesus and mentioned in the Gospels of Mark and Matthew. A "Joses" also appears in lists of Epiphanius ("Josis") and Eusebius ("Joseph") of the early bishops of Jerusalem (i.e., leaders of the Jerusalem Assembly). Eusebius lists Josis as the third bishop of Jerusalem after James the Just and Simeon of Jerusalem.

Tau'ma (Judas Thomas; Jude, Brother of Jesus; Thomas Didymus)

Jesus's younger brother Jude was nicknamed Tau'ma (or "twin"), perhaps because he looked exactly like Jesus. Interestingly, the names Thomas and Didymus also mean "twin." He's believed to have traveled through today's Middle East to Kerala, where he reputedly founded India's first church in AD 52. I've chosen to call him Tau'ma, the Aramaic version of Jude, to separate him from Judas Iscariot, Judas Thaddeus, and Jesus's son, Judas. Because of the nickname meaning "twin," I've made the assumption that Judas Thomas and Jesus's brother Jude were the same person.

Mentioned: Yudah (Judas Iscariot)

According to the Gnostic Gospel of Judas, discovered in Egypt in the 1970s, Judas was one of Jesus's closest allies. There was no betrayal. Jesus asked his dear friend to point him out to the Romans in order to save the rest of the disciples. Read more in my novel *The Transmigrant*.

Fictional characters:

Michal, Yakov's wife

Abram, Iosa's partner

Talitha, Yakov's servant and lover

Shemuel Bar Azai

When Were the Books of the New Testament Written?

In the second century, there were dozens or maybe even a hundred gospels in circulation, all with their own flavor of Jesus and his message. This, of course, caused a problem for anyone who wanted to claim their version of Christianity as the correct one. The twenty-seven books that make up what we call the New Testament were decided upon in the year AD 331, when the emperor Constantine sent a letter to Eusebius, bishop of Caesarea, instructing him to prepare fifty copies of the "Divine Scriptures," to be sent as a royal present to the Christian churches of Constantinople and surrounding districts.

AD 50–57: The Seven Authentic Letters of Paul

Thirteen of the letters in the New Testament are attributed to the apostle Paul, but most scholars and historians consider only seven of them authentic. These are the most contemporary sources of information we have from the time of the disciples.

- First Thessalonians (c. AD 50)
- Galatians (c. AD 53)
- First Corinthians (c. AD 53–54)
- Philippians (c. AD 55)
- Philemon (c. AD 55)
- Second Corinthians (c. AD 55–56)
- Romans (c. AD 57)

AD 70: Gospel of Mark. Written in Rome or Southern Syria by a second-generation Christian (one of Paul's disciples), shortly after the fall of Jerusalem in AD 70.

AD 85–100: Gospel of Matthew. Written in Antioch (Roman Syria) by several different Jewish Christians, possibly second-generation followers of Peter. Partially based on the Gospel of Mark and on the Q Source (the assumed original gospel).

AD 90–110: Gospel of Luke. Written in Greece or Asia Minor by an educated follower of Paul. Like the Gospel of Matthew, it draws from both the Gospel of Mark and the Q document, but it also has several unique parables. It's generally believed this same author wrote the Acts of the Apostles. The level of Greek used in both the Third Gospel and the book of Acts is highly advanced, and not the kind of language a poor disciple would use.

AD 90–110: Gospel of John. Written in traditional Greco-Roman biography style at Ephesus, in Asia Minor, by a Greek Christian. It's generally considered less historical, as it is quite distinct from the three previous gospels and includes several (probably inauthentic) stories about Jesus, including the wedding in Cana and the resurrection of Lazarus. The first part, "In the beginning was the Word…" is almost identical to a section in the seventeenth-century BC Sama Veda.

AD 80–90: Acts. The same person likely wrote the Gospel of Luke and the book of Acts. He was probably a physician and associate of Paul in Antioch. Given these books were written so long after Jesus's and Paul's deaths, we can dismiss them as hearsay, and it's unlikely that they hold a lot of truth.

Other Questions You May Have

What about the "Twelve Disciples"?

Traditional Christianity claims that Jesus had twelve disciples. For centuries, theologians and historians have tried to come to a consensus about who belonged to this exclusive group, but so far they have failed. Why? Because there was no group of twelve. It makes little sense that Jesus would have felt it necessary to have an exact number of disciples instead of letting anyone who made the cut join his group. In fact, an Eastern Christian tradition derived from the Gospel of Luke holds that Jesus had as many as seventy apostles during his ministry.

What happened to the disciples after Jesus's death? Nobody knows for sure. Apart from the seven authentic letters of Paul (First Thessalonians, Galatians, First Corinthians, Philippians, Philemon, Second Corinthians, Romans) and the books of the historian Flavius Josephus, there are no factual sources that mention most of the disciples. We know only that no one initially connected the disciples in Jerusalem to Jesus, and the persecutions of Christians didn't start until Emperor Nero came into power in AD 54.

Why isn't there a mention of John in the novel?

It is my belief that John the disciple and apostle did not exist or was possibly a combination of a minor disciple and Mary Magdalen, who was the true Beloved Disciple. Some of the Gnostic Christian writings of the Nag Hammadi Library and evidence from the text of the Fourth Gospel itself support this theory. Eventually, Mary Magdalen was discredited as the (unnamed) prostitute in Luke 7:37–38 and also male-washed into John by some early church leaders, who were uncomfortable with the idea of a woman having such power and wisdom.

Were Jesus and his disciples vegetarian?

Jesus's moniker, the Nazarene, did not allude to his being from Nazareth, because the village did not exist in Jesus's day. The first-century historian Flavius Josephus does not mention Nazareth among all the towns and villages of Galilee, and archeological evidence suggest the town was founded after the Jewish revolt in AD 70. However, Jesus was a Nazarene, having taken the Nazarite vow of abstaining from meat and intoxicating drinks, such as wine. This particularly irritated Paul, who in one of his letters to the Corinthians emphasized that there's no sin in eating meat. "Eat everything that's sold in the marketplace. There is no reason to raise questions of conscience" (1 Corinthians 10:25).

What was the Jerusalem Assembly?

Contrary to common belief, Jesus did not create a church. His disciples were just followers of Jesus. They did not refer to themselves as anything in particular, except possibly Ebionites ("the poor") or the Jerusalem Assembly. Why they moved to Jerusalem from Galilee after the crucifixion is unknown.

Why doesn't this book include any post-crucifixion sightings of Jesus?

Paul is the first source of the tradition that Jesus was raised on the third day after his death. In fact, there were no mentions of Jesus's Easter morning appearances until after AD 85 (when the gospels of Matthew and Luke were written). The original gospel, called the Q source, does not mention Jesus's resurrection from the dead.

Was Paul in love with Mary Magdalen?

There's no proof of this, but reading between the lines of Paul's letters, this could explain why Mary Magdalen's reputation was sullied and why she was later portrayed as a prostitute. Paul preaches that women must keep silent in churches and be in submission. He says, "it's good for a man not to touch a woman" and that men should remain single and celibate. This is where the "priest must be celibate" comes from, which has caused harm to people for centuries. Everything Paul says sounds like a man who had his heart broken.

Were Mary Magdalen and James the Just married?

This is a purely fictional love story. I have found no evidence of such a relationship.

Dear Reader,

PLEASE LEAVE A REVIEW!

These days, all authors rely on reader reviews to spread the word about their books, and reviews are especially important for independent authors like myself. If this book moved you, please take a minute to leave an honest review on Goodreads, BookBub, Amazon, Apple Books, Kobo, Barnes & Noble, or wherever you hang out.

A simple phrase, a few words, or just a star rating… It would mean the world to me. Thank you!

Much love,
Kristi Saare Duarte

For more information about the author and upcoming works and events:

www.kristisaareduarte.com

Twitter: @kristisaare
Facebook: KristiDNYC
Instragram: AuthorKristiSaareDuarte
YouTube: Kristi Saare Duarte
Pinterest: KSaare00

Acknowledgments

I could not have written The Holy Conspiracy without decades of thorough research, studies, and explorations by the many magnificent theologians who put their massive knowledge on paper. It would have been impossible to create a credible account of the disciples' lives without their hard work and diligence. Special thanks to Barrie Wilson, author of *How Jesus Became Christian* and *Paul vs Jesus*; Robert H. Eisenman, author of *James the Brother of Jesus*, Bruce Chilton and Jacob Neusner, authors of *The Brother of Jesus: James the Just and His Mission*, Patrick Goggins, author of *James the Just: Jesus's Brother, Paul's Superior*. A full list of the more than one hundred sources that influenced this novel is posted on my website: www.KristiSaareDuarte.com/research.

A great big heartfelt cheer to all readers who have connected with me in any way: you brighten my world! And a monumental thanks to everyone who has left reviews on Goodreads, Barnes & Noble, Apple Books, Kobo, Amazon, Smashwords, etc. In today's publishing market, an author cannot be even slightly successful without reader reviews. I owe you big-time.

A huge thanks to Laurel Robinson, my brilliant editor par excellence: Your keen eye and straightforward comments have saved me from many embarrassing mistakes in this novel. And to the fantastic editor Daia Gerson, who gave the novel a last once-over pre-publication. I take complete responsibility for any remaining grammatical errors or typos.

I owe a mountain of gratitude to the kind, patient, and sometimes brutally honest beta readers who pointed out all the stuff that made little sense, needed reworking, or was just plain bad: Susan B. Stavropoulos, Patrick Andersen, Khalima Bolden, and Barrie Wilson.

I'm beyond grateful to have met the fantastic authors in my writers' group: Marc Clark, author of *The Princess and the Parakeet*; Mary Sheeran, author of *Banished from Memory*; and the future best-selling authors Laura Jokisch, Amy Lau, Anne Smith, Stephanie

Cochinos, Jennifer DeMeritt, Kerri Lee, and Tori Luce. Your inspiration and support are priceless.

A shout-out to my incredible fellow spiritual authors whom I've met through *The Transmigrant*: JB Richards, author of *Miriamne the Magdala*; Patrick Andersen, author of *Second Born* and *Acts of the Women*; and Keith Forrest, author of T*he Spiritual Fruitcake: Written from the Heart for the Soul.*

Finally, my family. I couldn't do this without you. Especially my lovely sisters: Tiina, for all the support, laughs, and for always being on my side. And Anne-Pii, for being my sister and for loving me.

And last, but absolutely not least, my husband, Eduardo: I'm so lucky to have met you. You're my soul mate, the life of my party, my travel buddy, my greatest love.

ALSO BY KRISTI SAARE DUARTE

THE TRANSMIGRANT

ISBN: 978-0-9971807-0-1 (Paperback)
ISBN: 978-0-9971807-1-8 (ebook)
ISBN: 978-0-9971807-2-5 (audiobook)

What if Jesus was once just an ordinary boy seeking enlightenment?

AD 8, at the Temple of Jerusalem. Twelve-year-old Yeshua thrills his audience when God seems to communicate through him. But while his listeners gush, the priests scoff and say that no carpenter, however wise, can ever enter their holy ranks. Humiliated and robbed of his only dream, Yeshua resigns to a dreary life as a simple laborer. Until the day he meets a Buddhist pilgrim who invites him along to his country Sindh (Pakistan), where anyone can become a monk. An irresistible portal of hope opens and now Yeshua must choose between honoring his father or selfishly chasing his dream.

"An inspired narrative that humanizes Jesus in a sensitive and delicate way, which we have not seen since Hermann Hesse's tale of the Buddha, Siddhartha, or Kahlil Gibran's The Prophet."
    —Paul Davids, Writer/Producer/Director of "Jesus in India" from NBCUniversal

"A beautiful story, deeply touching and very inspirational."
                                                                    — Reader's Favorite

"If you liked The Alchemist and The Celestine Prophecy, you will love The Transmigrant. Read this inspiring coming-of-age novel about Jesus travels in India and Nepal."
                                                                    — Inspirational Storytellers

www.KristiSaareDuarte.com

Made in the USA
Las Vegas, NV
16 December 2024

14279536R00173